The Snow Dragon

THE SNOW DRAGON

Three Variations

by S.P. Somtow
illustrated by Mikey Jiraros

Diplodocus Press
Bangkok • Los Angeles

The Snow Dragon
Three Variations

copyright © 1982, 1986, 2015
by Somtow Sucharitkul

The short story *The Fallen Country* originally
appeared in *Elsewhere, Volume II,* published by Ace
Books, in 1982

The novel *The Fallen Country* was originally
published by Bantam/Spectra in 1986

The Snow Dragon opera libretto appears here
for the first time.

published by
Diplodocus Press • Bangkok • Los Angeles

trade paperback ISBN:
978-1-940999-11-1

hardcover ISBN:
978-1-940999-10-4

FIRST EDITION
1 2 3 4 5 6 7 8 9 0

A new incarnation
and a new dedication

to Mikey
who now hopes
to live happily ever after

Variations:
Three Incarnations of the Snow Dragon

You're holding in your hands three incarnations of a single story. One, a piece of short fiction written in the late 1970s by a young Asian author, was one of my first attempts to write a fantasy story, but even then I wanted to defy the fairytale conventions and the escapism of dragons and princesses.

For a long time *The Fallen Country* was a monumental disappointment to me because I was under the impression that I'd had some kind of "breakthrough". Then, all the magazines to whom I submitted it rejected it for reasons they would never make quite clear to me. There are reasons that in hindsight are clear to me, but they were not the reasons given. I think that people somehow didn't (or wouldn't) believe in the story's essential truth.

I ran into Harlan Ellison for the first time at some convention and he said to me, "Somtow, I've been following your work. I absolutely *must* have you in *The Last Dangerous Visions.* Send me a story immediately!"

This is the short story I sent him. Harlan rejected it in a phone call filled with such scathing criticism that I didn't dare show the story to anyone for several years.

Of course, *The Last Dangerous Visions,* an iconic projected anthology that has been accumulating its legendary status for decades, is still not out, which means that had Harlan loved the story, it would still not be in print yet.   Which means that the subsequent novel, the second incarnation, would also not be, and in turn that I would never have turned the story into an opera.

The Fallen Country sat in a drawer for a few years and finally one day there came a request from the editor Terri Windling, who was assembling an anthology called *Elsewhere,* for me to submit something. This was supposed to be a gathering of "high fantasy" tales, and I rather sheepishly sent her this story even though I was sure it was not what she would want.

She told me, "I understand this story ... I've experienced something like it."

I didn't pry. *Elsewhere* grew and grew as well, like *The Last Dangerous Visions.* But it got published and my story made it into the second volume of a much expanded anthology.

The story was liked enough after it came out and even made its way into other anthologies.

But a second incarnation came about when Bantam-Spectra told me they wanted to do a line of young adult novels, and asked me if I had anything to offer.

I said, "I have a short story I could adapt."

The novel is really about a completely different set of people despite its underlying elements being the same.

I learned from my editors that YA novels had to be written with a protagonist a bit older than the children who would read the books, so that the readers would have "a protagonist they could look up to."

I learned that Dora Marx, who is by no means a secondary character in the short story — indeed the story is really about the relationship of the boy and the therapist and about their shared journey —

couldn't be allowed to play a major role by the conventional wisdom of YA writing, "because she is too old."

A younger, sexier Dora came into being, but she could no longer carry the burden of being Billy's co-conspirator. Instead, I cooked up a bunch of stalwart friends who help Billy work through his trauma, with Dora basically more of an observer.

It is really a completely different work. In this book, you will get a chance to compare them and decide for yourself which story you prefer.

Both stories came out in the 1980s. Even if dragons really existed, the events would not have unfolded the same way today, a time when therapists now have to observe mandatory reporting laws; Dora Marx's dilemma would not be the same today.

Although one imagines that dragons are perhaps not quite amenable to human legislation....

●●●

A long time passed. In fact, something like thirty-five years since the original idea first came to me.

A daring American conductor of Tamil descent was asking me for a new opera. It had, he said, to be something to do with fairy tales, because the Skylight Theatre in Milwaukee was doing an entire season based on fairy tale. Having a dragon in it would be nice. Did I have any adaptable stories containing dragons?

I sent Viswa Subbaraman two stories, one an oft awarded and oft anthologized work called *Dragon's Fin Soup,* and this one. I was sure he would go for the former, which is really wild and really operatic, and really exotic as well. Viswa chose *The Fallen Country.*

Thus, I came to revisit this territory once again, a lifetime later, from the point of view of a different career.

Opera is the most powerful artistic medium. In the hands of a Mozart, a story that otherwise come off like an episode of *I Love Lucy* can become a profound paradigm of the human condition — this is clearly true of *The Marriage of Figaro.* Conversely, the greatest literary material can end up a bit trivialized, as witness certain versions of *Faust* and *Hamlet.*

Great librettists, like Arrigo Boïto who adapted Shakespeare's *Othello* for Verdi, understand that in a opera the music must do the talking. The words are like clotheshangers: they must be sturdy and well balanced to take the weight of that designer gown or upscale tuxedo. As one of the few composers since opera began who writes his own libretti, I have the great fortune to be allowed to conceive the musical and textual structures as a single entity.

An opera with a 12-year old boy as a protagonist, whose part must *absolutely not* be "dumbed down" in any way, is already a challenge. Putting a gang of teenagers around the hero would perhaps be an insurmountable one; I certainly thought so. So I ended up throwing out the novel and returning to the original short story, the one about the abused innocent and jaded therapist who has issues of her own.

The libretto has none of the linguistic frills that characterize my early writing. The minimalism is essential in order to provide a framework of utter clarity through which the music may speak. And since the music was going to be designed for an orchestra of only 14 people — a prospect more frightening to Somtow the maximalist than orchestrating for 100-piece band would be — I knew that there would be a lot of chiseling and honing involved.

The opportunity to produce a significant mezzo role was irresistible and pairing the boy soprano and the mezzo provides a different color palette for the duets.

The Snow Dragon is my eighth, ninth or tenth opera depending on which ones you count and how you count them. But it's the first one to use a contemporary setting and I had to evolve a more conversational style of vocal writing. At times, the opera's music is barely elevated above the rhythms of normal speech, so that when the occasional passages of "operatic" lyricism burst through they are firmly anchored in a kind of reality.

Viswa and the Skylight made me reach all the way back into the earliest moments of my literary career for the source material for this piece which seems to represent the Indian summer of my "late period". For this opportunity I am humbled and grateful.

S.P.Somtow

PART ONE

THE SHORT STORY

The Fallen Country

He had blank, sky-blue eyes and confused blond hair. He had a wry, dry voice with just a lemon twist of longing in it. He was small for his age, almost as though he had willed himself not to grow. As I closed the door behind us, my hand brushed against his and he flinched away violently in the split second before willing himself to smile; from this I pegged him as a victim of child abuse.

"Hi," I said, answering him. "My name is Dora Marx." I eased him into the brown, wombish chair that faced my desk. "You may call me—" I sat down myself, with the stuck-record-in-a-groove smoothness that comes from seeing a thousand children a year for twenty years, "—either Dora, or Mrs. Marx. Whichever makes you feel more comfortable."

"I think I'd prefer Mrs. Marx," he said. "But," he added, "you can call me Billy." Touche. He didn't look at me. I went to the window to slam out the eleven o'clock yelling from the schoolyard. God damn it, they should never make you work under these conditions ...

I said, "You're the one who—"

"They found at five in the morning, dinging to the steeple of Santa Maria's. You read the papers?" "Sometimes," I said, flicking the dipping out of his file.

BILLY BINDER. AGE 12—

"Where'd you get that scar?" — like an albino earth-worm, wriggling into the sleeve of his tee shirt.
"Fell off my bike." Sure.

—FOUND HALF-DEAD ON THE LEDGE, HIS ARMS AROUND THE STEEPLE ON THE SIDE OVERLOOKING ANGEL PLAZA. FATHER EPSTEIN, SUMMERTIME PASTOR STANDING IN FOR FATHER SANTINI, WHILE TRYING TO RING THE BELL—

"It says here," I said, "that you were suffering from severe frostbite."
"Yes. From the snow."
"It doesn't snow in Florida in the middle of August—" No point trying to argue with him yet. My job was to listen, only to listen. I wasn't trained to root out traumas. It wasn't up to me to pronounce the kid an attempted suicide either, or to solve the mystery of how he got to the topmost turret of a locked historical monument, or to elucidate the medical wonder of frostbite in a hundred-degree heatwave - I was only a counsellor in a parochial school too poor and stupid to afford an expert.
I wouldn't get anywhere by questioning his story. Perhaps I should start with something else. "How often do they beat you up?" I said.
"What?" Terror flecked his eyes for a second. Then they went dead. He said, "Almost every day." It was in the same tone of voice.

"Who?"

"Pete, my Mom's boyfriend." "What?"

He told me about it, never raising his voice. I had been doing this for twenty years. After a while you grow iron railings round your brains. Nothing hurts anymore. I listened, staring at my hands and wishing a ton of Porcelana on them. I knew I would sit there and endure until the catalogue of beltings and poundings had dissolved into incoherence, into tears, into hysteria, and then I would flow into the cracks in the kid's soul like epoxy glue and make him seem whole for a while ... but he didn't give me a chance. He went on in that same monotone, detail after detail, until it was I who was ready to crack. I held up my hand. He stopped.

"Don't you ever cry?" I said.

"Not anymore," he said. "I've promised." "What do you mean, you promised?"

"The Snow Dragon."

"Tell me about him."

"I knew it!" he cried. Now he was exultant, taunting. I wasn't prepared for the change in mood; I started most unprofessionally. "You're supposed to be trying to help me or something, but all you want to do is listen to me lie!"

Shifting gears to accommodate his outburst, "Is that why he hits you?"

"Yes! Yes! But I won't stop!"

"It's all right," I said. "You can lie if you want. You can tell all the lies you want in this room. Nothing will ever escape from here ..."

"Like a confessional? Like a black hole?"

"Yes." Imaginative imagery, at least. This kid was no dummy. "Like a black hole." He looked me in the eye for the first time. His eyes were clear as glass; I could read no deceit in them.

"Good," he said firmly. I waited. I think he had begun to trust me.

"So what were you really doing, then, up there. Straddling the steeple, I mean."

"Rescuing a princess."

That's how he started telling me the stories. The stories! They would have been the envy of any clinical psychiatrist with a pet theory and a deadline and a paper to be churned out in a fury. To me they were only stories. Of course I did not believe them; but my job was to listen, not to judge.

Billy had been adopted by one set of parents after another. He couldn't remember the first few. After the divorcees had played musical chairs for a while he had settled with the third or fourth mother, Joan, and they'd moved to our town, a spiderweb of brash fast food places that circled the Eighteenth Century Spanish church that was the town's one attraction. Billy shed pasts like a snake sloughing its skin or a duck shaking off canal water. The only thing he kept was the name, Billy Binder. He'd always been adamant about his name. He'd always gotten his way about it somehow: throwing tantrums, whining, running away. It was the only part of him he'd ever kept successfully. Days his mother typed accounts in a doctor's office; nights she went to school, dreaming vaguely of a softer future. As I grew to know Billy I would go over and meet her sometimes at the doctor's. She was a dark-haired, tired, cowering, rake-thin woman; I never got much of a feel for her. And somehow I never met Pete. I never went to their house, except once, at the end of my association with Billy; and I shall never return there.

Pete came on a motorcycle and took over their lives. He and Billy exchanged a single glance and understood each other to the core: enemy. But Pete was the stronger, physically anyway. He wielded his leather belt like a lion tamer in a circus. Nights, after it was over — and it almost always happened, every night — Billy went to his closet of a room and lay down choked with anger. He never tried to disguise his weals. He flaunted them in school, never offering any explanation for them. And no one dared ask him for one. They saw him shrouded in anger as in a burning forceshield, and they were afraid to touch his loneliness.

A night came when the anger burst at last. It was long past midnight and the pain had died down a little. Billy got out of bed, wriggled into some old cutoffs, pulled on a tee shirt, wincing as it raked against new welts. He tiptoed out of the house. He found his old bike leaning against the front door, and then he hiked like a maniac into the burning night. He did not know what drove him. A quick twisty path rounded some shadowy palms and crossed an empty highway and skirted the beach for some miles. It was a night without stars, the heat wringing moisture from the blackness. At first he heard the sea, but the surf-shatter faded quickly. In the distance rose a wall of luxury hotels, distant giant's tombstones. In a while he made a left turn into the town. He was not hiking with any particular purpose. It began to snow.

He didn't take it in at first. His anger was everything. But it didn't stop. Fragments of cold were pelting his face, and then great sheets of white, but Billy had never seen snow before, and he was too busy being angry to realize that this was a blizzard....

(I'll kill him! he was thinking, forcing the pedals against the ever-piling snow ...)

And then it thinned. He came to a stop, stuck against a rock or a drift. A dead, sourceless light played over vistas of whiteness. It didn't feel like the world at all. The snow didn't stop. Sometimes it tickled his face. Sometimes it swirled in the sky, its flakes like stars in a nebula. There was no sun or moon. Misty in the horizon, an impossibly far horizon, Billy saw white crenellated castle walls that ran behind a white hill and emerged from the other side of it; they went on as far as he could see, twisting like marble serpents. Billy began walking towards the hill. He did not wonder at where he was. The cold didn't touch him, not like sticking your hand in the freezer. He walked. By a strange foreshortening or trick of perspective he found himself facing the hill—

The hill's wings flapped, eyes flared briefly, fire-brilliant blue. It was a dragon. Again the eyes flared, dulled, flared, dulled ... Billy gazed at the dragon for a long time. In a rush that sent the wind sighing, the dragon spread its wings, sweeping the snow into fierce sudden flurries. Billy saw that the dragon had no scales but little mosaic-things of interlocking snowflakes; when the dragon's eyes flashed, the flakes caught rainbow fire and sparkled for a few seconds.

The dragon said, "Billy Binder, welcome to the fallen country."

Billy was afraid at last. "Send me home!" he cried. And then he remembered Pete and said nothing. When the dragon spoke, its voice was piping clear, emotionless, like the voice of a child's ghost. It wasn't a booming, threatening voice at all.

"What are you thinking?" he said. "That I don't sound fierce and threatening the way a dragon should? That I don't roar?" He did roar then, a tinny, buzzing roar like an electric alarm clock.

Billy said, "Who has stolen your roar?" He felt a twinge of pity for the dragon; but then his anger slapped it down.

"This is the fallen country. Billy. Here there is no emotion at all. We cannot love or hate. We cannot utter great thunderous cries of joy or terror...the world is muted by perpetual snow. That is why you are here."

"What do you mean?" Billy was scared and wanted to go back to his bike. He looked behind him and saw it, impossibly far away; it seemed strange that he could have walked this far, through the trudge-thick snowdrifts, in only a few minutes. Perhaps time was different here. He knew that time was different in different countries.

The dragon said, "You are here because you are full of anger, Billy Binder. In the fallen country we need such anger as yours. Anger is strength here ... if I could feel such anger, such love, such hatred as you can feel, I would die. Billy...."

Wrenching his feet out of the knee-deep coldless snow, Billy forced himself to walk toward the dragon. Even the dread he had been feeling had passed away now. "But who has done this to you? Who has stolen your feelings?"

"You know. You have touched his shadow. His shadow has come pursuing you. The Ringmaster. With his whip of burning cold."

Pete! "You should kill him!" Whiteness burned all around him, making the tears run.

"He cannot be killed. He slips from world to world as easily as you have done." Again the pitiful whinebuzz that passed for a roar. "But we can work against him. Slowly, slowly we can sap him of his strength. Your anger is powerful here. Your anger can build bridges, can burn pathways through the snow. Try it, Billy."

Billy clenched himself, feeling the rage course through him, and when he opened his eyes he saw greenery poking through the snow for a few seconds, but then it was misted over by white again."Do you see?" the dragon said. "You are Binder." "That's my name," said Billy, "but—"

"Your roots are in the fallen country. That is why you have never felt truly at home in your world, why you have been tossed from household to household, taking only the name Binder with you."

Thunder shuddered through the cloud-haze. For a moment the sky parted. A whip cracking, halving the sky, retracting into the grayness, a burst of sound that could have been applause or a circus band starting up or a crowd deriding a fallen clown
—

"Pete!" he blurted out.

"No," said the dragon, "only the shadow; the Ringmaster has a thousand shadows, and it is only a shadow of his shadow that has followed you all the way to your distant world."

Billy nodded, understanding suddenly.

Then he saw a red weal open on the dragon's neck, blood trickling in slow motion onto the snow, blood that stained the whiteness like a poppy-duster — "He's hurt you!" he said. They were akin then, he and this alien creature. Both were at the mercy of — "Can't you cry out?" he cried into the howling wind, "Can't you feel anything?"

"No." The dragon's voice did not change. "Here one need feel no pain at all. It's better to feel nothing; isn't it? Come now. Ride me."

He extended a wing; it fanned out into a diamond-speckled staircase. When Billy stepped onto it he realized that he felt no cold at all. He should be freezing to death through his worn sneakers, but he felt only numbness. It was less real than a dream.

"Let's go now. We'll have adventures, rescuing princesses, fighting monsters and such. Isn't that what every child wants to do? A lot of children find their way into the fallen country. And they find a use for themselves here ... one day we'll have a whole army of them."

"But I want to find the Ringmaster himself! I don't want him to hurt you and me anymore. I want to kill him."

The dragon only laughed; a wretched ghost of a laugh. Billy clambered up the wing.

"Every child who comes here dreams of reaching the Ringmaster. Of shaping his anger into a bridge that will touch the very heart of the Ringmaster and topple the circus where he wields his whip. They learn better, Billy."

"I want to kill him!"

Again a specter of a laugh. Billy settled on the dragon's back; it was ridged with soft dunes of snow. The dragon flapped his wings, not resoundingly, but with a thud like a cellar door slamming shut in a next-door house.

The dragon said, "You'll never need to cry again, Billy. From now on you will have to save your grief, your anger, save it for here where it will be of some use. Listen! I am the Snow Dragon, the last surviving dragon of the fallen country. I survived by purging myself of all that made me dragon: my fire, my rage, my iridescent, sparkle-flashing scales that gleamed silver in the moon and gold in the sun. Now sun and moon are gone. And I have

waited for a thousand years, so long that I have lost
the capacity to feel any joy at your coming... I, me
Snow Dragon, tell you to dry your tears for the last
time. Promise me."

"I promise."   Billy found himself acceding, on
impulse, without thinking it out. Already his eyes
felt drained. Only the melting snowflakes
moistened his cheeks. He felt no motion, but saw
the ground fall from the dragon's claws. They were
rising.

They flew through snowstorms into landscapes
overcast and lightly puffed with snow. Here and
there the outlines of castles, here and there a spire
poking through the whiteness. There were oceans
frosted with vanilla icing. There were cities full of
silent people, trudging listlessly, never pausing to
watch the dragon swooping in the sky, never lifting
their glazed-dead eyes from the snow. At times the
sky opened, the whip cracked once, twice,
thunderclap-swift,   raising fresh welts in the
dragon's hide. They flew on; and the Snow Dragon
never seemed to notice the Ringmaster's capricious
punishments.

"Do you still want to kill him?" said the dragon.
The air streamed past Billy's face, and yet he felt
nothing, as though he carried around him a bubble
of utter stillness. "After what you've seen he can do
—"

"Yes! Yes!" Billy cried fiercely. Anger pounded
inside him. "I see what I have to do now; I see why I
was brought here!" And he closed his eyes, thinking
of the bridge of anger. And again and again the
lightning-whip cracked. Although he didn't feel its
wetness he saw he was sitting in a pool of
congealing blood. Dragon's blood. Purple, smoking
in the chill air.

I pushed myself into a nice, controlled, professional posture. "I liked your story," I said, noting from the silence through the window that the forty-five minutes were over.

How can he sit there and spin such a haunting w e b of dreams — I was shivering in my chair. So was Billy, as though from terrible cold. I thought, He has plucked, out of the septic tank of the human unconscious, an image of such precision, such startling profundity, an image of the dark country we all carry inside us ... I checked myself, knowing I was beginning to sound like a pretentious academic paper. Get a grip on yourself.

"Billy," I said, trying to gauge my tone, to show just the right blend of concern and unconcern. His story cried out for involvement, for belief, the way poetry does even when it lies. But my job was not to sit back and revel in the mystery and the beauty of his delusions. It was to help him find reality ... to shatter the crystal goblet with my sledgehammer of platitudes. "I liked it," I repeated-

"It wasn't a story." "Of course not."

Pause. "See you next week," I tried a noncommittal half-smile.

"Sure," And suddenly he was gone, leaving me alone to hunt for shadows in the shadowless sunshine.

The following week, Billy said, "I wait until it builds up, until I can't stand it any more. And then it bursts out of me and I'm free to enter the fallen country. And afterwards, I find myself in bed or maybe in some strange place, and sometimes I'll be blue with cold and my joints will feel like icicles and I'll be shaking all over ..." I found the mother, Joan, at a desk in an office in a huge building, coffined in by expanses of naked glass, always reaching for the phone.

I said, "You know there's at least one way of ending the problem, don't you?"

She said, "Yes." When she looked at me she reminded me of myself, and I was unnerved by this. She was a dark-haired, slight woman, who didn't look like Billy at all — well, that was only to be expected. Unlike her stepson, she did not hide her feelings well. I saw her guilt very clearly.

I said, "Then why don't you get rid of the man?"

She paused to take an appointment A crisp, mediciny odour wisped by for a moment. Outside, palm-fringed concrete paths criss-crossed a carpet of harsh, brash green. But I was thinking of snow, of cold, numbing snow. Finally she answered me, speaking with difficulty.

"I can't, I can't!" She was crying a little, and I found myself turning away, embarrassed- "What can I do, Mrs. Marx? He's a force, not a person — he's not human. And what about Billy's lies? Will they suddenly end?"

"By imagining that Pete is not human." I said cruelly, "you make it a lot easier on yourself, don't you?" Mustn't lose control...

Feeling very foolish, I turned around and walked out. I don't know what I was trying to accomplish. All I knew was that I was well past my good years, and that I longed for the snow, for the fallen country that we all keep locked in our hearts. I wanted to be like Billy. I was looking forward to his next appointment, even as I felt guilty, because I had been spying on another's pain.

Then there were the princesses: some were in dungeons, buried neck-deep in the snow; others were chained in the topmost turrets of candy cane castles of intertwisting tourmaline and olivine, half-veiled by the clinging whiteness.

Billy saved a princess the second or third time he came to the fallen country.

They were swooping down from where the sun should have shone, and Billy saw the castle, a forest of ice-caked spires, mist-shrouded, dull grey in the unchanging cold light of the fallen country.

"Time to rescue a princess!" said the dragon.

They circled the tower, for a minute Billy reveled in the rushing of the wing-made wind. The dragon's flight was a dance that almost seemed like joy. But when Billy asked the dragon, "Are you happy, Snow Dragon? Has my coming done this to you, then?" the dragon's swooping seemed to lose its passion.

The dragon said, "Now, Billy, isn't rescuing princesses one of the oldest compulsions of your world? Isn't it what every earth creature longs to do?"

"I wouldn't know," said Billy, who didn't always do too well in school, and did not know of such things as myths. "Where's the princess?"

"In the castle, of course. And now—" they were skimming the turret's edge, almost, and the windrush had become still — "you must do what you know best how to do."

"I don't know what you mean!" "Your anger, Billy ..."

And Billy understood, then, what he was capable of doing. He took the anger inside him, he thought of Pete and of terrible nights lying awake and burning for vengeance, he concentrated all this anger until it took shape, took form... a bridge sprang up where the dragon had hovered, clawing the emptiness — a bridge of thin ice, as though someone had sliced up a skating rink and slung it into the sky. The bridge ran all the way to a round window, gaping with serrations like a monster's mouth, at the top of the tower. Billy sprang lightly from the dragon's back. He looked down for a moment, thinking I should be scared but I'm not, I'm too angry.

Beneath him the whiteness stretched limitlessly. He could not be scared; you could not gauge the distance of things at all, the ground seemed cushiony-soft, not a death-trap at all. He took a couple of steps on the bridge. It was slippery. He looked at the dark yawning jaws of the window, feeling no fear, fuelled instead by his terrible anger, and he began walking.

He leapt gingerly from the bridge into the room; he expected it to be dark but it was lit by the same depressing sourceless light mat illuminated the world outside. The princess was-chained to the wall. He closed his eyes and shattered the chains with a swift spurt of anger, and the princess came towards him. She was a typical blonde, boyish, unvoluptuous princess like the ones in Disney cartoons, with kohl-darkened eyelashes fluttering over expressionless glittering eyes that seemed almost faceted like an insect's. She did not smile, but walked towards him stiffly and thanked him.

"That's all I get?" he said.

"What did you expect?" said the princess. Her voice was like the dragon's voice: thin, toneless, uninterested.

"But I expected—"

The princess laughed. "Expected what? Something strange and beautiful and romantic? How can that be, with him up there, watching, watching? He'll catch me again, don't you fret."

"I want to kill him."

"I know you want to kill him," the princess said, seeming to read his mind. "But you won't, you know. He is more real than you will ever be."

And then she stepped out of the window and left him stranded; for the bridge was gone, melted into the air. And it was because he had lain aside his anger for a moment.

"That's how I ended up on top of the church," Billy told me. But how could I believe such a thing? And yet it was so neat, so cleverly paradigmaticized. That the real world and the fantasy should have such interfaces of confluence: the church, the castle. Piety and passion, authority and rebellion, father-shadow and princess-anima, superego and id. An amateur analyst's dream.

I said to Billy, "Let's work together now, you and I. Let's come out of the fallen country into the real world, let's fight this inner grief of yours." The words sounded so false. They were false.

"You know what he told me?" said Billy. "The Snow Dragon, I mean."

"What?"

"He told me that I would never have to leave if I didn't want to."

That bastard Pete! But it's people like him who pay my rent. I too am a vampire, feeding myself on children's emotions. Would Billy understand, if I told him, how we all have a piece of Pete inside us?

Billy said, "Our time's up, Mrs. Marx."

"Wait a moment—" I had no business going on longer than the allotted time. "Billy, won't you stop and just let me help?"

He paused at the door. We confronted each other for a moment, an innocent child who daily harrowed hell and a middle-aged, middle-class, middle-grade counsellor jaded with trivialities who must supposedly know all the answers.

His face was trusting. He was a pathological liar, a liar of frightening vividness, but all I saw was a frightened kid who yearned for something I did not have to give. He said, "How can I let you help me if you won't even believe me?"

I said — I couldn't lie, even to reassure him — "No, I don't believe you." "But until you believe me, Mrs. Marx, we'll never get anywhere."

To my surprise I found myself longing to agree with him.

When I looked up he was gone. I saw that carefully, methodically, I had been shredding his file with my fingernails. Hating the sunlight, I found myself walking through the schoolyard, wishing it would snow.

I live in a luxury condominium — there are dozens such in our town — where children cannot come. There the old people hide. There I am protected from the nightmares that I must face every day.

Usually I do not remember any dreams; but that night — the fourth week of Billy's visits with me — I do remember things: dragons' wings, leathery, hung with icicles — Did my father ever beat me? I couldn't even remember, damn it!

Waking up. Outside — a hurricane building up? Beating of giant wings?

I sat up on the bed. Through the mosquito netting of the open window I heard night-sounds, insects, the ocean hidden by a dozen Hiltons and Ramada Inns. I thought of calling Pop, whom I hadn't thought about in years, but I knew it was too late to patch up my life now—

There was a knock on the door.

Not the buzzer, not the little loudspeaker I use to force strangers to admit that they came in peace. I did not move. It came again, and then that voice, that heart-wringing voice: "I'm cold, Mrs. Marx."

Children may not enter this domain.

How had he gotten past security? Unless he had just materialized, like in his stories... I pulled on a bathrobe and went, through the dusty little living room, to the door, opened it—

He collapsed into my arms. It was like...when I was a kid, hugging a snowman. "For God's sake, Billy."

"I killed a monster today!" His voice frail, defiant. "But now I'm ready for him." "Don't try to attack Pete, he's too strong for you—"

"Pete? Screw Pete. I mean him."

He's going into fugue. Got to keep him here, got to keep him warm, or God knows what he'll try— "Look at me, you bitch!" He ripped his tee shirt open. I saw blood. I saw scars. I saw blue bruises.

Red, white and blue, like the goddamn American flag. But his eyes were dry. And blazing. "Now try to believe. You're all I have, Mrs. Marx. I'm going back like me Snow Dragon says, maybe forever. Or until I kill the Ringmaster."

"No!" I tried to hold on to him, but he twisted away from me. Somehow he had warmed up, as though the very fever of his anger could melt away the cold. I knew how unbearable the real world was, I knew the cold hard beauty of his imaginary one, but I couldn't let him run away from reality, I couldn't let him hide inside himself, I was conditioned to helping the children face the truth —

"Believe me!" he shouted. "Come with me!"

Grasping at straws, "All right, all right!" Quickly I was pulling on an old dress, not caring that he could see my sagging breasts — we had come too close for modesty now — I was shepherding him out of the door, down the steps, into the car, thinking Hospital, doctor, shrink, anything, just anything ...

I am ashamed to admit that I was also afraid that seeing me walking through the condo grounds at midnight would jeopardize my rental agreement, would force me out of my own fallen country.

As we pulled out onto the highway, it began to snow-

I panicked, fumbling for the wipers. Billy watched me solemnly, with a kind of I-told-you-so superiority. The snow grew from powder-fluffy to blizzard sheets; I stomped on the accelerator and slithered, I couldn't see the road at all.

"I knew it," Billy was saying softly. "I knew you had it in you to come with me."

He understands, I thought suddenly. About my secret fears, about the pain I think I hide so successfully. And all the while I thought I was taking the lead. We ploughed through the thick whiteness, until—

I stalled out. I pushed hard on the door handle, cursing old clunkers. When I got the door open the snow flew in, whipping my face and flooding the car floor with chalky ice.

"Out of the car now," Billy said.

"We'll freeze!" I didn't want to lose control of the fantasy, didn't want to relinquish myself into the hands of a demented kid.

"No we won't," he said firmly. He scooted over me, a bony bread crust of a boy, and then he was walking out into the billowing whiteness, was striding, oblivious to the cold, had become a grey shadow ghost streaked with white.

I tried to remember the things he'd told me. Be angry! I told myself - Anger will warm you.

Why didn't I wrench myself away? Why didn't I think I was going mad? I must have known all along, the realness of Billy's fantasy must have touched me all along....

I followed the kid cautiously. Soon I too felt nothing. The wind lashed my face and I could have been in a shopping mall buying shoes. I called out the kid's name but he was too intent to answer. I fell into the fallen country's strange detachment; it lured me, it drugged my pain, I knew that I could live there forever.

The snow whirled around me and I saw nothing but eye-smarting toothpaste commercial dazzle-white, and then, through the burning white, two pinpoints of blue fire.

The Snow Dragon!

The storm subsided a little. There he hovered. I watched him, believing in him completely. The wings were not leathery - my nightmares had lied to me — but like a thousand layers of crystal-stitched gauze. He landed, shook a snowdrift from his back — whiteness peppering whiteness — and I saw the sky open and the whip crack and I saw the blood trickle down him, and he did not even tense in pain. I called his name, "Snow Dragon."

"You have brought another one?" The dragon spoke only to Billy. I was here only as an observer, then.

"She's been hurt, too, Snow Dragon! Only she doesn't see it; sometimes she hides it too well."

"You are back too soon. Something is wrong with things. The fallen country is all disordered." "This time I've come to kill him!"

"You cannot kill him." He sounded resigned. "You haven't energy enough." "I am energy enough! She's seen! She can tell you!"

The dragon seemed not to hear. The wing came down; lashing the snow and making it dance for a moment. Without hesitating Billy leapt up. I followed, searching in vain for my fear.

And then we broke through the thick mist, and still there was no sunlight, only a kind of grey clarity in the air. I sat hunched into a ridge on the dragon's spine, my shapeless blotchy dress fluttering a little. I saw the castles blanketed with white; I saw the distant ice-sea, the snow-forts ringing the snow-hills.

"My bridge of anger," Billy said. His voice did not waver. The dragon circled slowly, I felt the kind of unease you feel on a plane in a holding pattern, but only for a second; then I felt nothing again. It was good to feel nothing.

Billy stood. The dragon braked in mid-air, an eerie, weightless feeling. And then Billy began to dream his bridge into being.

At first nothing. Then the whip, cracking in the sky, over and over, the dragon shivering himself into stillness as though concentrating the pain deep inside himself, and I was sitting in fast-hardening purple blood, and the dragon's breath came harder, clouding the chill wind- And as the cloud cleared I saw that a bridge was growing in the air, a suspension bridge with great columns of ice sprouting up from the mistiness below, pathway of living ice, thrusting in a rainbow-curve across the sky, reaching for the crack in the sky where the whip still cracked, from which great thunder-howls of laughter burst forth now, shrieks of a blood-lusty crowd.

The bridge hung there. Girders, rainbow-fringed from the sourceless light, a boy-wide road that thinned in the distance into a point.

"Your anger," the dragon said, "you are exhausting your anger, see, it will soon be gone, Billy Binder."

"Never!" the boy cried resolutely. "Only when he dies, that'll kill my anger, only that." He stepped out onto the ice. Again I felt a second's anxiety, and then the fallen country's spell drug-dragged it from me.

"Let me come too!" I yelled after him. Already he was tiny in the distance. Space and time seemed to work differently in this country. An adventuress now, this old woman who had made nothing of her life, I ran after him, my low-heels clicking like castanets on the thin ice. I had to be with him. I was angry too, angry because of all the times I'd listened to the kids and done nothing while they bawled their guts out onto the floor of my little office - I was going to kill one child abuser in my lifetime! I was going to crush this dream-Pete that Billy had created, to throttle him to death with my twenty years of rage! Already I felt my fury fuelling the bridge, making it firmer, easier to run on.

I was getting tired fast. But Billy still ran ahead, relentless as a wind. With a burst of anger I caught up with him, we ran neck and neck for a moment, and I saw that he wasn't even tired yet, and I knew I was wrong to think I could help or that I had anger enough in me — I who had never been hurt like that, who experienced the hurt only vicariously.

The bridge soared up, steep in the strange foreshortening, and now even Billy was gasping. Then I was lurching forward, seeing the bridge telescope contact between my eyes, seeing the splitting sky.

A circus tent now, walls of flapping canvas painted sun moon stars shivering sheep-cloudlets,

floors of mist-steaming packed snow, countless rings where bone-bare children leapt through fire-hoops, their faces tense with terror, frightened seals with planets whirling on their noses, scared to drop them, elephants trampling with earthquake feet, toppling skyscraper building-blocks, trumpeting thunderstorms....

I stood there, panting, exhausted, couldn't take anything in. But Billy ... he strode through the chaos, single-minded, seeking the centre of things. And then I saw him, a little man with a whip, and he was dancing as he waved the whip, his eyes were as cold and expressionless as tundra-snow that has never thawed. And I knew his face. My face, Pete's face, even Billy's face, a template of human faces, always changing. I even saw Pop. I swear it, even Pop - Pop whom I couldn't remember beating me, until tonight.

The Ringmaster bowed to the audience. The cacklebuzz that had been a constant background, soft-brush percussion to the raucous band music, died down. He spoke very quietly. I recognized a little of Snow Dragon in his voice, and I was chilled by it.

The Ringmaster stepped out of his ring. He advanced towards Billy; again I saw that I was being ignored, that I was a watcher in another's confrontation, that I might as well have been sitting at the desk in the office listening to the screaming children in the yard.

The Ringmaster cracked his whip. Once. Worlds whirled! Children leapt! Blood spattered the sand! And then, like clockwork winding down, they sank into slow motion.

"You came, Billy Binder," said the Ringmaster. "I've been expecting you."

"You bastard!" Billy cried. "But I'm strong enough to get you!" Laughter echoed from the stands; I spun round to watch, and I saw that they all had his face, his face that was also mine and Billy's and Pop's and everyone else's and they all laughed in unison, as though animated by a single hand.

"So come and get me!"

Billy reached out with his rage, a fireball burning tracks in the snow. I saw grass for a split second. "You've got it all wrong!" the Ringmaster said. "You haven't come here to kill me at all! I sent for you. I bred you to be another shadow, another Ringmaster even — that's how you were able to find me. I granted you this gift of anger so you could build a way to me."

"No!" he shrieked.

"A shadow of my shadow," said the Ringmaster, raising his whip but never his voice, "You too are to become a shadow of my shadow, like Pete, like all the others.

"Billy, Billy ..." the Ringmaster said. "You could be just like me, I have no pain, I only give pain now; I've been freed ... Hate me, Billy. Hate me! Your anger only makes me greater, only binds you more to me! For you are my son, Billy Binder, be free, Billy, be free, like me."

Billy stood, catapulting firedarts of anger, and the Ringmaster absorbed them all and grew tall, and snow-tempests swept around him, blurring him. Once I tried to step in, to add to Billy's store of rage, but I was frozen to the floor of snow.

The Ringmaster went on, "Oh, Billy, how can you turn your back on this? We are alike, you and I. You too can wield the whip and make a thousand universes dance with pain, and never feel the pain yourself."

"I'll never be like you! Never, never, never—" Billy screamed, and then I saw a final blast of rage explode from him and the canvas wall split open for a moment and I saw for an instant another whip, and another face of another Ringmaster up in the sky above us, and behind him another and another.

Then I looked at Billy, saw him shrunken, spent, the anger burned from him. I looked at the Ringmaster, panicking, thinking: We're stranded here now, we'll never get back to the real world; we'll stay and rescue princesses and fight monsters and see the princesses get recaptured and the monsters get reborn, for ever and ever.

I began to yell hysterically at the Ringmaster. He stood for everything I'd ever been angry about. I shouted: "I hate you! There's no reason for you to be; you're senseless, you screw up the whole universe!"

But Billy said, very quietly, "I don't have any anger left." And the Ringmaster's face grew pale, and he said, "But you must hate me! I bred you to hate me! I followed you and beat me hatred into you ..."

Billy turned and spoke to me at last. "Don't you see?" he said, "I could have been like that, He's not the real Ringmaster at all. You glimpsed it, didn't you? I was so angry that I opened up ... another country, the fallen country behind the fallen country, and I saw that the Ringmaster was only a shadow himself, that he danced to the whip of a higher ringmaster... How can I hate him?"

"Don't..." the Ringmaster said. I saw anguish cross his face for the first time. Or maybe I was just imagining it. It was only for a second.

Deliberately, quietly, Billy turned his back on him.

I followed the boy like an idiot. The dragon waited by the bridge, the bridge was already dissipating into mist; the dismal, cold light was brightening into sunlight, and— by the car, patches of green.

Billy said to the dragon, "It's true, isn't it? What he said. That he's my father."

The dragon said nothing. I knew, though, that he did not disagree. And then Billy said, "It's strange, isn't it, how he plants in all his kids a little shred of something ... that could destroy him, like he was dancing for his Ringmaster and secretly working to sabotage him at the same time."

The dragon said, "I too am part of the shadow, Billy, the part that seeks the shadow's own death, the left hand that does what the right hand dares not know about. You have killed us both: him by your compassion, me by compelling me to feel love for you ...

"The snow is melting. The fallen country will be closed to you now." He did not speak again, but uttered a roar that rent the sky as sunlight broke the cloud-veils, a cry both of heartache and of joy, and he spread his wings and soared upwards with a heart-stopping whistle-rush of wind.

And then he was gone, disintegrated like a windgust, like a dream, like a half-stirred memory. There was the car. I drove like a madwoman, churning up snow, bursting suddenly into the known world of concrete roads and forests of hotels and condominiums bleached lifeless by loneliness —

Police sirens! Lights! "The house!" Billy cried. We rounded a turn, he sprang out and sprinted towards the house, red blur of revolving sirens everywhere, swirling ... We watched, silently. They brought Joan out, shaking, and then a stretcher, a covered one, I heard the onlookers muttering, looking curiously at Billy, avoiding his eyes, heard them say how Pete had gone crazy and just gone and crashed his motorbike into the house.

"I killed him," Billy said softly, for me alone. And I believed him. For he had found the way into Pete's soul, and in understanding it, in giving it peace, had destroyed it. The inner and outer worlds are congruent in a thousand places. Wherever we stand, we are within a hair's breadth of the fallen country.

Billy had understood things which I had never understood, I, whose job was understanding. I'd been so sure of myself, coaxing traumas out of children, beating on their little minds until they danced out their pain for me in my office- But where was my peace? My suffering was trivial, and so was my reward — to be beset by little things only, to be a watcher, not one who can compress the shadow-substance of her dreams until they become diamond-hard, like truth. I moved closer to him, trying irrationally to shield him from the screaming sirens. Quietly, but openly, without shame, he had begun to cry.

If only we could wear our griefs as lightly as the snow wears the sneaker prints of children's dreams.

I went closer to him, almost touching him now, and began to do what I am trained to do. At first no words would come. Damn it, Dora Marx, I thought — Who has stolen your roar? I groped—

"Sure," I murmured. "Sure." I wondered if he would flinch if I tried to hug him.

PART TWO
THE NOVEL

Chapter One
The Steeple

Billy Binder and Charley Moore lived in the same town and went to the same school and played in the same concrete schoolyard under the same sun. But they didn't come from the same world. Charley's world was the one most of us think of as normal: a world of friends, of occasional quarrels with parents; of dreams about beaches and cars and money and girls. Billy's world was cold and terrifying. He wished he could fall off the edge of the world into another country. One day he did just that. It could have been called madness; it could have been called magic. Billy called it the Fallen Country.

And though they lived in the same town and went to the same school and played in the same schoolyard under the same relentless Florida sun, it was in that other country that Billy Binder and Charley Moore were destined to meet.

There's an old church in Boca Blanca, built more than four hundred years ago by the Spanish. It's the Church of the Sacred Something-or-other. No one ever pays much attention to it, although it is the only tourist attraction here, and not much of one since about ten years ago. That's when they built the turnpike and passed the town by. After that, as far as the rest of the world was concerned, it didn't exist. It was just the kind of town where you'd expect a kid like Billy Binder to end up.

Charley Moore saw him first. It was the day that began with doing the worst thing he'd ever done in his life. He and some of his friends were up in the old belfry where they shouldn't have been. They often came there, even during the week, after school. No one ever used this side of the church, and there was a back way up, a stinking, dank, winding stairwell. It was Sunday morning and their parents were socializing in the church hall. It was either stand around, slouching in the corner while the parents talked of their plumbing or their computers, or hang out in the street where the summer sun could get you. When tourists think of the South Florida sun they think of the winter sun, warm and comforting, an escape from their own gray winters. They don't know the off-season sun, sweltering and unpleasant.

Charley and his friends were crouching in one corner of the belfry, their arms against the cool stone. "It's so damn hot," Charley said. Because he was sixteen years old, the others stopped to listen to him. "I wish I was somewhere else, far away."

"Yeah." That was Walt Alvarez; a tall kid with his hair impeccably spiked. "Like maybe New York."

"Los Angeles."

"Paris." All the kids were chiming in now.

"I'd settle for Fort Lauderdale right now," Charley said. A palmetto bug crawled across his hand and he watched it idly. It gave him a dry tickling sensation. He wondered whether he ought to crush it. "But anyways I got something to like take our minds off the heat."

"And summer school," Walt said. "Summer school starts in a week."

"And our parents."

"And the fact that we're all broke." Charley liked it when they spoke one at a time like that, imitating him. That was all that could be said for younger kids, really. They knew when to be worshipful.

"And the heat." Charley reached into his cutoffs, fumbled, pulled out something, held it up for the others.

"Where'd you get *that?*" Walt said admiringly.

"I'm surprised you even recognize it," Charley said, brandishing a small bag of dope. "But since you ask . . . I met this really cool dude. In the mall. He showed me his bike. I got a good deal. His name's . . . Stark, I think. Just Stark. No first name, no last name." Charley didn't want to tell them how the man had hypnotized him almost. Something about his eyes . . . you couldn't resist him. He'd found himself reaching deep into his shorts pocket and pulling out the last five dollar bill and handing it to the man. Suddenly he wished the whole thing had never happened. But there he was and there were the other kids and he thought, "I'll look stupid if I don't go through with it."

"Does he go to our school? said Sean Gish. He was only thirteen but he always had more money than the others.

"School?" Charley said. "No, he ain't no kid, he must be like twenty-five, thirty. He told me he's a . . . a circus trainer."

"There's no circus in town." Walt seemed suspicious.

"No, he doesn't do it anymore, he told me." Charley said. "But he used to be. His kid goes to our school, he told me. He's got these weird eyes." That was as much as he was willing to say about the effect the man had had on him.

"He was just bullshittin' you. He's just a pusher," Walt said.

Charley didn't say anything. He just fished a matchbook out of his cutoffs and lit up, while the other boys stared at him in a mixture of awe and dismay. He took a deep drag and passed it on.

"I don't know," little Sean said.

Charley laughed at him. He knew Sean would succumb to him; everyone always did. Charley was a born leader even if he didn't always know the way. But in the end, though they were all giggling like elementary school kids, Charley felt dirty somehow, inside.

"But it's so damn hot!" Walt was saying between spasms of laughter. "Why are we doing this?"

"I can't breathe," little Sean said in a tiny voice.

Charley looked at his watch. "Time to cool it." He looked at his friends. Why did they have to act so hysterical? "Calm down, dudes!" he said. The uncomfortable feeling inside him was growing. Sean was still gagging. "Here. I'll drag him over to the window."

He lifted the young boy easily off the stone floor and half-carried him to the window which overlooked the roof. East, toward the sea, was the more modernized part of the church, with an odd-looking steeple they'd added in the nineteenth century which looked as if it had plucked from some completely different church and just planted there.

They were all groggy from the dope and they clustered around the window, clowning around and trying to get at the fresh air. It wasn't that fresh, though; it was oppressive and smelled of rotting fish. Charley was slightly high from the dope but it wasn't the great feeling he'd expected from what Stark had told him. He held Sean against the window and felt him coughing into the outside air.

As he stood there, he glanced idly at the ugly Victorian steeple.

"I'm seeing things," he said to himself.

"Seeing? What seeing?" Walt said, standing just behind him, not quite tall enough to see past Charley's head.

"Nothing. No, nothing." Maybe this was what getting high was all about? He blinked, rubbed his eyes, and looked again. It was still there.

It was snowing on the steeple.

"Lemme see," Walt said, elbowing him aside a little.

"Yeah." Charley stared. When he was a little kid he'd seen a cartoon like that . . . was it Bugs Bunny? . . . with a cloud hanging over his head, raining on him alone. That was what the steeple was like. And there came a sound from it too, a spooky whining.

Walt said, "I coulda sworn I saw—"

"What? What?" Charley said, almost hysterical for a moment.

"Nah. It's stopped now. But it looked kind of like a blizzard."

"Yeah. Right. Uh huh." Doubtful voices came from behind them.

And then Charley saw what the snow had left behind. "Wait a minute. There's a kid there. Look. Clinging to the steeple."

"That ain't no kid. Look, he's pale, marble maybe," Walt said. "Just one of the statues. That steeple's crammed with statues and stuff. See, it's got a pale blue face. People don't get to be that color unless—"

"Unless they're frozen," Charley said. "And look, you're wrong. That kid's wearing jeans and a tee shirt with holes in it."

For a long moment he gazed at it, not knowing what to do. At last he said, "We're gonna have to tell someone." It was there still, refusing to go away: a blue-white boy, hugging the stone and metal, not moving.

"You think he's dead?" little Sean said. "You think he's been up there, maybe, for days? Like murdered or something?"

"No. He just appeared. Just like that. In a snowstorm." Charley agonized for a few moments, then said, "I'm going downstairs to tell Father Santini."

The others stared at him in horror. Walt said, "But we've been smoking! They'll be able to tell. You know how parents are. We'll get in trouble if—"

"Kid's maybe dying, can't you see?" Charley said. They didn't answer. Now—as I had come to know over the last few years—Charley was really a good person at heart; he only played at being bad. So when he said, "All right. You guys slip away. I'll take the rap, or something. But I can't just do nothing."

The others slunk away. Charley feverishly gathered all traces of what they'd been doing, stuffed the evidence in his pocket, waited a moment, and followed them.

He found Father Santini coming out of the vestry. "Ah, Charley," the priest said, slightly bewildered to see the boy emerge from the wrong end of the building. "You have a problem?"

"Come on! There's something you've got to see."
He spoke with such urgency that the priest followed
him without hesitation. They stepped out onto the
lawn, into the blazing sun. "Look! Up there, stuck to
the steeple—"

"Is this one of your pranks? I don't see anything
except . . . wait a minute. But what could it be?"

"It's a boy, I'm telling you."

"How can you tell? You couldn't possibly tell
from down here. Unless you've been . . . upstairs . . .
have you?"

"Never mind," Charley said, hoping he could
wriggle out of that one later. As it happened, in the
excitement that ensued, he didn't have to.

When Father Santini had squinted at whatever it
was for long enough to determine that maybe he
should believe Charley after all, he went inside to call
the fire department. People were streaming out of
the church hall now; someone had been spreading
the word. They were standing, pointing, staring.
Charley thought of just getting into his car and
driving on home, but something compelled him to
stay on as the fire truck pulled up and firemen raced
up to the disused belfry and crawled painstakingly
along the shingles of the roof. After all, he thought,
maybe they'll think I'm some kind of hero because of
all this.

They brought the kid down on a stretcher.

Charley pushed forward through the crowd to get
a look. He saw his mother up ahead; she was
covering the eyes of his little cousin Stephanie. Was
the boy already dead then? Charley found himself
right next to the ambulance. The sun was so bright
you could hardly see the crimson lights flashing.
They were hauling in the stretcher now, and he saw
that Father Santini had come up to stand beside him.
The priest seemed, as always, distracted.

"Do you know him?" Father Santini said.

"I don't . . . wait a minute. He goes to our school, I think. I'm not sure about his name . . . wait, it's Binder, Billy Binder." He remembered it with startling clarity because he'd heard the name only that day. But he couldn't remember where.

For a second his hand brushed against something stone-cold, ice-hard. He snatched it away. "Frostbite," he heard someone say. "Impossible! It's ninety degrees out here," someone else said. "I tell you the kid was frozen solid," the first voice was insisting, "like one of those woolly mammoths you read about, in Siberia, you know."

Charley remembered that he and Walt had seen snow on the steeple earlier. I must be crazy, he thought.

"Excuse me," someone was saying, prodding him. He saw that it was a nurse. "Do you know who his next of kin are? Does he have insurance?"

"Yes," Father Santini said, "you know him, don't you."

It was then that Charley remembered, suddenly, where he'd heard the kid's name spoken.

("I got a kid in your school." A smooth voice that issued from a scarred face. The smell of leather and gasoline. "Billy Binder. He ain't my kid, though. I inherited him. You need drugs? I got good drugs: anything you need." The mall, empty, Saturday evening.) Charley said, "His father's name is Stark. He's a lion tamer or something."

Everyone seemed to be looking at him. The boy was half in, half out of the ambulance; Charley could still make out his face. It was still a little blue. Charley looked defensively at Father Santini and the others. "I don't really know him," he said lamely. "I just saw him, that's all. And I met his dad once."

But he suddenly knew that there was some kind of bond between him and the strange kid. Maybe it was because Charley had risked being caught to save him. Or maybe it was something to do with meeting his stepfather yesterday in the mall and hearing his name.

"Are you his friend?" the priest said. "Maybe you can think what we should do with him."

The ambulance was pulling out now, and the crowd was dissipating. He didn't answer Father Santini at first. He was thinking quite seriously about how Billy could be helped. He didn't know how he could have climbed up there by himself, didn't know how he could have gotten himself frozen solid like that. The snow had probably been just a hallucination; maybe there was something in the dope. But you had to have superhuman strength to get yourself in a position like that. And who had strength like that? Maybe if you were really angry. Or maybe if you were insane. A madman has the strength of ten, where'd he heard that before? "A shrink," he murmured.

"What's that?" Father Santini said. "Oh, a psychiatrist? Maybe they can't afford one."

"I know. He can go and see Dora. Dora will talk him out of it."

"Are you sure?" said the priest, who had misgivings about non-religious counsellors.

"Dora's helped me a lot," Charley said. He thought about the young counsellor, fresh out of college it seemed, who had turned up only a few months before, a sudden replacement for old Father Madigan who'd had a heart attack. She'd seemed so incongruous . . . like a spring breeze in a graveyard.

Father Santini sighed. "I suppose our Dora will have to do. He'll probably be out of commission for a day or two, but . . . when he comes back to school, do you think you can take him in to see her?"

"Sure," Charley said dubiously. Now that he brought up the idea he had to go through with it. Maybe it was a way of making up for the terrible thing he'd made the others do. He wished he could go back in a time machine and start the whole day again from scratch.

"I'll give you a note for his home room teacher."

"We don't have home rooms, Father . . . we're in high school, remember?" Charley and the others went to a small parochial school with junior and senior buildings on the same campus, affiliated with the church.

"Oh. Of course," said the priest. But he seemed already to be thinking about something else.

"I'll take him to see Dora then."

•••

The story about the kid frozen to the church steeple had made the front page of the Boca Blanca supplement to the <u>Post.</u> Even Charley's dad, whose breakfast conversation was generally confined to caveman-like grunts, looked up from the paper and asked Charley if he knew who the kid was.

"Yeah, for sure, I've seen him," Charley said. He was thinking about how he'd promised Father Santini that he would take the kid in to see Dora Marx. "Maybe he'll refuse to go," he thought. "Maybe it'll be really difficult." And Charley wasn't quite sure about just approaching him in the hallway. He was sure Billy wouldn't remember him; hadn't he been delirious with cold?

"You're quiet this morning," Charley's mother said.

"I'm thinking."

"That's a new one," his father said.

Charley thought, "At least I won't have to do it for a few days. He'll be in the hospital or something. I'll have plenty of time to think of some way of broaching the subject." He was starting to resent Father Santini for making him agree to do it.

Charley's mother said, "I think you should try to help him. There's got to be a reason behind all this. He must be really unhappy."

"Of course he's unhappy. His stepfather's a pusher," Charley said. "Anyway, what could I do for him? He's probably got a million problems. The counsellor can do it. It's her job."

"Do I detect certain lack of compassion in you, Charley?" his mother said. He realized she was only half kidding.

"I'll help him, I'll help him!" he said grudgingly. "But like, he's a nerd. It'll be embarrassing."

"But good for the soul," said his Dad's voice from behind the Post. The newspaper vibrated like a kazoo. Charley sighed. As if he didn't have problems of his own.

●●●

As it turned out, Billy was in school the very next morning.

At first, Charley didn't believe it was him. He walked right by him a couple of times. He was leaning against one of the lockers, a frail kid, stunted almost.

The third time Billy stopped him and said, "You're the one who saw me, aren't you?"

Charley was taken aback at being addressed directly by Billy. The kid was really small. He had to be a freshman, Charley thought. He said, looking around nervously to make sure his friends wouldn't see him talking to such a geek, "How could you be back in school already?   You should be in bed or something."

Billy said, "Did you see? Did you believe?"

Charley said, "What are you talking about?" He wished he hadn't bumped into Billy so soon. Somehow Billy made him feel uncomfortable. He didn't have any *give* in him. And he stared you down. Charley went on, "I still think you shouldn't have come in today."

Billy said, "I heal real quick."

Charley said, "How?"

"Dreams can fuel anger. And anger can make dreams real."

Charley was getting more and more perplexed. But he thought, "I might as well get this over with, so I can be rid of this kid and whatever his problem is." Aloud he said, "There's someone I have to take you to."

He waited, anticipating resistance.

But instead, Billy only said, "Oh, another counsellor. What the hell, I've seen it all." And he followed Charley meekly into Dora's office.

Chapter Two
Billy Binder

Billy wasn't too surprised at being dragged in to see another one of those counsellor types. It wasn't the first time it had happened to him. Sometimes it was his schoolwork, sometimes it was some kind of attitude problem. Charley knocked on the door marked "Ms. Marx" and charged in without waiting for a reply, shouting "Dora, Dora, it's him." And then he bolted. The thermometer on the wall read 90°F.

Billy thought, "I can dance rings around these people. I can play games with their heads. She'll never touch what's inside me, never, never. None of the others ever did." And he stood there, waiting for Ms. Marx to make the first move.

"Hi, Billy. You're back from the hospital already?"

("She's beautiful," he thought suddenly. "She's not old, not tired. She looks like she really might care." But he buried the thought deep in his mind. Under a snowdrift.)

"My mother works there. They had me checked out."

"Who?"

"Stark. And my mother."

Billy looked at her from across the desk. "I won't tell her a thing," he thought. He imagined the desk stretching on and on, like in those dreams where you're running down a corridor and you can never reach the end. He knew what she saw: a pale boy with blank, sky-blue eyes and confused blond hair. Small for his age, almost as though he'd willed himself not to grow.

She got up, closed the door behind him. His hand brushed against his. Damn it! Why did they always try to touch him? He flinched away violently as though he'd had an electric shock. He forced himself to smile, but when their eyes met, he knew that she knew. She *knew!* "She's got me pegged already," Billy thought. "Yet another victim of child abuse."

He sat down in the huge brown armchair that faced the desk.

"Hi, Billy. My name is Dora Marx. Most of the kids just call me Dora." Oh yes. Billy knew all about the ones who acted like they wanted to be your friend.

"I think I'd prefer Ms. Marx," he said. "But," he added, "you can call me Billy. If you like." Touché!

The air conditioning clunked. Billy felt a gust of warm, medicinal air in his face. "The heat can't touch me," he thought. In his heart he felt the wind from the Fallen Country, infinitely cold. Ms. Marx got up to slam out the noontime yelling from the schoolyard. (Again, Billy thought: "She's not cold inside like the others. Maybe she's the one I can tell." But he didn't want to let go of his secret yet. It had been part of him so long. He was afraid to be healed.)

"You're the one who—" she began.

"Yeah. They found me clinging to the steeple. Did you see it in the paper?"

She took a file from the desk and opened it. Billy could see she was trying to look casual. She took the clipping out. "Billy Binder, age fifteen . . . where'd you get that scar?"

"Fell off my bike," Billy lied.

"Was found half dead on the ledge—" she read from the <u>Post,</u> "his arms around the steeple on the side overlooking Angel Plaza. Father Santini, pastor, while trying to ring the bell—"

"That part's not true," Billy said. "Some kids were up in the belfry smoking dope. That's who noticed me for the first time."

"It says here you were suffering from severe frostbite."

"Yeah. From the snow." Billy wasn't going to give away anything, not anything.

"It doesn't snow in June in Florida."

"So I'm a liar," Billy said. That was the most important thing about these counsellors. They always thought you were lying. They even had a term for it. Pathological liar—someone who can't tell truth from fantasy.

Then she said, "How often do they beat you?"

(He thought: "I mustn't give myself away, no, not until I'm sure.") He forced himself to go dead, to appear infinitely cold. "I don't know," he said. "Every day, I guess."

"Who?"

"Stark."

"Who is Stark?"

"He is—" and Billy suddenly found himself blurting it out. "The Ringmaster. The Ruler. The Master of the Fallen Country." No! How could he have said those things? She was a stranger. The secret kingdom wasn't for her to know about. No. "Stick to the kind of things they like to write reports about," Billy told himself.

"Tell me," she said softly. She reached across the table. Her hand flicked across his. He flinched again.

He started to tell her about the beatings. ("She thinks I'm going to break down and start crying and then she'll comfort me and then I'll be cured," he thought. "But I'm not gonna break down. I'm gonna wear her out instead.") He started to catalog the beatings, the poundings, in cold clinical detail. Finally she held up her hand for him to stop. He felt that he'd won, in a way. Grownups were so predictable.

She said, "Doesn't it hurt you inside? Doesn't it make you cry?"

"Not anymore. You see, I promised."

"What do you mean, you promised?"

There it was again . . . he had almost given away the secret! Oh well. There was nothing wrong with tantalizing her with a few scraps. "The Snow Dragon," he said.

He looked straight into her eyes. What was she thinking? An imaginary companion, maybe? Of course Billy had had those . . . a long, long time ago. She said, "Tell me about him."

"I knew it!" he cried out. "You're supposed to like help me or something. But all you want to do is listen to me tell those lies. Then you'll smile and tell me how creative I am . . . but you'll try to pull me out of it into what you call the real world. But that's not the way it really is. You'll tell me it's my overactive imagination. I've been through it all before, I've been through real shrinks too. There's nothing new you can tell me."

"Is that why he hits you? Because of your lies?"

"Yes! Yes! But I won't stop!" He felt the great anger building up inside him. Could he trust her? Did he dare?

"It's all right," Ms. Marx said. "You can lie if you want. You can tell all the lies you want in this room. Nothing will ever escape from here."

It was only then that Billy realized how much he needed to tell someone. "Like a confessional? Like a black hole?" he said.

"Yeah," she said. "A black hole."

"That's a star that has collapsed into itself, I heard. Where gravity is so strong that not even light can escape. Where it's dark. Yeah. That's how I want it to be. Dark, dark, dark. And safe."

"Safe. That's how it'll be."

But he'd been promised that many times in his life. He couldn't just come out and tell her the big secret. Not yet.

"So what were you doing then, up there? Straddling the steeple, I mean."

Keep her guessing . . . "I was rescuing someone."

"Who?"

"I don't remember." He tried to make his eyes go completely dead, like the eyes of a zombie. "Oh, what the hell. A princess."

That was how he began telling Dora about the Fallen Country and the Snow Dragon, about the other kingdom he inhabited, his dark and terrifying vision. "If it disturbs you," he said, "you can pretend I'm making it up. You can file it away and look it up in psychology textbooks. Then you can some long word for whatever schizo . . . schizophr—"

"Schizophrenia," she whispered.

"If only she could see what I've seen," Billy thought. "But she doesn't. She's just listening to me because it's her job." He went on with the story of his life, but his mind was on something else altogether. He was thinking, "Maybe she's the one I'll finally get through to, maybe she's the one who will be with me at the very end of my quest."

He watched her; she was sweating away, even with the air conditioning going full blast. "But I'm not sweating at all," Billy thought. He rubbed his hands together and they were cool, like metal almost.

The reason was that they were in two different worlds. Dora sat in sweltering South Florida in the off-season; Billy in the feelingless cold of the Fallen Country.

Chapter Three
The Lion Tamer

Billy's journey to the Fallen Country had begun when he was only about seven years old. He had a completely different set of parents then, and they lived in a different small town. He couldn't remember exactly where it was, but from his description it had to be somewhere up north, maybe in upstate New York. Although he was only seven, he had already changed parents a couple of times. He couldn't even remember the first set, and he didn't know why he wasn't with them anymore, whether it was divorce or death. By the time he reached Boca Blanca he had been through a few more sets of parents.

If he had to say what those years had been like, he would have said only that it felt like floating . . . like not being anyplace at all. He had only one vivid memory from those early years. It was of meeting the lion tamer for the first time.

There was supposed to be a circus in town that week. And that was strange, because it was still winter. Maybe it hadn't really been winter, maybe which was just how Billy remembered it.

Billy walked home from school through the snow and turned on the television. He saw a commercial for the circus. There was a kid on a flying trapeze. He was soaring through the air, barely holding on. Then he let go! Billy was afraid he would fall, but no, he swung upward, tucked his body into a ball, somersaulted in the empty air . . . and then his arms flew out and the catcher caught him. It only lasted a few seconds. But for those moments Billy really wanted to be that kid, to feel those moments of fierce, ecstatic freedom. He poked at the TV, trying to get the scene to come back. But it didn't. Instead he saw the camera pan over the audience, rapt, cheering. And then he saw, through the tent flap, a view of the world outside the circus . . . sunlight. Trees. In the distance, a lake. Wind. He could almost feel it if he put his face against the television set. It was warm, and he wanted so much to be warm.

Then he heard a voiceover saying that the circus would be playing down at Karney Park. Billy knew where that was. It was only a few blocks away. Then the voice said that today was the last day. He just had to go. "Maybe," he thought, "if I go there I'll become like the kid in the commercial. And when I leave the tent, the sun will be shining."

But how could he get there? Getting there was the most important thing in the world right now. He knew that there was a $20 bill hidden in the remote control box of the TV set, in case of an emergency. He picked up the phone to call his Mom at work, but when it started to ring he got the feeling that she wouldn't think it was an emergency.

He went outside to see if any of his friends were there. But the street was empty, and none of the identical townhouses on the block showed any signs of activity. "They've probably all gone to the circus," Billy thought. "Except me."

Billy was the only latchkey kid on the block.

"I know!" he said. "I'll leave a note."

He found a screwdriver in the toolbox in the kitchen and opened up the TV controller. There it was, scrunched around some naked wire. He took it, uncreased it, and stuck it into his jeans.

Then he tore a page from his notebook and painstakingly scrawled out a letter to his mother:

Dear Mommy

I went to the
            Sircus.
                        Bill

He stuck it on the refrigerator with one of those magnet things, threw on his coat, and started walking down to Karney Park.

There wasn't much snow in the Park; most of it had been shoveled into dirty white heaps. There was the circus tent. It was bright green canvas, and a rainbow flag flew from the top, and there were pennants hanging all around it. There was a ticket booth converted from a pickup truck. He went and bought a ticket.

"Your parents say you could come?" said the vendor. He was an old guy with a patch over one eye.

Billy shrugged. "Yeah." He smiled and tried to look cute, the way you try to look when you want a grownup to give you your own way. It worked. He clutched the ticket in his hand.

"But the show isn't for another hour," the old man called after him.

"I'll just look around."

"Well, just don't bug anyone. Or I'll have to call your parents."

"Uh huh." Billy doubted that his parents would come, anyway.

He started walking around. There were some clowns. He watched them for a moment and laughed. He peeked into the circus tent but they wouldn't let him in yet. He saw a couple of people cleaning the aisles.

Then he sneaked around to the back of the big tent.

There were some trailers parked in the back. They were brightly colored; against the gray sky they almost hurt his eyes. There were also some cages, too. A growl. He jumped. It came from the cages.

He went over there. Most of the cages were covered. But there was one that you could look inside. It was all dark. He went up to it. The growl came again, closer now. There was a lion inside the cage. It was hard to see him, though. Billy had seen lions in cartoons. They were fierce. They prowled. They leaped. They roared. The lion in the cage wasn't like a real lion. He was huddled in one corner of the cage. His fur was wet and untidy. A rank smell of dung clung to Billy's nostrils.

He looked into the lion's eyes. There was a sound like an engine idling in the distance, and Billy knew that the lion was purring.

"Hi," he said. The lion looked curiously at him. "I'm real sorry you're in the cage. You want to be friends? You want to be . . . free?"

Suddenly Billy heard a loud banging noise from one of the trailers. He crouched down, pressing himself against one of the wheels of the cage. He heard footsteps in the slush, getting closer and closer. There was something absolutely terrifying about those steps.

He heard a kid's voice. "I won't go on!" The kid was crying.

"What do you mean?" A dark, angry voice. "It's just a sprained ankle. You don't do flying with your ankle, damn it! You'll go on."

"But—"

Billy heard a sharp, slicing sound. Like a whip whistling through the air and hitting flesh. The kid screamed. "Shut up!" The man said. "Or you'll get more. And more. And more." Billy couldn't move. He heard the whipping noise over and over. Each time the kid's scream grew fainter, as though he were losing the will to fight back. At last the screaming subsided into a soft sobbing. Then Billy heard the man go up the wooden steps into the cage, he had a glimpse of jeans and spurred boots as he went up. He heard the cage unlatch with a crash. Then he heard the whip crack again, directly over his head, and he heard the lion's paws pounding on the wooden floor as it sprang up to obey.

He couldn't stand it anymore. He straightened himself up and started to leave. Then he saw the other kid. They oractically collided into each other.

It was the kid in the circus commercial. He had seen him flying through the air . . . he had envied those moments of supreme freedom. Now he saw him, a little boy maybe a little older than himself. He stood in the slush, in the damp wind, with only a torn tee shirt on. A purple bruise ran down his cheek, down his neck. There was blood on the tee shirt. Billy could tell that it was fresh.

The kid didn't seem to see him at all. Billy looked at him for a long time. At last the kid said, "I'm gonna kill him. I'm just gonna kill him."

Billy didn't know what to do. He wanted to help the kid, but the kid didn't even know he was there. Finally Billy pulled out a grubby handkerchief from his pocket and handed it to the young circus flier, and he said, "Please don't cry. Here. Use my handkerchief."

The boy saw Billy now. He looked at him. He seemed embarrassed that he'd been caught crying. "Get out of my way, get lost," the boy said. Billy just stood there. The kid punched him in the chest. It was a feeble blow, more of a gesture than anything. Billy wasn't hurt.

Billy said, "Who are you? What's your name?"

The boy just stared at him.

"I'm Billy Binder."

"They have no names there!" the boy said. "No names! Not in the place you're going to."

"What do you mean? The circus?"

"No, stupid! The other place."

"I don't know what you're talking about."

The boy said, "When you get there, you'll know. But remember that this is where you started." He held out a hand, grubby, slender-fingered. "I'm sorry I hit you, brother."

"Brother?" Bewildered, Billy gave the other boy five and extended his own hand.

"Come as soon as you can," he heard the boy say, "I can't hold out much longer. It's too cold." The boy seemed to fade away, like a shadow into a flurry of snow.

"Come where?" Billy said. But he was talking to thin air.

•••

When Billy got around to the front of the circus again, he saw that people were starting to pour into the tent. He decided to go in. Maybe it would help make him forget about what he'd just seen.   He joined the crowd and the show started.

It wasn't that much of a circus. There were a few clowns and things, and a woman to turned cartwheels on the back of an elephant. Then there was a magician who pulled colored handkerchiefs out of the air, and a couple of jugglers who would juggle anything the audience threw at them. They started to throw the wildest things. At the end they were juggling a rubber chicken, a pocket stereo, and a bra that had been rolled into a ball. Billy started laughing hysterically. At last he was having a good time.

Then it was time for the lions. The steel gratings were lowered into the ring. Then, about a half dozen lions and tigers entered. They seemed gloomy. They didn't roar. They didn't seem fierce at all.

"The greatest lion tamer in the world!" said the announcer. "Stark the Terrible!" And a man, dressed entirely in black, stalked into the ring. He cracked his whip. The big cats trotted around the ring. The audience applauded. But Billy didn't. He knew who that man was.

The man looked up. It seemed to Billy that the man knew he was there, in the audience. That he was seeking him out. Billy tried to push himself lower down on the bench, to hide behind the people in front of him.

"Scaredy-cat!" A voice behind him. He whirled around. He recognized the kid; it was one of the Sullivan kids who lived across the street. Billy didn't know them too well—he didn't know anyone too well.   But he thought of them as friends, or almost friends. He didn't want to look chicken in front of them, so he forced himself to look, peering between the shoulders of the adults who sat in front. All he saw was the whip flying, and now and then the brown body of a mangy lion. "Stop!" he said softly, "stop, stop." For a moment he almost thought it was him down there, he could almost feel the sting of the whip.

Then there was only one lion . . . it was the lion he had seen in the cage. He sat up and watched him move, circling the ring, warily eyeing the lion tamer. There was a hoop of fire on a metal stand. The lion tamer cracked his whip again and again. Billy could see that the lion was afraid. He saw that the whip was going to hit the lion's flanks, and he squeezed his eyes tight shut. He just couldn't look. He heard the audience murmur, and then burst into a deafening roar of applause. He looked again. He saw the lion circling . . . a small red welt on his side . . . "I'm gonna kill you!" Billy whispered fiercely. They had been the words of the young circus flier.

He couldn't stand it anymore. He got up and started to leave, elbowing his way down the narrow aisle toward the exit.

As he reached it, he heard the circus band blaring. The lions' act was over. He heard the shuffling and clanking as the railings were taken down. Wild applause now. He turned. Everyone was looking up. Billy did too. "And now," the announcer said, "direct from Romania . . . the Flying Andrescu family!" He saw a man and a woman climbing the rope ladder toward the roof of the tent. He saw the net being lowered into place. The young boy followed them up the ladder, moving slowly. But no one seemed to notice that he was hurt. Only Billy knew.

The fliers reached the top and launched into their act. At last the boy took off, swinging back and forth . . . then he let go, twisted himself into a knot of energy, exploded into the curve of falling . . . it was so beautiful that Billy was transfixed. And then he saw the boy's face, which had last seen contorted in anger and hurt. There was no pain in it at all. There wasn't any kind of emotion. Where had it all gone? Billy stared into the kid's eyes and saw utter emptiness.

And Billy longed to be like that, to be able to change pain into something beautiful. He watched the kid fall slowly into the net, a time that seemed forever. Then he walked out into the freezing air, astonished for a moment that it was not warm and green outside like it'd been in the TV commercial.

He saw a car pull in. His parents. There was going to be trouble. His Mom opened the door and came toward him. "Mom!" he cried.

"Just what do you think you're—" his mother began.

Just then the show ended and people began pouring out. His mother seemed confused for a moment. Billy wondered how he was going to get out of this fix. He saw the Sullivan kids emerging from the tent, and their mother with them. He waved frantically to them.

"Oh," his mother said. "I didn't realize you'd gone with the Sullivans. For a moment I thought you'd run off by yourself! Silly me. Why didn't you call me? You got me all worried." Billy heaved a sigh of relief. "Well, come along now. Oh, you can say goodbye to the Sullivans first, if you want."

"That's okay, Mom," Billy said, and followed her obediently to the car.

•••

As he went to bed, it suddenly occurred to him that his mother hadn't even asked him whether he had enjoyed the circus. He lay awake half the night thinking about the lion tamer and the circus flier.

Around midnight or so he heard voices. They were fighting again; he didn't know what about, but it was almost always about something stupid.

"I think I'll count lions this time," he thought.

He imagined lions: sleek, tawny, strong-smelling, leaping through a hoop of fire. What was behind the circle of flame? Perhaps it was another country, where the lions would feel no more pain.

His parents' voices shattered his not-quite-dreaming. Years later he would be unable to remember those parents' faces or even their names. But he would never forget their voices, shrill in the darkness.

Lately, the fights had been getting longer and louder than before, and Billy realized that things were probably going to come to some kind of crisis. "I'd better stop thinking about my parents," he told himself as he drifted into sleep.

He knew that he'd be getting new ones soon.

Chapter Four
Charley Moore

After taking Billy in to see Dora, Charley tried to forget about the time he'd seen him on the steeple. It made him nervous just thinking about it. Now and then Charley would see Billy in the hall, but he avoided him. They didn't hang out with the same crowd. In fact, he didn't think Billy hung out with anyone at all. Charley never saw him at the mall, for instance, where on a good day you could catch pretty much everyone you needed to see. Charley was getting more wary of the mall these days, because now and then you could see Stark there, and Stark was bad news.

The mall was a good place to go because you could generally rely on the air-conditioning. But today it wasn't working that well; the outside heat seeped in even though it was going full blast. It wasn't much of a mall, really, just one corridor of boutiques with a department store on each end. Charley and Walt and a couple of others—and Sean, when his parents let him—would usually hit the mall after school. There was a video arcade where half the machines were always out of order, an oriental knickknack store where you could gaze longingly at throwing stars and ninja outfits, and a movie house with six tiny tube theaters where you were always blasted by the soundtrack of the next movie. There was also a bookstore with a large selection of fantasy roleplaying aids. That was where they were at that very moment. Some of them were leafing through the latest issue of a gaming magazine. Charley was standing a little apart from the others when he saw Dora Marx peering into the front of the bookstore.

He said, "Hey, you guys. Dora's here."

The others looked up. Sean said, "Huh? Are we in trouble?"

Charley said, "Of course not. Wait. She's waving at me. Let me go and see if she wants something." She came into the bookstore. Charley said, "I think I know what this is all about." Before Dora could open her mouth, he said, "I guess you want me to help him, right, Dora?"

She said, "How did you know?"

"Just a hunch," he said, and frowned. "My parents said the same thing. You figured out what's with him?"

She said, "Sometimes, when things around you get really bad, do you wish you were somewhere else?"

"I guess so."

"Well, things are really bad with Billy," she said. "And he's started to wish so hard that . . . well, maybe he think that somewhere else is really coming into being . . . he's wishing himself into another world."

"It's just in his mind, then?" But Charley knew he had really seen the snow on the steeple, though he had been trying as hard as he could to forget it.

"Just in his mind."   But Charley saw the uncertainty in her words. "You know anything about him?"

"I've met his father.   He's a lion tamer or something."

"Oh? That part is true, at least. That surprises me."

"He's also . . ." Charley wondered whether he should tell her about the dope pushing. But that reminded him of that awful Sunday, and he didn't want to think about it. He said, instead, "He really hits on him, doesn't he? I never really noticed the kid before, but when I brought him into your office I saw, like, scars on him."

"Yes," she admitted.

"I used to think that Stark was a pretty cool dude, but now I think there's something sick about him," he said.

"What do you think we should do about Billy?" she said. "I mean, to help him without . . . you know, coming on too strong."

"Well, you're the expert," Charley said. "You sure helped me a lot when I felt like committing suicide over that girl." It was a painful memory for him. To drive away the thought of it, he quipped, "Actually, fantasizing about you was what got me over her, if you want to know the truth." Why had he said that now? He reddened.

"You shouldn't joke about that," Dora said, very seriously, "because you're getting big now, and I keep seeing in you the man you might become, and, well, I like what I see." And she kissed him on the cheek.

"I'll do anything!" Charley said, almost meaning it. "Even for the geek. If it's what you want."

She said, "What he needs is some kind of anchor on reality. I mean, something that isn't his home or some teacher like me. After all, the summer vacation is coming soon, and I won't be around."

"Is he a psycho or something?" Charley said.

"I don't know. Does he have any friends?"

"I don't think so."

"Listen, Charley, you're the one I trust the most. I don't think he's completely crazy, but he's on the brink. Do you know what I mean? He needs . . . someone to be with him." She seemed pretty nervous about it and Charley had a feeling she was more disturbed by all this than she let on.

"We'll take care of it, Dora," Charley said. "My friends and me. Somehow."

"But subtly."

Yeah."

"I don't want him to know I talked to you."

"Hey! You really care about him, don't you?" Charley said. "I'm jealous!" To his own surprise, he realized he wasn't quite joking. He had never seen Dora go out of her way like this. What was it with this Billy Binder? The one time he'd talked to him, he had seemed cold, untouchable, the kind of kid who sits in a corner at a party and mopes. But Dora was all worked up. The odd thing was, Billy and Dora were alike in some ways, Charley thought. They were both different somehow, fish out of water, square pegs in round holes, whatever. Billy had his problem, of course. Dora, Charley had learned a long time ago, was Jewish by ancestry and an atheist by conviction, and yet she was working for a Catholic school. She'd once explained to him that it was something to do with the school having to keep with the times, it was kind of an affirmative action sort of deal. Charley said, "Why can't you help?"

"Because . . . I'm not a kid."

"Nor am I—" Charley began. "Well, if you say so."

"Give me a call when you turn eighteen, though!"
she said. "Oh, what am I saying? I'll get fired one of
these days." Rather embarrassed, she turned and left
the bookstore.

"That is one foxy teacher," Walt said.

"She's more than just a teacher!" Charley said.
"She's something else!"

"Come on, forget about her," Walt said, laughing.
"I got a heavy date set up for you tomorrow."

"Huh? Who with?"

"My sister."

"Maria? All right!"   Charley had had his eye on
Walt's sister for weeks.

Charley, Sean and Walt left the others and went
across to the video arcade. "There's this radical new
game," Walt said, tweaking the safety pin in his left
ear. "They brought it in yesterday. Look."

Charley had a weakness for new video games,
and when he saw the new *Dragonrider* machine he
was astounded.   It was one of the new laser-
hologram ones.   It was one of the ones where you
climbed inside and it surrounded you completely. A
sign flashed above it in neon green and pink. "You sit
down inside it, see?"   Walt said, pointing.   "And it
really gives you the feeling of being on a dragon's
back and flying over this secret continent. The day it
came in, I reached maybe the tenth level.   Each
continent is different, they got like desert one and a
jungle; one with lakes and one with mountains . . .
and castles and monsters you got to try to zap with
your dragon's breath."

"Dude!" Sean whispered, awed.

"You got quarters?" Charley said.

"Got a dollar," Walt said, elbowing his way
through to the change machine.

"Someone's in it," Sean said. He took a couple of
dollar bills from his pocket. He always had the most

money.   That's why the other guys suffered his presence. "We'll have to jam in."

"There ain't no jamming spot," Walt said, walking around the machine in search of a ledge or something where you could plant your quarter and reserve your turn. "Maybe you can reach in and stick a quarter on his dashboard." But he had already lost interest and had wedged himself in among a group of people who were watching a screen that showed two really punked-out guys slugging it out. It was one of the new martial arts type games. The guys in the video looked exactly like Walt. Their hair stood on end and one of them had a safety pin in his ear, the other one had a razorblade dangling from it.

"Hey, Walt, they made a video game about you!" Sean said, and followed him into the mass of people clustered around the game. Charley was by himself for a moment. He turned to the *Dragonrider* game. There was a rear window in the cubicle that gave you a glimpse of the screen inside. A bunch of people crowded around it. Charley couldn't see past them.

He heard someone say, "Must have turned it over by now, he's been in there for like maybe an hour."

"Yeah," someone else said, "but he's totally stuck in this level, he can't seem to get past it."

The first kid said, "Maybe it's the last level. I never saw that level before."

Charley tried to squeeze in, but there were just too many people. Instead he knelt down by the entrance to the cubicle, got out his quarter, and eased it onto the control board, as inconspicuously as possible so he wouldn't distract whoever it was who was playing.

Then he looked up at the screen.

White, nothing but white. Here and there an aerial view of a city steeped in snow, or a lake covered with ice. Part of the screen was obscured by a holographic image of a dragon's neck, its scales glistening like snowflakes. There was a whole array of control buttons for moving in different directions and for firing what looked like laserblasts from the dragon's jaws. Now and then the dragon roared and the whole cubicle shuddered from the high-decibel output of the game's stereo speakers.

It was dark inside the cubicle and Charley couldn't see who was playing. But then he saw a round burn mark on the back of the kid's left hand, like a cigarette burn maybe, and he suddenly knew who it was.   It was freaky, because of the conversation he had just had with me. Charley didn't know what to say.   He got the feeling he was intruding on Billy's private world somehow. That was the feeling people always got from Billy. He was about to retreat with his quarter when Billy spoke to him, never once taking his eyes off the video screen.

"You're the one who always looks the other way when I come along. Do you hate me?"

Charley was startled. He thought Billy hadn't noticed. He was too surprised to answer.

"You're the one who saw me on the steeple," Billy went on.   "You're the one who took me to see Dora Marx."

"Yeah."

"Thanks," Billy said.

They didn't speak for a while. Charley watched the game. The dragon roved relentlessly over the desolate landscape.   Now and then a monster clambered out of the snow, and Billy zapped it with a deft flick of his wrist.   Most kids who are really jamming on a game seem to be actually living it out, using fierce body language and cussing when they miss.   But Billy had a look of complete detachment. He didn't seem involved at all. And he never missed.

And it was chilly in the cubicle. It felt good, comforting, numbing.

At last Charley felt impelled to say something to break the tension. "You want to hang out with me and my friends sometime?"

"Did Ms. Marx set you up for this?"

"Yes. But I would do it anyway."

"What do your friends think?"

"They'll do whatever I tell them. I'm the one with the driver's license."

Billy went on playing for what seemed like a long time.

"Don't you ever move on to the next level?" Charley said at last, frustrated. "It might get boring after a while."

"For some reason, when I play, it's all I get."

"Oh. Like the snow."

Billy went on playing the game.

After another long while, Billy said, "Sure, I'd like that very much," answering Charley's invitation. "But I don't know if I can get away."

Charley said, "I don't want to push myself on you, but, like, I feel responsible in a way. Because you might have died up there, if no one'd seen you."

"So what?"

Again Charley felt the curtain of ice between them. But he persisted. "School will be over soon. You got summer school?"

"Yeah. I'm flunking algebra."

"Me too." Charley smiled ruefully, hoping to break through the barrier. "But there's a week in between school and summer school and we're all going to take my Dad's car and go off somewhere for a few days. Thought you'd like to come maybe."

"You're going nowhere." It was a low voice, quietly menacing. Charley looked across the cubicle and saw the bottom half of a leather jacket, and rough hands reaching in to grab Billy. He saw Billy's eyes go dead, like a zombie's. Stark pulled Billy out. The screen blinked and flashed GAME OVER GAME OVER GAME OVER.

"Come on, give him a break," Charley said.

"It's none of your business!" Stark shouted so everyone in the arcade could hear. For a moment Charley thought Stark was going to punch him in the face. Charley could see people scrunching harder against their video games, trying to block out the embarrassment. "Cub's got to be broken. Got to be beaten down, got to learn who's the master. That's the way it is." To Billy he said, "I told you to come straight home."

Billy didn't answer, but he looked Stark straight in the eye, defiant. And he snarled at him. Charley could have sworn he sounded like a beast, an angry lion.

"I don't like your attitude," Stark said. "You're going to get it. As soon as we get home. Or do you want to get whipped right here in the mall?"

Charley said, "For God's sake, Stark—"

The arcade manager, a shapely woman in her twenties with an apron full of change, came up and said, "What's going on?"

"Never mind," Stark said. "Sorry to impose." Charley watched helplessly as he dragged Billy off, down the main corridor of the mall, in the direction of the exit. In the few seconds that he and Stark had confronted each other, he had felt violated. *Violated*! He was trembling with rage. He wanted to run after Stark, to pull him away from the boy who was in his power. But he knew he couldn't fight him. Besides, Stark had something he could hold over him . . . he had sold him drugs that other day. Charley didn't want his parents to find out. He was trapped! He knew now he should never have spoken to Stark, he

should never have been enticed by the glamorous motorbike and the leather and the silver skull-and-crossbones that dangled from his ear.

Walt and Sean came up to him. Walt said, "What was all that about?"

Charley was too confused to answer for a moment. Then he said, "I don't really know. But me and you guys, we're gonna do something about it."

"Even if we get in trouble? That Stark dude, he looks *mean*," Sean said. "And since when did our gang turn into a geeks' counselling service anyways?"

"Shut up," Walt said, "like just because we're cool doesn't mean we shouldn't help the uncool."

"His life's in danger," Charley said. He'd never really thought about dying before he met Billy Binder.

Chapter Five
Stark

Billy told Dora more about himself:

After another round of divorces, Billy came to Florida with a new mother whose name was Joan. They moved to Boca Blanca. Billy shed his past like a snake sloughing off its skin. He loved the new town because it was warm, because it never snowed; he loved the spider web of brash fast food places that circled the old church that was the town's one attraction.

The only thing he'd kept was the name: Billy Binder. He was always adamant about his name, and he'd always gotten his own way about it, either by throwing tantrums or whining or even running away. It was the only part of him that seemed truly his.

Days, his mother typed accounts in a doctor's office; nights she went to school. He hardly saw her. When he did, she always seemed to be sitting at the dinette table in the kitchen furiously guzzling black coffee or diet cola. Sometimes she took her caffeine straight up, in pills. She'd be sitting straight up in her chair, and her knee would be trembling, trembling. She was a dark-haired, rake-thin woman. Billy would sit there staring at her for a while, waiting for the school bus maybe. They didn't speak much to each other, although now and then she'd start talking to herself and he'd only half understand what she was talking about, stuff about night school and about the guys she was meeting there. It was never anything Billy was interested in.

Sometimes she'd bring someone over for the night, and then she'd make Billy stay in his room, because she didn't want them to think she was too old. In the morning Billy would sneak out of their duplex house through the back, across the neighbors' back yard. He wouldn't get breakfast when there was a man staying over, so it wasn't something he looked forward to. But they never remained more than a day or two. Billy's new mother would always become frustrated. Sometimes, at breakfast, he would see her sobbing quietly to herself. He wanted to reach out to her but he didn't really know how.

Billy was twelve when they moved to Boca Blanca. His mother Joan wanted him to go to the parochial school that was associated with the famous church, that attraction for nonexistent tourists. She could afford it because she had money coming in to pay for Billy's education from the divorce settlement.

Life went on in the same sort of way for a couple of years.

Then, one evening, Joan brought home someone different.

She'd been talking about him for several days; Billy never listened to her much. One time, though, she said, "And you know, he's been to so many places and done so many things . . . he's even been a lion tamer."

Billy tensed up at this.

"I went to a circus once," he said.

"Oh, really?" she said, momentarily surprised that Billy had said anything at all. "Anyway, this guy, I told him I had a kid and he said he didn't mind at all, and—"

Billy didn't want to hear more about it, so he got up and went to his room. He could still hear his mother talking out in the kitchen. He turned on the television as loud as he could, and got dressed to go to school.

That evening, Billy was in his room when he heard the roar of a motorcycle outside. He knew he was supposed to stay inside, so he didn't go anything when he heard the key in the front door and the footsteps inside the house.

He was surprised when they opened his door and came inside. When he looked at them he realized who the man was. Because he had never forgotten the man's face. And the face of the young circus flier, knotted in grief and anger.

"I know you!" Billy shouted at him. "You're bad!"

But his mother was smiling, and looking at the man adoringly. "Bad means good, in kids' talk," Stark said, ignoring Billy's expression of horror. He was a handsome man, black-haired, stoutly built. He wore an open leather jacket over his bare chest, and his arms were tattooed with dragons. A silver skull dangled from his left ear. He was the sort of guy many kids Billy's age might hero-worship. But Billy's heart was pounding. "Go away," he said, "go away now!"

Billy's mother said, "This is Stark. Just Stark . . . he doesn't have a first name, isn't that neat?" She looked up at him and said, "I brought him in to see you because I think he might be staying for a while, a long while."

Stark said, "I thought I'd better get a look at the kid. Because, from now on, I'm going to be sort of like a father to him."

"You're not my father!"

Joan said, "Now. Billy, be nice."

Billy said, "I don't want to be nice! I don't need a father! Leave me alone!"

Joan started to say something, but Stark stopped her. "I'll deal with this," he said. "Kids, they're like lion cubs, you gotta train them. In the jungle they're just wild things, mindless. But a man can mold 'em, make 'em do tricks. Let me talk to him a moment. Man to man."

Joan sighed. "Yes. I haven't given him enough attention. I guess. I've just let him run around too much." She smiled at Stark. "You two make friends now, see?" Then she turned and left the two of them alone together.

Stark locked the door. Then he said to Billy, "Drop your pants. I'm going to give you a licking."

"No," Billy said.

Stark said, "I'm stronger than you. And I'm going to be the boss around here. And I want you to know it now." He unbuckled his belt and moved toward the boy. "Now!" Billy felt the belt cut across his arm. He remembered the lion and the hoop of fire, so long ago . . . and the circus flier arcing through the air. He turned and tried to escape but he was being pushed against the wall, and then he felt more pain, and cloth tearing, and lines of pain bursting across bare flesh. "I can't give in, I can't cry," that was his first thought. He clung to that thought.

"I am your father," Stark said. "Say it. Believe it. When I'm through with you I'll have you dancing at the end of the whip, I'll have you leaping through fire."

There was nowhere left to go. Billy's body was being slammed against the wall. "Say it," Stark said, "say I'm your father."

Billy tried to make his mind go blank, to block out the humiliation and the awful pain. He saw Stark's face, contorted, demonlike. But there was something even worse in his eyes: worse than the senseless, relentless rage—

Billy could see that Stark really *wanted* to be his father . . . that in some twisted way he was trying to force Billy to love him.

He knew that this would go on and on, day after day. There was a war between them. Stark had strength on his side, and the power to inflict pain, a lot of pain. The only weapon Billy had was not to yield. He knew he would end up saying whatever he had to say to get the beating to stop, but even so it wouldn't always stop right away, because Stark would know that Billy didn't really mean what he was saying.

When it was over Billy would lie down choked with anger. At school he didn't try to disguise his weals. As the weeks went on he flaunted them and never offered any explanation for them. And because his scars made him seem different from the other kids, he became even more isolated than he'd been before. He encased himself in anger. It seemed like he'd burn you up if you tried to touch him. And so everyone ignored him and did not dare touch the loneliness within.

At breakfast his mother no longer drank endless cups of coffee. Stark put a stop to it, because he said it made her look sallow and undernourished. One morning she had tried to say something about Billy's scars, but Stark had only said, "Just growing pains, honey.   Kid's been without discipline so long, it's hard at first.   But we'll soon have him shaped up. Right?"

Then he got on his motorbike and drove off.

Billy's mother never figured out exactly what it was Stark did for a living. Billy saw how completely he had hypnotized her, and he grew more and more angry. And he buried his anger deep inside himself.

The beatings happened almost every night. Billy figured out ways of lessening the pain. He tried to will his body into being very cold, because he'd heard that cold could deaden pain. He thought a lot about the young circus flier and tried to imagine where he was and what he was doing, and whether he too had searched for a way to make the pain go away. Did he throw all his energy into making that perfect curve of falling? Perhaps that was the reason you tried to make beautiful things. To numb pain.

Before Stark came, Billy used to dream a lot about leaping through that hoop of fire . . . of finding adventure in colorful lands beyond the flames. But now, as he drifted into sleep every night, he only thought about being cold . . . about the cold of winter stealing up over his wounds and taking away the feelings from them . . . about a winter that lasted forever.

Sometimes he would wake up wiping away hoarfrost from his lips.

As the school year started to come to an end it started to get hotter and hotter. Billy edged closer to his fifteenth birthday. And the anger, which had been building up inside him and which he had tried to bury under layer upon layer of cold, was ready to burst out.

Chapter Six
The Snow Dragon

There were times, though, when Billy and Stark seemed to have an unspoken truce. Stark wasn't an ogre out of a fairy tale. Often he seemed to snap out of whatever was possessing him. There was a Jekyll and Hyde quality to him, and Billy sometimes didn't know what to expect.

Once Stark came home in the afternoon, after school, before Joan got home. He bounded into the house and dragged Billy away from the television and said, "Come on, come on, kid, we're going places today!"

And he made Billy sit behind him on the motorbike and they zoomed away. It was cool that day, and breezy. As they rode along the beach they made their own wind, fierce, smelling of the gasoline and seaweed. "Where are we going?" Billy shouted. He dug into the back of Stark's leather jacket with his hands.

"You like this? You like going fast, kid?" Stark said.

"Yeah!"

Stark accelerated. The bike roared. This was how Billy imagined the circus flier must have felt as he soared over the net. He hadn't thought about the flier in a long time, but the memory returned, startlingly clear. He remembered the anger in the boy's eyes. Panicking, he wanted to escape. But he couldn't let go of Stark's jacket without being hurled onto the concrete. They belonged together, Billy and Stark, they needed each other. But he could not bear to think the thing they shared was love.

"We'll go to the club!" Stark shouted.

"But we're not rich!"

"I can get in! I know magic!" The cycle roared; they zigzagged over the sand itself, through clumps of palms, and Billy felt the sharp grit on his face and hands. But he didn't care. Though he was holding on to Stark he felt free as an uncaged lion.

They pulled up beside a wire fence.   Billy recognized it dimly: it was the back of the ritzy club that all the rich people belonged to.   Beyond the railings he could see bushes sculpted into the shapes of animals; he could see a lawn that stretched out, out toward the sea.   An awning that led up to an entrance.   There was a gate; a man in uniform guarded it.

"Hey," Stark said.

The man looked at him, winked, and let them both in. Stark said, "This is my kid Billy." Billy winced at this. It was getting dark, and if Stark noticed he didn't say anything about it. "Let's go exploring, kid," he said. He grabbed Billy's hand and shoved him through the bushes and it was like stepping into another world.   "Keep low!" Stark whispered.   Wide-eyed, Billy saw old people reclining in deck chairs, sipping cocktails, conversing in low voices.

"You think I'm gonna be like that when I'm old?" Stark said. "Sitting around doing nothing, surrounded by an iron cage that says keep out. No way. Me, I'm going places, I'm flying high."

"By selling dope?" Billy said. He knew he shouldn't have. It slipped out because Billy's guard had dropped, because Stark had been acting so friendly.

"You daring me to whip your butt?" Stark said softly. Billy didn't say anything. "I'm not fighting you today. It's a good day today. I made a thousand bucks in ten minutes. Don't spoil the day for me."

Billy shrank away a little. He still didn't say anything.

Stark said, "Yeah. We're gonna be rich. And I'll give you anything you want. I'll give you your own car when you turn sixteen. I'll buy you a computer and a stereo and clothes and all the dope you could ever want."

Billy thought, wonderingly, "He's trying to buy me! Hitting on me didn't work and now he's trying bribery."

"It's good to be a kid," Stark said, his eyes distant. It seemed to Billy that Stark must never have been one.

"What was your childhood like?" Billy said.

Stark slapped him hard across the face. Billy felt blood oozing from the side of his mouth.

"I was only asking. . . ."

"I had the greatest childhood in the world!" Stark shouted, so loudly that some of the club members looked up from their bushes. "Don't talk to me of childhood! Don't you dare question my childhood."

One of the patrons said, "Say, shut up and just finish clipping the bushes, will ya?"

The man in uniform was standing behind them. "No scenes, buddy," he said to Stark. "Come back another time." He pulled an envelope out of his pocket and handed it to Stark. "But . . . hey, thanks for helping me out. These society types, you know, they can't deal with guys like you directly."

"Because they don't want to touch my greasy fingernails . . . because they think I'm scum!" Stark shouted.

"Don't raise your voice!" the guard said.

Roughly Stark pulled Billy forward and shoved him through the gate. "You shouldn't have asked about the past," he said.

"Why?" Billy cried.

"It's none of your damn business! I didn't ask to be what I am!" Stark yelled as he jumped onto his bike and motioned Billy to get on behind. Billy was too scared to. But he had to. He gripped Stark's jacket hard as they rode into nightfall. He could feel Stark's body quaking, like a volcano about to erupt.

He got the worst beating he'd ever had that night. And it was time for the anger to explode.

•••

It was long past midnight, and the pain had subsided a little. Billy lay awake. He was thinking of the first time he'd seen Stark. It was almost as though he were there again, standing in the slush in front of the circus tent . . . and the circus flier was saying, "Come as soon as you can . . . I can't hold out much longer . . . it's too cold."

Come where? Suddenly he had a vision of the circus flier with his hands outstretched, his body spinning dizzy, out of control, hurtling toward the net, only there was no net. . . .

And Billy screamed and sprang out of bed and knew that he had to get away. He had to go where the other boy had gone before. This thing went beyond than one boy battling one man. There was something else . . . something to do with snow, with neverending snow.

He wriggled into some old cutoffs and pulled on a teeshirt. He winced as the shirt raked against new welts. He tiptoed out of the house. His mother and Stark were asleep. Billy's battered bike was leaning against the front door, and he hopped on and rode like a maniac into the burning night.

He had some vague idea about running away.

A path twisted around some shadowy palm trees and crossed an empty highway. He realized he was going in the direction of the beach. He didn't want to go back to where he'd had that appalling scene with Stark, so he turned resolutely away from there. There were no stars; the air was dense; it seemed that the heat was wringing moisture from the blackness. Every bump in the road sent a sliver of pain through his whole body. There was no one around at all. He rode beside a low wall where the sand began. At first he could hear the sea, but the shattering of the surf began to fade. In the far distance, on the other side of the bay, he could see luxury hotels, white, like tombstones.

In a while he made a left turn back into the town. He had long forgotten the idea of running away; he was just riding now, letting the rhythm of the pedals propel him randomly.

It began to snow.

He didn't notice at first. All he was aware of was the anger. But the snow didn't stop. Little pieces of cold were pelting his face. They became great sheets of white. But it had been so long since Billy had seen snow . . . perhaps not since the day he had gone to the circus, more than seven years ago . . . and he was too busy being angry to realize that he was bicycling straight into a blizzard. Each time he pushed the pedals he thought, "I'll kill him," over and over, forcing the wheels against the ever-piling snow.

He rode on, forgetting time.   At last the snow thinned. The bike was stuck in a drift, against a rock perhaps. He leaned the bike against the mound of snow.

A dead light played over vistas of white.   It seemed to have no source. It didn't feel like the real world at all. Billy thought he must be dreaming. The snow never stopped completely.   Sometimes it tickled his face. Sometimes he could see it swirling in the sky, its flakes like the stars in one of those photographs of distant galaxies. There was no sun and no moon. The horizon was impossibly far away.

"Maybe it's another planet or something," Billy said aloud to himself.   His own voice sounded muffled, as though he were hearing himself speak from inside a locked closet.

At the horizon there was a hill, and the walls of a castle rose out of the mist. Billy started to walk toward the hill. He didn't wonder where he was anymore, or whether it was a dream. He knew that all his life he had been travelling toward this place. Maybe he'd find the other kid there, the one who had called him "brother."

The strangest thing was, he couldn't feel the cold at all.   It wasn't like sticking your hand into the refrigerator. The hill seemed really far away at first, but in this place things weren't the way they looked, and in a very short time he was standing right in front of the hill.

Suddenly he realized that the hill had wings. And eyes that flared briefly with blue fire. The wings flapped once. Again the eyes flared, dulled, flared, dulled. It was a dragon. Billy watched it for a long time.

In a rush that sent the wind sighing, the dragon spread its wings and swept the snow into fierce flurries. It had no scales, Billy saw, but its skin was a mosaic of interlocking snowflakes; when the eyes flashed, the flakes caught rainbow fire and sparkled for a few seconds.

And the dragon said, "Billy Binder, I welcome you to the Fallen Country."

At last Billy was afraid. "Send me home," he said, "please."

But then he remembered what was waiting for him there, and he said nothing.

After a while the dragon spoke again. Its voice was clear, piping, emotionless, like the ghost of a child. It wasn't the booming, threatening voice Billy had expected at all.

"What are you thinking?" the dragon said. "That I don't sound fierce and frightening the way a proper dragon should? That I have no roar?" Then it lifted its head and a tinny buzzing sound, like an electric alarm clock, came from its throat.

Billy said, "Who has stolen your roar?" He felt pity at first. But anger overwhelmed it, as it had overwhelmed all his other feelings.

"This is the Fallen Country, Billy. We don't feel things the way they do in the world above. We cannot love or hate. We cannot utter great thunderous cries of joy or terror. The world is muted by perpetual snow. That is why you are here, Billy Binder. The Fallen Country has been waiting for you."

"What do you mean?" Billy was scared and wanted to get back to his bike. He looked behind him and saw it, a tiny speck in the distance. It seemed strange that he could have trudged this far through the thick snow in only a few minutes. Maybe time was different here. He had heard that

time was different in different countries.

The dragon said, "You are here because you are full of anger, Billy Binder. Here in the Fallen Country we need such anger as yours. Anger here is strength. If only I could feel such anger, such hatred as you can feel, Billy Binder! Then I could die gladly. But I cannot."

Billy wrenched his feet out of the knee-deep snow. He forced himself to walk toward the dragon. Even the dread he had been feeling was passing away now. "But who has taken all this from you, dragon?" he said softly. "Who has stolen your feelings?"

"The one you know. You have touched his shadow. His shadow has pursued you across what you call time. He has many names. He is the strongest of all. We call him the Ringmaster here, because of his whip of burning cold."

Stark!

"You should kill him!" Billy cried out. "That's what the circus flier kid said. That's what I say. I'm *going* to kill him. When I'm older."

Whiteness burned all around him, making the tears run.

"You cannot kill him. He cannot die."

"I've got enough anger to kill him," Billy said.

"No. He slips from world to world as easily as you have done." Again the pitiful whine that passed for a dragon's roar. "But slowly we can work against him. Slowly, slowly we can sap him of his strength. Do you understand how powerful you are here, Billy? Your anger can build bridges, can burn pathways through the snow. Try it, Billy Binder."

Billy clenched himself. The rage coursed through him. He concentrated his anger into a bolt of energy . . . he felt it exploding from his fingertips. When he opened his eyes he saw a few spots of shabby greenery poking through the snow. But they were soon covered again, for the snow never stopped falling.

"Do you see?" the dragon said. "You are Binder, the one who will chain the Ringmaster."

"My name is Binder," Billy said, "but—"

"You come from the Fallen Country. Your roots are here. That's why you've never felt truly at home in the world above, why they have tossed you from household to household, only taking the name *Binder* with you—"

Thunder shuddered through the cloud-haze. For a moment, the sky parted, and Billy saw a whip cracking. The sky split in half. The whip retracted into the gray. There was a burst of sound that could have been applause or a circus band starting up or a crowd laughing at a clown—

"Stark!" Billy screamed.

"No . . . the one you call Stark is only the shadow of a shadow, and the Ringmaster has a thousand shadows, and it is only a shadow of his shadow that has followed you all the way to your distant world."

Then Billy saw that a red weal had opened on the dragon's neck. Blood trickled in slow motion onto the snow. "He's hurt you!" Billy said. They were akin, he and this alien creature. Both were at the mercy of . . . "Can't you cry out?" he shouted at the howling wind. "Can't you feel anything?"

"No." The dragon's voice didn't change at all. "You see, there *is* no pain in this place. It's better, isn't it? To feel nothing at all. It's what you've been longing for all these months. Now come. Get on my back, and I will show you your new kingdom."

The dragon stretched out a wing. It fanned out into a staircase. When Billy stepped onto it he hadn't felt the cold for a long time. He should be freezing to death through his worn sneakers and teeshirt. But he felt nothing. It was less real than a dream.

"Let's go now!" the dragon said. "We"ll have adventures. We'll rescue princesses and fight monsters. Isn't that what every kid wants to do?"

"I guess."

"A lot of you find your way into the Fallen Country, Billy Binder. Here they have a use. They can turn their anger against the power of the Ringmaster. One day we'll have a whole army of them."

"But I want to find the Ringmaster himself! I don't want him to hurt you and me anymore. I want to kill him."

But the dragon only laughed, a wretched ghost of a laugh. Billy climbed up the wing.

"All of you want the same thing at first, Billy Binder," said the dragon. "Of shaping his anger into a bridge that will touch the Ringmaster himself and topple the circus where he wields his whip. But the desolation of the Fallen Country finally steals into your hearts . . . you lose your anger, the one weapon that you have."

"I want to kill him!"

Again that thin laugh. Billy settled on the dragon's back. It was ridged with soft snow. The dragon flapped its wings, not resoundingly, but with a thud like the slam of a distant cellar door.

"You'll never need to cry again, Billy. From now on you'll have to save your grief, your anger, save it for here where we can use it."

"When will I know I can come here?"

"You will know. Listen! I am the Snow Dragon. I am the last dragon to survive in the Fallen Country. I am alive because I have purged myself of all that made me dragon: my fire, my rage, my shining scales that once gleamed silver in the moon and bright gold in the sun.   Now even the sun and moon are gone from the Fallen Country. Billy Binder, I have waited for you for a thousand years. I have waited so long that I have even lost the capacity to feel any joy at your coming. I, the Snow Dragon, tell you to dry your tears for the last time. Promise me."

Billy said, "I promise."

From that moment, Billy never cried again. He tried to, but his own promise bound him. Already his eyes felt, dry, drained.   Only the melting snowflakes moistened his cheeks.   Afterwards he wouldn't even think of crying.

The ground was slipping from the dragon's claws. They were rising now.   They flew through snowstorms into landscapes overcast and lightly puffed with snow. Here and there were the outlines of castles. Now and then a spire poked through the whiteness. There were oceans frosted with vanilla icing.   There were cities full of silent people who trudged listlessly through the slush. Sometimes they paused to point at the dragon swooping in the sky, but usually they never lifted their glazed, dead eyes from the snow. It was a huge country.

Sometimes the sky would open and the Ringmaster's whip would crack, once, twice, like thunderclaps, raising new welts in the dragon's hide. They flew on.   The Snow Dragon ignored the Ringmaster's punishments, but Billy shrank back against the cold leather.

"Do you still want to kill him?" the dragon said. "After you've seen what he can do. . . ."

"Yes! Yes!" Billy cried fiercely. The air streamed past his face. But he didn't feel it. It was as if they were flying around in a bubble of utter stillness. "I have to kill him, that's what I came here for!" Anger pounded inside him.

He closed his eyes, thinking about that anger. "I could build a bridge of anger," he whispered, "I could reach him."

Again and again the lightning-whip cracked. Although he didn't feel its wetness Billy saw that he was sitting in a pool of congealing blood.

Dragon's blood, purple, smoking in the chill air.

Chapter Seven
The Princess's Tower

"What about the steeple?" Dora Marx asked him when he visited her the next time.

He started telling her about the princesses then. He wasn't sure if there was only one of them or whether there were several. They had different colored hair and eyes and clothes, but there was the same look about them.

After a few times in the Fallen Country just scouting the terrain, there came a day when he rode the Snow Dragon into mountain country; there was a princess in a dungeon, buried neck-deep in snow. There were lots of princesses, Billy learned. Sometimes they were chained up. Sometimes they were just standing there, and all Billy had to say was "You are free." And it would work. Until the next time. There was always a next time.

Once they were swooping down from the where the sun would have been, if the Fallen Country still had a sun. Billy saw the castle, a forest of spires, mist-shrouded and caked with ice. It was dull gray in the unchanging, cold light of that pervaded the Fallen Country.

The dragon said, "Time to rescue a princess!"

Billy said, "Again?"

They circled the tower. For a minute Billy reveled in the rushing of the wind of the dragon's wings. The dragon swooped; its wings flapped; it soared in a dance that seemed almost full of joy.

"Are you happy, Snow Dragon?" Billy said.

But as soon as he asked, the dragon's dance seemed to lose its passion. "Happy, unhappy . . . those things are for you to feel. Doesn't it please you to be rescuing princesses? Everyone wants to rescue a princess. Don't you know any fairy tales?"

"No," Billy said. It was true. None of his parents had ever told him a fairy tale, and they did not have them on television. "But I guess it's good to save them."

"It works against the Ringmaster's power," the dragon said.

"Where is she this time?"

"In the castle, of course." They were almost skimming the edge of the turret, and the rushing wind had become still. "But now it's up to you."

"You always do this to me!" Billy said. He was getting frustrated now. "I don't know anything about rescuing princesses. I can't even rescue myself. And you're not telling me what to do."

"It is a pity you do not know the tales every child knows. But you seem to have a good instinct for them."

"I don't know what you mean!"

"Your anger, Billy. . . ."

And Billy understood suddenly what he was capable of. This was to be a first real test of his powers in the Fallen Country. He took the anger inside him, he thought of Stark and of those nights lying awake and burning for revenge . . . he concentrated on the anger, balled it up, rolled it into a shape, sent it spurting toward the castle.

He blinked. There was a bridge in the air now, a bridge where the dragon had hovered, clawing the emptiness. It was made of thin ice. As though someone had sliced it from a skating rink and slung it into the sky.

In the distance Billy could see a round serrated window like the mouth of a monster, gaping from the topmost tower. The bridge ran all the way towards it.

Billy leaped off the dragon's back. He kept thinking, "I should be scared but I'm not, I'm not. I'm just angry, angry—" He landed squarely on the bridge. It was rock-hard. "My anger is strong," Billy thought.

Beneath him stretched whiteness without end. He wasn't scared. You couldn't gauge the distance of things, and the ground seemed cushiony soft. He thought of the young circus flier poised to spring. "I'm like him," he thought.

He took a couple of steps, tentatively, on the bridge. It was a little slippery, but he firmed it with a burst of anger. He looked at the yawning jaws that were the window, feeling no fear, fueled instead by his overpowering anger. He walked. He reached the window.

He leaped gingerly from the bridge into the room. He expected it to be dark, but it was lit by the same depressing sourceless light as outside. There wasn't really any outside and inside here, he realized. It was just for show.

The princess was chained to the wall.

"I'll save you," he said. He saw bruises on her cheeks, and with a sharp spurt of anger he shattered the chains.

The princess came toward him. She was a cartoon princess in a flowing dress of snowflakes. Her eyes glittered; they almost seemed faceted like an insect's. And they were dark and expressionless.

She did not smile, but walked toward him stiffly and said a quick, whispered "Thank you."

Billy said, "That's it? That's all I get?"

The princess said, "You're the new one, aren't you? Yes. I feel the warmth around you. It charges the air and reminds me that I too was once as you. You're surprised I don't seem more grateful?" Her voice was like the dragon's voice, thin, toneless, uninterested. "What did you expect? I'll marry you and you'll inherit half my father's kingdom?"

"Something like that, I guess."

"That's not how things happen in the Fallen Country. The new ones, they keep expecting something strange and beautiful and romantic. They came here for escape, didn't they? But how can they, with <u>him</u> up there, watching, watching?"

He started to speak. She leaned over and gave him a single icy kiss on the cheek. "My store of emotion is but a tiny one, Billy Binder," the princess said, "but I will give you a small piece of what is left." A single tear glistened in her eye; but as it fell it turned into an icicle. "You don't know how much that cost me. But I still have a few tears left, and you are young."

"What will you do now?" Billy said.

She laughed. "I will go back to my father's kingdom. And then he'll capture me again . . . don't you worry, we'll see each other again."

"You mean I haven't really saved you at all?"

"Oh, you're all alike, you battered children who end up in the cold kingdom. Until you understand the Fallen Country completely, you keep thinking you can really do something to save the world . . . but one day you'll suddenly realize that it's all you can do to slow down the advance of the endless cold a little . . . and you'll never expect anything again."

He thought, "I want to kill him!" but could not bring himself to say it aloud.

She said, "I know you want to," and he knew from this that she could read his mind. "But you won't, you know. He is more real than you will ever be."

"I am real!   I have to be real, because I can feel pain!"

"Can you? There is no pain in the Fallen Country."

Billy waited for her to continue.

"And you know what else?" she said. "You can stay here forever if you want to. You never have to leave. You never have to feel pain again."

"And the world outside? There's a Billy Binder out there who's getting beat up on, who's suffering."

"When you come here, the one that remains behind in the world above is only a shell of Billy Binder. Our secret selves, our real selves, are here."

"But princess, princess . . ." Billy could barely speak. "How can you say that your true self is here when you've given up all your feelings?"

"It is the self I want to be!" For a split second Billy thought he could see rage color her cheeks. But it subsided immediately. The princess said, "There you go, wringing from me the last droplets of my emotions. You are only hastening my end."

"That's what you want? To feel nothing?"

"Isn't that what you want?" the princess said. "That's why you came here, isn't it?"

She stepped out of the window and left him stranded. The bridge was gone, melted into the air. It was because he had lain aside his anger for a moment.

He climbed up to the ledge, stood there watching the princess as she dissolved into the gray clouds. "Princess—" he shouted. He didn't even know her name.   Later he would find out that they had no names in the Fallen Country.

He tried to summon up his reserves of anger. He thought of Stark, wielding his leather belt like a lion tamer's whip; of the welts in the hide of the lion as it leaped through the circle of fire. But it all seemed so far away now.   And the Snow Dragon?   He could barely see the dragon, no larger than a seagull, skirting the edge of a cloud, white against white. It was snowing hard. Pretty soon he couldn't see end of his arm if he stretched it in front of him. He wanted to find someone—the dragon, the princess— a friend.

He turned. The jaws of the window had snapped shut. There was no way back into the castle. The tower walls stretched up and down into mist. "If I climb higher," he thought, "maybe I'll burst through the mist and I can see out and call the Snow Dragon."

He found a toehold in the wall, carefully felt along the ice-coated bricks for a handhold, and hefted himself up a couple of feet. And again. And again. The wall seemed to go on and on. Until, at last—

"I found myself clinging to the steeple." Billy told Dora Marx.

"Clinging . . . to the . . . steeple," she said.

He nodded and waited for her to go on. When she didn't he said, "You want to tell me I'm lying, don't you? But my eyes don't lie.   You're thinking, 'How innocent he looks, I've never seen a kid with such innocent-looking eyes.' Either I'm one of the world's greatest con artists, or his suffering has driven me insane, hopelessly insane . . . but which is it? You don't dare guess, because if you guess wrong. . . ."

"It's not my job to decide."

"I don't need help!   Leave me alone!"   Billy was feeling hostile. He should have known it was useless to tell the truth. It had always been useless before.

"And tonight," Billy thought, "I'll go home and face the same thing I always face." Aloud he said to her, "But there's a third possibility, one you don't even want to think about."

"That it's all true?" He could tell she was floundering. "Yes, well. . . ."

"That it's all true," he said. "It scares you, doesn't it?"

She didn't answer him. She seemed to freeze up. That's what the Fallen Country did to people. It drained them of their emotions. Maybe she had, somewhere inside her, that same anger, locked away.

"What should I do?" Dora said.

"If only I could make you see it! If only I could pull you in!" Billy said. "It gets stronger and stronger all the time. Sometimes I feel that all I need is to hold someone's hand and I'll take them inside with me. Then there'd be one more person who could cross from this world to the other . . . a person besides me and the Ringmaster. An adult who could maybe fight the Ringmaster on his own terms."

Dora said, "You're the only one who can do it, Billy."

"I don't want to do it alone!" There. He'd admitted it. The loneliness.

"Billy," Dora said, "have you ever read any of those fantasy stories where there's a troubled kid, and he escapes from his problems into a never-never-land and has neat adventures?"

"No." Billy didn't know any stories.

"Your story is so much like one of those stories," she said. "But life's not like that. You have to play the cards you're dealt. It's the hardest thing I have to tell you, but it's true. But maybe, just maybe . . ." and she smiled, and her smile gave Billy so much pain because he wished so much he could have a mother who would smile at him like that, and she said, "maybe when you finally do battle with the Great Evil One, you'll save me a seat?"

"Right in front," Billy said. "Right by the ringside."

"Try not to be afraid, Billy."

"I'm not afraid!" But already he felt the fear, and he longed to return to the Fallen Country where fear was as foreign as warmth, as love.

Ms. Marx leaned over and touched his cheek, once, very lightly. "Cold, isn't it?" Billy said. "Like I was already dead."

Chapter Eight
The Hospital

It had been freaky enough to see Billy at the mall when Charley knew that Billy *never* hung out there. And then to see that scene between Billy and Stark, to *know* what must be going on at their house . . . all this after Charley had thought that he'd probably never say two words to Billy for the rest of high school.

But the next day Charley couldn't help noticing that Billy wasn't in school. He could feel it even without looking around for him. Because when Billy was anywhere nearby it always felt cooler . . . as if the air-conditioning was actually working properly for a change.

During a break he went into Dora's office. He had to tell someone.

He said, "I think something bad has happened, Dora. He wasn't in any of his classes." Then he told her about what happened at the shopping mall after she'd left.

Dora buzzed the school office. The sister on duty said, "We called the house, but there was no answer."

Charley said, "I got a bad feeling."

Dora said, "Maybe we should go down to the hospital." There was only one in Boca Blanca.

"I've got the same feeling about it too."

"Let's go."

"But what about sixth period?"

"I'll write you a pass."

"It's only shop anyway."

They went to the parking lot. It had to be a hundred degrees. Charley noticed that the counsellor was pulling out the keys to a battered old VW. He said, "Let me, Dora," and steered her toward the student lot, where he opened the door to his own gleaming, brand new Datsun. "You can be my date." He smiled. He was pleased at leaving school early even though he was a little nervous about what they might find at the hospital.

"I had forgotten," she said, "that you'd gotten your license. I guess you really aren't a kid any more, are you?"

"It happens," Charley said. Then he added, "Don't worry. I doubt *you're* over the hill, noways."

She laughed. Charley wondered if she'd mind if he held her hand. But he didn't move toward her. He concentrated on his driving. Women!

They drove to the hospital and pulled in at emergency. They were shown into a ward. Billy was in a bed in one corner, propped up, with an IV bottle suspended over his head. There was a bandage over his left eye. There was some blood. A nurse was scribbling something on a clipboard. Billy was conscious. He lifted a hand weakly and waved.

"What happened?" Charley asked the nurse.

She said, "A few stitches, not that serious. Here's one kid who won't be riding his bike into trees for a while!" She patted Billy's head, filled a syringe, and started to inject it into the IV tube.

"What's that?" Charley said. He was unnerved by the blood, more than he wanted to admit.

"Demerol," Billy said faintly. "Five ccs."

"Clever boy!" the nurse said. "You must have been in before."

"I'll say! And he didn't ride his bike into a tree," Charley said. He was trembling with anger.

The nurse lifted an eyebrow. "Do you want to file a child abuse report?" she said.

"God damn it, it's obvious!" Charley said. He didn't care about being overheard. "Why haven't you reported it already, Dora? You're the one who's supposed to be grownup, not me."

The nurse said, "We can get you the paperwork." She looked at the two of them with concern. "But maybe you should talk to his mother. She works here, you know. She's Dr. Seymour's secretary. You can ask reception how to find her."

Charley said, "I'll stay with him awhile."

When Dora left he sat down beside Billy. He said, "We're going to get it to stop. Somehow. And you're going to come on that trip with us. I promise."

Billy said, "You're going to come on a trip with me, too. Very far away. I know a place where they'll need you. Because you're angry. For my sake."

Charley didn't know what Billy was talking about. He thought it must have something to do with what Dora told him, how Billy had wished so hard for another world that he was drifting into it, he was making it come true around him. Charley thought, "This is the kind of thing I have to try to pull him out of." Aloud he said, "Sure, Billy. I'll go to your place far away. But only after you come on *our* trip."

"Promise?"

"Sure."

"You just committed yourself to a lot. More than you know."

"Sure," Charley said, as Billy drifted off to sleep. Then he went off to look for Dora Marx.

•••

He asked for Dr. Seymour's office, and when he got there he saw Dora and another woman seated behind a desk, surrounded by expanses of naked glass, always reaching for the phone. Charley didn't go up to them. They were obviously squaring off for some kind of confrontation, and Charley didn't want to interfere. "When adults fight," he thought, "they never seem to make up. It's such a big deal to them."

Dora was being vague, talking about the heat wave, going around the problem.

Joan was a dark-haired, slight woman who didn't hide her feelings well; Charley could see her guilt very clearly.

He couldn't stand to see the two adults beating about the bush. He just charged up to them and said, "You know there's at least one way of ending the problem, don't you?"

"Yes." Billy's stepmom noticed him for the first time.

"Then why don't you get rid of the man?"

She paused to jot down an appointment. A crisp, medicinal odor wisped by. Charley looked away, past the two women, to brash green grass crisscrossed by palm fringed paths of concrete. The sunlight on the bumpers of the parked cars was blinding. He was burning up. The image of snow sprang into his mind, of cold, numbing snow.

Finally Joan answered, speaking with difficulty. "I can't . . . I can't," she said. She was crying a little, and I found myself turning away. She addressed herself to Dora, too ashamed or embarrassed to face Charley's direct accusations. "What can I do, Ms. Marx? He's not just a person . . . he's a force. Sometimes it feels like he comes from another world almost, like he's not human. And Billy <u>does</u> lie. He used to lie before Stark came. Will the lies suddenly end, if I get rid of Stark?"

"You love him," Charley said. "You're completely under his spell." At the same time he was wondering: "Why am I sticking up for the geek so much?" He knew he was trying to impress Dora with how mature he was . . . but there was something else too . . . he had stood at the edge of the Fallen Country . . . and felt the shadow of the boy's despair.

"Yes! I love him . . . I need him . . . and Billy's not my kid. And Stark's right, he does need discipline." She took a sip of her cola.

"I think you've been brainwashed, Joan," Dora said at last. "You say it's like he comes from another world . . . does that make it easier on yourself?"

"He does come from another world!" Joan said.

"Snow! Snow!" Charley thought.

He couldn't stay. And walked down the stairs together.

"I feel like a flailing idiot," Dora said. "I don't know what I was trying to accomplish. All I know is that . . . I'm longing for snowfall." Then, a little diffidently, she added, "I'm glad you were with me, Charley."

"For sure," Charley said.

"You don't seem . . ."

"Why should I be?" Charley said. He was angrier than he'd thought he was. "You're the one who's crossed the boundary, turned into a grownup, able to fix things. But you were—"

"Floundering like a fool?" She touched him lightly on the shoulder. "But Charley, you're wrong about one thing. There is no boundary. There aren't any magic turnstiles."

"No boundaries at all? Then what separates us from the Fallen Country?" But the answer was already becoming clear to him. Nothing. Or almost nothing. The thinnest thread.

"What Billy sees," she said, talking to herself almost, "is something beautiful. Do you understand,

I'm starting to look forward to those crazy stories, and it makes me feel guilty as hell, because I'm spying on his pain, but I feel jealous of him too, because in his pain he's created an entire world, while I've created nothing."

Charley listened to Dora's ramblings. He never realized before that she could have such complicated feelings. "And I thought only teenagers were that confused," he said, half resentfully. "But I was right, see? You do care for him. A lot."

"Just being professional."

"For sure." He sensed that he might be pushing too far, so he said nothing until they reached the ground floor.

"How is he?" she asked him.

"When I left him he was asleep," he said.

"Maybe I should take another look."

They went back to the ward. But he wasn't in his bed. Charley cornered the nurse and said, "Where've you taken him?"

She said, "I don't know. Perhaps you should ask at the desk."

They stood beside the bed. A cold wind wafted through the bed sheets. "Look," Charley said. "Frost. On the bed."

Dora said, uneasily, "Stark has been here, checked him out, taken him away for more abuse."

"No," Charley said. "I think he's gone away . . . to that other place."

"That other place? What did he tell you about it?" Dora said.

"He told me there was another country he went to sometimes . . . that one day he would take me there," Charley said. "I caught a glimpse of it, I think. In a video game."

"You're not the kind of person who would believe in an imaginary world."

"But, Dora, I saw the snow on the steeple."

"You saw?"   But Charley could tell she wasn't ready to believe yet.   "We have to be strong, you and I.   We have to pull him out, not get sucked in ourselves."

Charley said, "But what if he needs us in the other place?"

"I had to tell him something really hard last time we talked.   I had to tell him 'No, only you can be there at the end.'   You're a really good person, Charley," she said.   "But you can't step over the line into madness, you can't feel his suffering for him. . . ."

Charley said, "Is it a better world, this secret kingdom of his?"

"He doesn't feel pain there. But there's a price."

Charley looked at the empty bed. Two drops of frozen blood remained on the pillow, bright crimson, clear as gemstones.

Chapter Nine
The Arcade

They drove away from the hospital. Charley asked Dora where she wanted to go.

"You'll have to drop me off at the school, I guess," she said. "My car's still there."

"What a pity. I was hoping to get to see your house."

"Some other time," she said uneasily.

There was something fishy about the way she said that. Charley had noticed it before, when he'd asked her where she lived. It was weird because he felt much closer to her than any of the teachers, yet he'd never been to her house. She always changed the subject when he asked. He'd often fantasized about it . . . corpses in the refrigerator, that kind of thing.

"Go on, Dora, tell me your dark mystery. It can't be that bad."

"Some other time, okay?"

Charley sensed that Dora didn't want to pursue the subject, so he said, instead, "What did you think of his mother?"

Dora said, "She's in way over her head. I'm sorry for her, in a way."

Charley said, "What about the next three months? You don't work during summer school, right? Where will you go?"

"I don't know. Far away. Somewhere cool."

"What about Billy?"

She hesitated, then said, "Charley, I'm going to have to leave it to his friends to help him. You know, there's only so much I can do. He needs people his own age around him to give him some sense that the real world is worth coming back to."

"You're thrusting the responsibility onto me, then." How could she do that to him? he thought angrily.

She said, "Look, I'm only a mediocre counsellor at a small parochial school that's too cheap and too stupid to afford a professional. It wouldn't be right for me to get personally involved."

"You mean you're scared to."

She was silent. He knew he'd seen right through her.

"Well," he said, "if we can, we're going to take Billy away from his home for a few days. You're right, us kids should take care of our own, there's only so much an *adult* can really do or understand." Dora flinched a little at his resentment, but she didn't say anything. "We're going on a trip and we're taking him with us."

"That'll help a lot," she said.

"Yeah. But before you give up all responsibility, maybe you can do one thing for us, huh? You can talk his mother into letting him go. Then, Dora, I'll let you enjoy your summer vacation."

"I'll try."

Charley let her off at the school parking lot. He watched her get into her car and drive off. Then, on an impulse—and because he was still angry at her—he decided to follow her. "I'll find out what this great secret is," he thought. "Maybe she's an heiress with a huge mansion or something."

Her VW crossed Federal (she drove that decrepit old car like a demon and Charley had to cut through a parking lot to keep up) and went down a side street. He hid behind a limousine, watching her out of the corner of his eye as she turned down more streets. And then, at the intersection of Williams and Massoglia, he saw a huge concrete wall loom up. A fancy gate with iron railings. "Hey," he thought, pulling up to the curb as her car disappeared through the gate, "maybe this is some kind of mansion after all." Then he read the sign at the entrance.

BOCA BLANCA MEWS
Luxury Condominiums
Adults Only: No Children Allowed

"So that's the big mystery!" he said, whistling. "She lives in one of those no-kids-allowed condos." There were dozens of them in Boca Blanca, of course, it being a retirement town. "So that's what she really thinks of us kids!" he thought bitterly. "She listens to all our problems by day, and by night she protects herself from us with garlic and crosses." How could she stand living there? How old was she, twenty-two, twenty-three? And there were times when you could almost forget she wasn't a teenager. "There is no boundary," indeed! There it was. Iron. Probably with uniformed guards. Kids were kids and grownups were grownups and never the twain should meet.

Still angry, he decided to go on to the mall. He was surprised not to see his friends' bikes on the rack. "I guess they must have gone off somewhere

without me," he thought.   But he didn't mind.   He
needed some time to think, anyway.   "She
manipulated me," he thought, "into making friends
with that Billy Binder. Into doing her job for her."

He wandered into the mall. They still hadn't fixed
the air-conditioning very well, and the sweat was
running down his forehead.   He stood over the
throwing stars in the ninja section of the knickknack
store for a while, thinking about how Billy must feel
about Stark.   Then he found himself drawn
inexorably toward the video arcade.   Past the
flashing neon of the glass front, he could see that
Dragonrider was unoccupied.   In fact the entire
arcade was deserted. As he entered he understood
why. The air-conditioning was completely off inside,
and a technician, his tee-shirt and jeans completely
drenched in sweat, was standing on a stepladder
working on one of the air vents with a screwdriver.
In the change booth, the arcade manager had
collapsed against his cash register.   There was an
electric fan inside the booth, but it was off, too. A fly
crawled up one of the blades.

A digital thermometer on the wall read 101°F.

Charley was drawn toward the *Dragonrider* game.
He knew it must be stifling to crawl up inside there.
But its sign kept blinking on and off, on and off, and a
mysterious, rhythmless music came from it.   Over
the top of the cubicle, in shimmering laser-
holography, a dragon pawed the air, its nostrils
flared, breathing rainbow-fringed fire. It seemed to
pull him in.

Before he knew it he was seated at the controls
and fumbling for a quarter.   It was so hot that he
could hardly breathe. He glanced at the sign on the
glass front of the arcade:

SHOES AND SHIRTS MUST BE WORN

"They can't be serious about that," he thought, "not when the air conditioning's off." He peeled his tee shirt and sat way back in the seat so that he couldn't be seen. He emptied both pockets. There was an assortment of quarters and game tokens from different arcades. He had been hoarding the tokens because there was this one arcade in Pompano Beach where you could get ten tokens for a dollar and they just happened to work in this place too.

He put one in, thinking of the last time he'd been here.

And he was riding the dragon's back, thrusting over an imaginary kingdom. The heat was suffocating. He could almost feel the dragon's breath. Screen followed screen: castles, oceans, deserts, jungles. How had Billy managed to reach that desolate, snowy landscape? Charley remembered how cool it had felt in there. How detached Billy had looked. And his dead eyes. "Come on," he said, sending forth blasts of dragon's breath against the trolls and beasts that were coming at him. There was a huge castle now, its drawbridge yawning wide, a many-headed hydra with thundering footfalls. Charley began to shoot at it madly—

Too late! He saw the teeth of the hydra closing in, he saw the slavering tongue inside its jaws. The screen flashed:

Thy Mission is over, Dragonrider
Put in another token within 3 seconds

to continue thine Adventure

Frantically he thrust another quarter into the slot. "I'm going to get there!" he murmured. He stopped to wipe the sweat that was pouring into his eyes. Then he charged right on ahead, sending a ball of fire into the hydra's mouth. The creature shuddered and disintegrated. He passed over the arid plain into a lush jungle. A more difficult level now, as another dragon veered toward him, its rider's black cloak flying behind him. The holography was so realistic that Charley gasped at the crimson eyes set in a skull's face.

He fired.   Lance met lance over the treetops. Thrust, thrust, parry, thrust . . . he shook his head to flick away beading sweat. "I gotta reach the cool screen," he thought, "so this heat will go away." He fought. His wrists started to ache, but he went on, pounding and pounding on the controls.

Another token. Now another. And another. The whole back of the cubicle was slick with sweat. He felt he was slipping, slipping into a dark, fiery place. Still he was fighting.   He was starting to get inaccurate now, loosing his firebreath almost at random. He took a wrong turn, rammed into the side of a cliff. An elementary mistake. What a pain! He reached for another token. There weren't any. It wasn't like him to get worked up over a video game, but he couldn't take it anymore. He slammed his fist down on the dashboard, hard. "I want the cold!" he whispered harshly, "the cold, the cold." He felt so much anger . . . it wasn't because of the video game, it was because of everything that had happened today, the horrible thing that had happened to Billy and his feeling that Dora had betrayed him.

At that moment he heard a sharp splintering sound. His first thought was, "God, I hope I haven't broken the monitor or something!" He stared at the screen. A spiderweb of cracks was bursting across the monitor . . . I have *broken it!* . . . and then he saw beyond the shattered viewscreen, saw the swirling mist and the flurrying snow . . . shards of holographic glass flew into the air . . . and a blast of cold: desolate, numbing cold. Fog was filtering into the cubicle. And beyond the mist, more and more snow, snow that stretched forever.

"I'm dreaming!" Charley thought.

He looked around. He wasn't in the cubicle with the video game at all now. He was standing in snow up to his knees. The cold was seeping into his pores. He was holding his tee shirt in his hand; he slipped it on to keep out the cold. It was halfway on before he realized that he wasn't feeling the cold the way he ought to have been. He couldn't feel anything at all.

He heard Billy's voice, immeasurably far away: "Help me, somebody, help me!" It came to him on the wind.

"Where are you?" he shouted. His own voice sounded tiny to him, muffled. The wind was roaring. Snow was flying in his face. Where was the sound coming from? Overhead somewhere. He looked up. And saw the Snow Dragon . . . not the terrifying beast of the video game, but a strange ethereal creature crusted with snowflakes. Billy stood on the dragon's back. He was wielding some kind of glowing sword.

The mists cleared and Charley saw the monster they were up against . . . the many-headed hydra from the video game . . . looming up, so huge that the dragon, darting between its firebreathing heads, seemed insignificant, a hummingbird or a darting dragonfly.

He knew he should be frightened, but there was something about this place that drove away your fear. He ran toward the monster. The dragon dived,

Charley raised up his arms, was snatched skyward in its sharp, robotic talons. Quickly he scrambled up, using the ridges in its flanks for handholds. He was standing beside Billy now. "Hurry!" Billy was saying. "There's no time!"

"This is one hell of a dream," Charley said.

The dragon whipped around to face the hydra. "It's no dream," Billy said softly. "Thanks for coming. I don't know if there's much you can really do, but . . . you don't know how much I've needed to see someone from outside . . . someone I know."

"What are you talking about?" Charley said. "What have you done, pulled me into your nightmares?"

Billy said, "No . . . your own anger brought you here. That's the only way you can get to the Fallen Country."

"Is that what it's called?"

"Yeah."

"I thought it was, like, the final screen of the video game. A reward for enduring the heat."

"You don't need a video game to come here. You don't need anything at all. You just need this blinding rage."

Charley watched as the hydra came nearer and nearer, belching its flames. As they got closer he saw that it wasn't much of a monster. It was held together with sort of Frankenstein stitches, and it moved like a zombie, without any purpose.

"Why are we fighting this thing?" he asked Billy.

"I don't know," Billy said. "It's just there, I guess. Anyways, we ain't having much luck with it." He leaped, sliced with the sword of cold blue fire. A head fell. There was no blood. Two more heads sprouted up in its place.

"You're doing it all wrong," Charley said. "Haven't you ever heard the story of Hercules and the hydra?"

"I've never heard any stories," Billy said softly.

"You're supposed to burn them at the stumps, to stop them from regenerating. That's what Hercules did. It was in an old movie, too."

"You're right! I'll do it!" Charley saw Billy close his eyes, concentrating hard on something. Then he twisted his whole body, thrust his arm out. Fire spurted from his fingertips to one of the hydra's neck stumps. A puff of smoke; the hydra groaned. The stump was cauterized. "Help me!" Billy said. "Use your anger!"

But Charley couldn't understand. He said, "It's one thing to burn off your excess energy by defending the galaxy at the arcade . . . but I can see that thing for real, and . . . I don't feel any anger at it, I don't really want it to die."

"But it comes from the Ringmaster!" Billy cried.

"Who?"

There was a thunderclap . . . and Charley saw, for a tiny instant, a whip cracking in the sky . . . or was it lightning? He couldn't tell.

"He's up there! He's causing all this to happen, he's making the whole world dance to his whip!"

"So that's how you're going to fight him? With your own whip? He beats up on you and you beat up on a harmless monster?"

Suddenly Charley didn't feel any anger at all. And as his anger left him, he began to drift away from the Fallen Country. His hands collided with the metal of the *Dragonrider* console. Billy's face shimmered, was fading. . . .

He heard Billy's voice: "But I need you! I need help . . . I can't do this alone anymore . . . I need . . . a friend. . . ."

Charley said, "I can be your friend. But not in there, not in that other world. Don't ask me."

And suddenly he the cold was gone and he could feel the searing, choking heat of the shopping mall all about him.

And still he heard Billy's voice: "Come and save me."

"Where?" Charley said softly.

In the viewscreen, dimly reflected over the words GAME OVER, Charley saw an image of a parking lot. An iron fence. A beach. A lone seagull in the sun. Or was it a dragon?   And snow.   He knew that beach intimately; it lay to east of the town, on the other side of Route 1.

The picture faded.   Charley wiped the moisture from his face with a fold of his tee shirt.

He looked out of the cubicle.   They'd finished working on the airvent and there was some air circulating now, but it was hot.

One or two others had come into the arcade and were playing. The manager was awake now and was handing some change to . . . Walt and Sean and Walt's sister Maria.

He went up to them.

Walt said, "I brought my sister. She wanted to see you." He added, kidding, "I don't know why." When Maria looked the other way, he nudged Charley in the ribs.

"She just broke up with Steve," Walt said, so softly that only Charley could hear.   "And I just gave her this whole shtick about how radical you are."

She smiled at him. She had short, dark hair with stiff bangs that angled over her forehead. She'd used just a hint of eyeliner and mascara, which made her clear blue eyes seem even wider. He realized that Walt had set the whole thing up, and that he was supposed to ask her out now. "It's Friday," she said.

"Oh, yeah.   I forgot," Charley said.   He thought: "Thank god for someone my own age . . . to take my mind off having a crush on the counsellor." He imagined the iron gate clanging in his face.

Walt said, "I thought we might all—"

"Go somewhere tonight. Probably a movie, right? In my car. And, as a reward—"

Maria smiled a little. "Afterwards we could go for a drive."

"It's an offer I can't refuse," Charley said, laughing.

"Awesome!" Sean said.

Walt said, "We'll be at my house. After supper. Around six, six-thirty? Except . . . I'm not too sure about Sean."

"You geeks!" Sean squealed. "If you don't take me you won't be able to afford popcorn."

It was a familiar scene; it happened most Friday nights. But Walt had not brought his sister along before. Charley was starting to look forward to the evening.

He was about to say something like, "Sure, see you later," when he found he was saying something else. "I may be late, you guys. I have unfinished business to take care of."

"What do you mean?" Walt said.

"I have to go somewhere."

"Where? Can we come too?" Maria said.

"I can't say."

"I love men with secrets," she said. The others giggled.

Now why had he said that? Charley thought. Absentmindedly he left the group and started to walk off toward his car. As he put it into drive, he realized where he was going and what his unfinished business was. He turned left at the corner, away from his house, and headed east, toward the beach.

Chapter Ten
Friday Evening

Charley pulled into the parking lot. It was exactly the image he'd seen reflected in the video screen. Part of the beach was private; it belonged to some snooty club. An iron fence separated it off. As he stepped out of the car the heat hit him all at once. He ducked into the shadow of a billboard that advertised Disney World. It wasn't much cooler.

He still wasn't sure why he had come here. He'd been playing that stupid game, and then he'd slipped into some kind of dream . . . probably the heat, seeping into his pores, driving him crazy, making him see things.   But he couldn't get rid of the irrational feeling that he was needed here.

He stood at the edge of the parking lot. There was a railing there, and some steps that led down to the private beach itself.   A sign warned against trespassers. There was hardly anyone on the beach. Only a tourist would want to be out in this weather; all the natives would be huddled in front of their air conditioners. And the tourists were long gone. The sun was low in the west, at his back. He stood for about ten minutes, feeling rather stupid, especially because he had abandoned a perfectly good opportunity to get close to Walt's foxy sister.

He was about to turn back when he saw, high in the sky, the same lone seagull he'd seen before. The image was complete. He stared at it, the brilliant sky hurting his eyes. But it wasn't a gull! It was a dragon! And the cloud that surrounded it wasn't a cloud . . . it was a snowstorm.

The dragon flew upward in an arc, an eye-smarting pinpoint of reflected sunlight—

And disappeared!

And a tiny figure was plummeting into the sea.

"Billy!" Charley ran down the wooden steps, flicking his sneakers loose, to the water's edge. He heard the splash, somewhere out there, started to run into the warm water.

There it was! A circlet of white foam, maybe a hundred yards out to sea. And a small figure bobbing up and down, like a broken rag doll. Charley started to swim toward it. Clouds of steam rose up, as though from evaporating ice. Charley threw himself urgently forward. When he reached Billy there was just a face, just above the surface. Charley felt for the boy's body, yanked it up, and forced its arms around his neck as he headed for the shore.

Billy lay unmoving on the sand. Charley slapped his face a couple times. He'd seen people do that in movies. Billy just lay there, dead weight. "You gotta come to," Charley said. "Please, don't be dead. You gotta wake up!" He kept shaking the boy. Water sluiced from Billy's mouth, his nostrils. What could Charley say? "If you don't wake up, the Ringmaster will win . . . you can't let him win, you just can't . . ."

"But I don't believe in all that," he said to himself, distressed at being pulled into Billy's fantasy. Were those the magic words? The boy stirred.

Charley said, "I gotta take you back to the hospital."

"Why?" Billy said softly. "I'm all healed now." He lifted his arm weakly and pointed to where he'd had the bandage above his eye. Charley saw that it was gone, and that the scar from the stitches had already faded.

"That's impossible. That fast?" Charley whispered.

"I've been in the Fallen Country. So have you. Only for a moment, but you and I were there together."

Charley tried not to think about his adventure in the video arcade, but now he saw everything vividly: the dragon, the hydra, the snow. "I had a strange dream," he said. "Two people can have the same dream, I've heard, sometimes."

"No dream. Feel how cold I am."

"In the middle of a heat wave. In the middle of Florida." Charley touched the skin, marveled at its coolness.

"I can't defeat him alone," Billy said, so quietly that Charley could barely hear him.

"Is that what you want? For me to go with you, to stand beside you?"

"Yes. Tell me you'll do it."

And because Charley so desperately wanted to free Billy from his unhappiness, he said, "I'll go." But he already knew that he would be unable to fulfill his promise. Because Charley was not an angry person. He'd never harbored anger in his heart for a long time. And he knew that anger was the key to entering the Fallen Country.

Billy smiled at him. "Can you help me up?"

"Yeah." Billy was small. Charley lifted him easily even though he was only a year older than Billy. He started to carry him up the steps, into the parking lot.

Someone—a lifeguard maybe—yelled over at them, "Hey, this is a private beach! You got a club pass?"

Charley shouted back, "You geek, you didn't even try to save him."

"Where are we?" Billy said. But Charley saw that he seemed pretty indifferent about it all.

"The club," Charley said, "the beach side. Members only, you know?"

"I know this place," Billy said. "The cage walls . . . to keep us out or to keep them in?"

"What are you talking about? You're delirious or something." He dragged Billy to the car and put him in the front seat and lowered it until he was almost fully reclining. Then he started the car.

"Not the hospital," Billy said. "I have to go home."

"Home—to *him!*" Charley said.

"Please."

"Okay. Which way?"

"I live on the other side of the mall, on the Broward County line."

Charley drove silently. His watch said six forty-five. He'd have to hurry if he was to make it to the Alvarezes by seven-thirty. As they crossed the railroad tracks into the town they passed a bank that had one of those digital time and temperature readouts. It was still almost 100°F, even though the sun was closer to the horizon. "It's so hot," he muttered, fiddling with the controls of his car's air conditioning. It was going full blast but he still felt warm. "So damn hot."

"Not for me," Billy said almost inaudibly.

It was true. Billy wasn't sweating at all.

"You're never really out of there, are you?" Charley said. "Not all the way, I mean."

"I guess not . . . left on Federal . . . right here, yeah."
Charley turned. "I used to think it was only a dream,
too," Billy went on.

"And now?"

"Now I'm starting to think that what we're in now
is a dream. When I think of it that way it hurts less. I
mean, you know, *that.* I can't feel it so much. There.
It's the third house."

Charley pulled into the driveway of a white duplex.
"Guess I'll see you in school."

Billy said, "Come on in?   For a second?   Just a
second?"   For a brief moment Charley saw naked
terror in the boy's eyes.

He thought to himself, "I'd better come in.   Maybe
he needs me to help explain something to the guy."
He followed Billy into the house.

It wasn't what he expected at all. For some reason
he'd always thought that guys who beat up their kids
lived in squalid surroundings.   He had this
preconception of a dump with empty gin bottles and
beer cans and junk all over the floor. And ketchup
stains on the curtains, that kind of thing. The whole
evil stepfather business.

Billy's house wasn't big, but it was tidy. Past the
living area Charley could see a small kitchen. Billy's
mom, who didn't look anything like him, was sitting
at a dinette table drinking coffee.

"He's not back yet," she said. Charley heard fear in
her voice.   "You've got a half hour maybe.   You'd
better straighten up your room."

"Mom . . ." Billy led me into the kitchen. "This is
Charley. He saved my life today."

She looked at Charley with upraised hands, and
said, "Is he always like this with you, too, with his
stories?"

Charley was about to say that it was true, but
Billy's mother went on talking without waiting for

him to say anything. "I have to study up on these charts," she said. "I'm taking astrology as an elective this semester in night school, isn't that something? I've got a Mars-Venus conjunction here, it means I'm a very aggressive woman but I have a streak of charm that prevents people from seeing how manipulative I am."

Charley wanted to say that he couldn't see any of these things in Billy's mom at all, but he was too polite.

"I'll show you my room," Billy said pointedly, causing only a brief pause in the stream of his mother's monologue. He dragged Charley off to the back of the house.

Billy's room was a normal boy's room, with bunk beds, a dartboard over the door, a torn poster from a science fiction movie taped to one wall with duct tape. There was an empty glass cage on Billy's desk. Charley looked at it questioningly.

"Oh, the tank?" Billy said. "I had a garter snake once. He throttled it. Because I was late taking out the garbage. Then he whipped me with it."

"The snake?" Charley said incredulously.

"The dead snake." Billy's voice took on a very matter-of-fact tone, the way you might talk about the weather or what you had for lunch. "It didn't hurt none. But he thought it was funny. When he saw it wasn't leaving any marks on me he got out his belt. He used the end with the buckle. That was the first time I went to that hospital."

Charley couldn't say anything. His first thought was, "I should never have gotten mixed up with something this weird . . . not even because of Dora." But then his mother had told him the same thing, had accused him of "a certain lack of compassion."

"They checked me out right away, though, because my mom works there."

"He seemed like such a cool dude when I first met him. He sold me dope, you know?"

"I know he does something like that. Mom doesn't know, though, doesn't suspect. All he has to do is smile at her and she comes to him. Like one of those lions in the circus. God, he's so charming, so likable sometimes."

"She lets him do all that to you?" This made Charley nervous; he remembered how he had become enticed so easily by Stark's cool demeanor.

"She doesn't care. She's not even my real mother."

"She has to care!" Charley said, thinking of what his own mother had said to him, even though she had never met Billy. "Everyone has to care about something like this—"

They heard the roar of a motorcycle outside. "He's here." Terror flecked his face. What was Charley going to do? He had to leave soon or he'd never make it to the Alvarezes. And he didn't feel like running into Stark. Not now, not after all he had learned about him. He heard a door slam. Too late. Unless he climbed out of the . . . He eyed the window, started to edge his way toward it.

Billy stood completely still. The fear was gone from his face. The temperature dropped a notch. He was quite pale. Charley thought he looked like a statue, a stone statue.

Voices: "There's a car parked out front! Who've you been seeing while I've been gone? I'll catch him, I'll kill him!"

"Oh, Stark . . . it's just one of Billy's friends . . . don't be mad- why would I ever see someone else. . . ."

"Friends! That kid's got no friends. He won't have any friends until he stops telling those lies. He probably stole that car! I can never whip him enough, he just keeps begging for more."

"Please don't, please leave him alone; he really has a friend here."

"Damn liar. Come out here, Billy! Come out and explain! Or I'll beat the crap out of you."

Billy didn't move. Charley froze. The door burst open. Stark was there. "You!" Stark said.

"Yeah," Charley said. "You remember me."

"Right," Stark said. For a moment he seemed undecided. Then he called out to Billy's mom, "See, I was right. It's not one of Billy's friends at all, it's someone I had . . . business dealings with."

"Damn it, I <u>am</u> one of his friends!" Charley said, affirming it for the first time. He felt a moment of embarrassment—after all, this was a kid he wouldn't have been seen dead with two weeks ago—but he realized suddenly that it was true.

There was a dead silence in the room.

At last Billy said, "Charley's spending the night here." He looked at Charley with so much silent pleading in his eyes. "Aren't you?"

And Charley U what would happen the minute he drove away from Billy's house. He had to prevent it, whatever the cost. Even if only for a few hours. He had to. He swallowed, thinking of Walt and Sean waiting for him at Walt's house. And Maria. And he thought of Stark belting Billy with the carcass of a snake. And because he <u>was</u> a compassionate person, in spite of how he appeared sometimes when he was with all his friends, he gave the only answer it was possible for him to give: "Yeah. That's right. I visited Billy at the hospital. And he invited me over. So I gave him a ride."

Billy's mother had come in now and was standing behind Stark. She had a bizarre expression on her face, bewilderment perhaps. Or awe.

Billy's parents left the room. Charley could hear them talking in the living room. Sometimes Stark was storming, sometimes he was soothing.   Billy's mom was going on about astrology.

"You don't know what I just gave up," Charley said.

Billy said, "Thanks.   Thanks a lot.   You're my best friend."

It seemed to Charley like a curiously childish idea, but flattering too.   He said, "I haven't had a best friend since junior high," but he didn't contradict the other boy's statement.

"I've never had one in my life," Billy said.

Chapter Eleven
Midnight Conversations

If someone had asked Charley, earlier that afternoon, what he thought and felt about Billy Binder, Charley would have said something like, "Not much." It was hard for anyone to get a sense of Billy, because he was so remote; when Charley talked to him it didn't seem as though Billy were really listening. But something changed when Charley told Stark he was Billy's friend. In a way, saying it made it true. Billy had shared the Fallen Country with him . . . they'd fought the hydra together . . . Charley's feelings first become clear to him in a country where people had no feelings.

They'd talked freely in the Fallen Country, where labels like geek or jock or cool or uncool had no meaning. But now neither Billy nor Charley knew what to say to each other next. They sat on the lower bunk for a long while. Charley tapped his heels nervously. What did they have in common? The conversation outside the door went on, becoming

noisier and more grating.   At last they heard the
vroom of Stark's motorbike.

"He's gone for now," Billy said. Charley saw how
relieved he was.

"Now what do we do?" A car started outside and
shifted from the driveway into the street.

"That's Mom. She's gone to night school. We have
the house to ourselves for a few hours."

"What time is it?" Charley didn't look at his watch.
He was asking just so that he'd have something to
say.

"Nine, nine-thirty."   Billy didn't have a watch.
Apparently you could tell time here by the comings
and goings.   "We've got maybe a couple of hours
before they start coming back. With Stark you can't
really tell. But I'll be safe if you stay here. Hungry?"

"Yeah."

"Come on. We'll see if there's any food."

They left the room. Even though Stark was gone
Billy walked on tiptoe.   Charley sensed the man's
presence everywhere. The house seemed suddenly
much gloomier; the favorable impression he had first
had was gone.   There were no air conditioners
anywhere, Charley realized, and the windows were
all shuttered. A 40-watt bulb shone in the living
room without a lampshade.   There were shadows
from a tall China closet and from one of those
standing lights that you could twist into bizarre
shapes; this one had no bulb.   More and more
Charley was beginning to wonder whether he'd done
the right thing, whether he was getting himself in too
deep.   As they went toward the kitchen Charley
stumbled against something.

"That's a wastepaper basket," Billy said, "made
from an elephant's foot."

They went into the kitchen and Billy opened the
fridge.

"Junk, junk and junk," he said. "What kind do you want?"

"It all looks alike to me," Charley said, looking over the array of TV dinners and canned foods in dismay. "Guess I'll have a coke, though." There were about five six-packs of cola on the bottom shelf. "Someone around here likes their caffeine."

Billy stuck a pizza in the microwave. Five minutes later it chirped; he took it out and began to eat it very methodically, one small bite at a time, in a very steady rhythm.

"You eat weird," Charley said. He was getting irritated, and the way Billy ate was unnerving, more like a robot than a person. "Look . . . you forced me to stay here, you made it look like it's a matter of life and death, you go on and on about being whipped in the butt with dead snakes and you made me miss a date with Maria Alvarez—"

Abruptly he realized he was making an ass of himself and stopped. Billy said, "Hey, it's difficult for me. Relating to real people, I mean. I scare real easy." Charley saw that even this small admission was a big confession for Billy. Billy was a proud person. That was something Charley could relate to easily.

"OK. I'll stay casual." They went into the living room, which somehow looked even creepier than before. That shape, behind the sofa—he hadn't seen it before, but wasn't it—a stuffed lion, maybe? "I think I'd better call the Alvarezes. I don't know how I'm going to explain any of this—" He picked up the phone on the coffee table. As he expected, Walt picked it up on the first ring.

"Like where the hell are you?" he said.

Charley said, "Look. I'm doing something important, I'm maybe saving this guy's life, tell everyone sorry for me, all right?"

"Well, we can't sit around watching music videos all night," Walt said.

"Why not? You do it every night anyway." Charley slammed the phone down.   "I didn't mean to do that."

"The anger . . . you do have it in you," Billy said softly. "Because he's touched you . . . he's changed you."

"I don't buy any of this crap!" Charley shouted. "I've had bad dreams before. This is just one of those things. You're not going to trick me into thinking I'm mad."

"Like me. Mad."

"I didn't say that!" Charley said, angry again.

"But you meant it."

It was true. What could he say? He picked up the phone once more to dial his parents. This was a lot easier than his friends; his parents trusted him. He said, "Dad? I'm staying over at Billy's house. Oh, you've met him. I think. Anyway, you'll meet him tomorrow, maybe. He goes to my school." He turned to Billy. "I stretched the truth a bit," he said, "but not that much."

Billy said, "You're only here because you're sorry for me."

Charley said, "Of course I'm sorry for you, Billy, but. . . ."

"You're just like the others. That Dora Marx will probably write an academic paper about me or something and become rich and famous. And you . . . you've heard of us battered kids. Seen it on TV, read about it in social studies. And you're curious, I'm just like a lion in a cage to you, and you've come to stare and to wonder who has stolen my roar." He turned to finish his pizza.

"Great," Charley said, "just great. I give up a great evening and it doesn't mean a thing to do. I pulled you out of the water; I went to the hospital to see you. . . ."

"Like those people who are drawn to the scene of a car crash.   They're just dying to see a mangled corpse.   You could have let me drown.   You could have let me be beaten tonight.   Can't you get it through your thick head?   I'm strong, I'm cold, I'm like the driving snow.   I don't have feelings anymore!"

"Yes you do, Billy," Charley said.

"No!" A blast of bitter cold came from around him, and his eyes glittered like crystals.   Charley didn't know what to say, so he just waited.   The gust died down after a while.   They went into Billy's room and Billy turned on the TV.

•••

"Well," Charley said after another long while, "we can't just sit around watching music videos.

"I'm not good at this, am I?" Billy said. "I'm sorry."

"No. Don't be sorry."

"Isn't there something we can talk about?" Billy said.   "We just seem to get madder and madder at each other."

The next video: lions dancing.   Billy shrank back into the bunk and wouldn't talk at all.   Charley knew, from talking to me, that Billy had a thing about circuses. He got up to change the channel.

Just then came another video: a beautiful girl flying through the air . . . splashing through a waterfall . . . tinkling synthesizer noises superimposed on a reggae beat.   Charley stopped to watch the girl. Billy noticed him.

"We could talk about girls," Billy said.   "Isn't that what guys do? I mean, friends. Like you and me."

He was really trying hard, Charley thought.   He said, "Like the one that got away. Tonight. I've been wanting to talk to her for weeks. Her brother hangs out with me."

"Tell me about her."

Charley didn't really want to talk about himself, especially to this guy he hardly knew. But there was nothing else to fill the time. So he started to tell Billy about the first time he'd seen Maria.

"It must be nice," Billy said, "to be able to talk to them. Be close to them." He got up suddenly and began to root around on the desk. Charley recognized the brown, leatherette-bound volume that he pulled out immediately. It was last year's yearbook. "Could you maybe point her out to me?" Billy said wistfully. He sat down again on the lower bunk beside Charley. They leafed through it together.

"There she is . . . no, there. They look so retarded when they're posing for these pictures, it's impossible to tell them apart."

Charley noticed something strange about the yearbook. It only dawned on him slowly. Everyone's yearbook always has these silly messages and signatures and weird poems scrawled all over it, but Billy's was completely unmarked. In fact, some of the pages still clung together, as though the book had never been opened. And yes, wherever he turned, no signatures at all, none.

Charley noticed that Billy had noticed what he'd noticed. It was another embarrassing moment. Billy laughed awkwardly. He said, "You're thinking I don't have any friends."

Charley thought, "It's almost like he can see into your mind, this guy, it's weird."

Then Billy said, "I just never got around to it, I guess." He was silent again, then he added, "I never get around to making any. People are embarrassed when they see me." He said it without a trace of resentment.

Charley half expected Billy to fly into another rage, like he'd done earlier in the living room. But he didn't. "He's used to hiding behind his rage," Charley thought, "but he's holding back. He's really trying." Aloud he said, "You're not too bad."

"Thanks."

They played roulette with the cable controller for a few moments. Eventually they settled on Channel 65's *Double Screamathon.* The first feature was a movie adapted from a Stephen King short story. Charley had read the story and was annoyed at some of the changes in the movie. He asked Billy if he'd read it too.

"Are you kidding?" Billy said.

Charley realized that, except for that yearbook, he hadn't seen a single book in Billy's house.

Billy said, "I've read no books, I've heard no stories."

"Then where do you get . . . I mean, that fantasy world you're always telling Dora about—"

"They're not stories. Remember, *you* had to tell me how to kill the many-headed thing—"

"Hydra." It was hard for Charley to believe that Billy had never heard a fairy tale. He must have just grown up glued to that TV screen.

"See? You're the one who knows what they're called and how to deal with them. You've read books and heard stories. Not me. I just go there. That's why I'm going to need your help. To go all the way to the center of the Fallen Country. To get to *him.*"

Charley wanted to tell Billy that he did not want to go, he wanted nothing more to do with the world Billy had made for himself. But he couldn't bring himself to say it. Maybe it wasn't even true. He turned away and just went on watching the movie.

•••

"Take the bottom bunk if you want," Billy said later. He started undressing to go to bed. There were scars all over his body. He just got into bed fully clothed and turned his face toward the wall.

It was long after midnight by then. The second feature was *The Creeping Terror*, a movie about a man-eating rug.

Charley watched it, laughing at the pretentious voiceover that narrated the whole movie. Billy said, from overhead, "Are you still thinking about that girl, and about how you could have gone on a drive with her, and maybe made out?"

"Yeah," Charley said. Then he said, "Do you ever think of them?"

"Huh? Oh, girls. But I have a girlfriend already."

"Tell me."

"She's different every time I see her. She sets her hair differently. Sometimes she changes its color too. But her expression is always the same. I do her these great favors, you know, like get her out of dungeons and torture chambers. But she never thanks me. Well, hardly ever. And she just walks away. And she's very sad, and she never smiles at all. And her skin is very pale, as though she were made of snow."

"She doesn't sound very friendly," Charley said, dozing off a little.

"Oh, but she's beautiful. Do you want to see her?"

Charley said, "Why, do you have a picture?" After all, he had just found Maria's picture in the yearbook.

"No," Billy said, "I mean, *really* see her. She's here, now, with us, always."

"He wants to lead me back to that cold, desolate place," Charley thought. He said, "I don't want to see her."

Billy said, "Are you afraid?"

The temperature in the room started to drop, slowly, evenly. "Can he actually do it?" Charley thought. "Can he turn the dreamworld on and off, like a television set?" He squeezed his eyes tight shut. "I'm not going to get sucked in," he said, "I'm not."

"When you are willing, you will come again." Billy's voice sounded groggy now. Sleep was catching up with him. "Because you're my friend. You said it, and now it's true."

"Yes."

Abruptly it was hot again, boiling hot. Charley felt stifled in his clothes, but he made no move to get out of bed to undress. He had the feeling that if he budged the slightest bit, he might slip away from his reality. He tensed into a rigid prone position and stayed like that until he passed out.

•••

They awoke to a tremendous shouting just beyond Billy's door. Charley sat bolt upright. He looked up at Billy, who had covered himself completely with a bedsheet, like a corpse in a morgue. Beneath the sheet the boy was trembling something fierce. Charley heard pounding footsteps up and down the hallway.

Then the outer door slamming and the roaring of the motorbike again.

Billy jumped down from the upper bunk. "We'd better find out what this is," he said. He threw on an old Spiderman tee shirt and led Charley out into the kitchen. A coffeemaker was perking wildly as they entered. Billy's mother was sitting there, her elbows shaking against the dinette tabletop as she raised a coke can to her lips.

"What's wrong?" Charley said.

Billy's mother looked accusingly at her adopted son. She said, "You shouldn't have pulled one over

on him like that, last night.   About your friend, I
mean. He's always got to be the boss, you know that,
those are the rules." She was sobbing furiously now.
"Now he's gone, I can't keep him." She pulled a paper
towel from the dispenser and dabbed at her eyes.
"It's your fault, you always have to fight him for
dominance, and you have to disrupt the stability of
the family unit."

Billy just stood there, not answering her.   He
looked like he'd heard this speech a hundred times
before.

Instead it was Charley who lost his cool.   He
started to shout at Billy's mom: "You're crying
because that madman walked out on you?   You're
blaming Billy?   You're totally out of your mind!
Stark's like crazy, a psycho, could have killed this kid,
and you're blaming the kid?"

"Don't, Charley," Billy said, very softly.

"What do you mean, don't? This bullshit has gone
on long enough."

"You don't understand, Charley. She is right. It is
between him and me, an ancient rivalry from
another kingdom."

"He said he wasn't going to come back," Billy's
mom said. "Not until you shape up."

"No great loss," Charley said, still fuming.

"He'll come back," Billy said.

Charley said, "Well, I don't think you should stick
around.   I mean, you may think it's natural for a guy
to come home and beat the crap out of you every
night, but it ain't! I'm taking you out of this house,
Billy Binder. At least for one more day." He couldn't
stand to be there for another minute. "Get in the car,
Billy. I'm gonna show you how it's supposed to be.
Come on." He pushed Billy out of the door.

Billy didn't protest; he acted completely passive
about the whole thing. As Charley sat down, though,

he said, "You *do* have the anger. You *will* come with me to the heart of the kingdom." There was a note of exaltation, almost of triumph, in Billy's voice.

"All this garbage," Charley said, turning the key in the ignition. "That's why I've gotta get you out of there. God, your house gives me the creeps, it's like the Addams Family in spades."

Just before he pulled out Charley had an idea. He ran into the house to get something from Billy's room. He was in and out before Billy's mother could speak to him. He threw his find in the back of the car.

Billy had no idea what it was. He wasn't even curious.

Chapter Twelve
The Moores

Charley's house wasn't that much bigger than Billy's, but it was detached and backed onto a canal. There was a little swimming pool in the back yard. And plants strung from the ceiling of the living room. The thermometer on the door read 102°F, but the air conditioning was going strong as Billy stepped into the house.   A faint odor of pancakes and sausage filtered into the living room.

"Good, we're in time for breakfast," Charley said. Then he called out, "Dad, Lydia, it's a friend."   He pointed Billy toward the kitchen, where Charley's parents were sitting down.   "These are my parents, Jonathan and Lydia," Charley said, "and this is Billy."

Billy was surprised that Charley called his mother "Lydia," and at first he thought it must be a stepmom, but they looked so alike, with their muddy blond hair and green eyes, that they could only be a mother and son.

The two older people looked up. Charley's dad put down his pipe. They stared at each other. Billy thought, "I embarrass them. They can see what I am. I'm wearing this filthy Spiderman tee shirt with holes in it and they can see bruises through the holes." He started to feel hostile.

"Hello, Billy," Charley's mother said. She put out her hand. Billy didn't know what he was supposed to do with it. At last, diffidently, he shook it. Then he retracted his hand immediately, as though he'd been stung.

Charley saw that things weren't going right and he said, "Lyd, I'd better have a word with you." And he steered his mother outside.

Billy thought, "He's telling her I'm a battered kid, he's telling her so she can feel sorry for me." He felt vulnerable, but he was determined not to give anything away.

Charley and his mother came back into the kitchen. Lydia came up to Billy and tried to hug him. He froze instinctively. Lydia said, "It's all right. No one will harm you here."

Billy stared accusingly at Charley, who said, "I had to tell her."

Lydia said, "Would you like some pancakes, honey?" to Billy. He didn't answer, but she started getting some more flour from the cupboard.

"What are you doing that for?" Billy said.

"Flour," Charley said. "For pancakes."

"Don't you have pancake mix?" Billy said.

"My mother always makes everything from scratch." Charley turned to his father, who smiled approvingly, patting his slight paunch and stroking his beard.

"Why?" Billy said. He didn't see the sense in it. The Moores were very eccentric people, it seemed. Lydia put a plate in his hand, and he realized how hungry he was. He hadn't had anything since the microwave pizza, more than twelve hours ago. The pancakes tasted funny, but they weren't bad, not what he'd expected.

"Dad teaches at Boca Blanca University," Charley said, "and Lyd's a writer." He seemed more cheerful now. Had his outburst really come from him, Billy thought, or was it somehow an effect that Billy's house had on people? "But right now," Charley went on, "they're collaborating no some monstrous book about . . . what it is, Lyd?"

"Mythography," she said, giving him his pancakes.

"Whatever that is," Charley said, shrugging.

Billy was astonished at the easy way Charley spoke to his parents. He longed to be like his new friend, and that longing made him act even more hostile. He wolfed down the rest of his pancakes and didn't say anything more. Charley's parents didn't seem to know quite what to make of him, and Billy thought, "People are always like this, they always smile and they're extra nice, but inside they're going tsk-tsk and feeling really embarrassed. It's like I'm showing them something about themselves, and they don't like what they see, so they just turn away and start going on about fixing their pancakes from scratch."

At last breakfast was over and Charley showed Billy the rest of the house. There were books everywhere, and the coffee table in the living room was laden with oversized books that showed famous paintings and foreign cities. The stereo was playing something very slow and soothing, all on strings. He was captivated by the music. Sometimes, on the back of the Snow Dragon, soaring over the Fallen Country, he had heard music issuing from one of the cities of ice below.

He stood for a long time, listening.

"Oh," Charley's mother said, coming in after them, "at least this one of your poor waifs has taste, Charley. He likes my late Beethoven string quartets."

"Enough of this!" Charley said, and dived for the stereo console. The music changed instantaneously to a steely, sharp-edged New Wave song. Charley's mom sighed. "Just when a thought we were going to have a little class around here." She turned to Billy and shrugged. "Ah well."

He didn't know how to take it. So he said, "Lot of books you got, Mrs. Moore."

"Yes," she said. "We have a lot more in the library. Third door on the left," she added, pointing vaguely toward the corridor that led to the back of the house.

"Let's go swimming," Charley said.

"I didn't bring my swimsuit."

"Those cutoffs will do fine. Or you can just skinny-dip, no one cares around here." Charley laughed.

"No," Billy said. He was so vehement about it that Charley recoiled for a moment. Why? For the first time since Stark had come into his life, Billy had the feeling that he didn't want people to see his scars. He wasn't proud to be different anymore.

It was because he had a friend now, someone who had stood up for him.

•••

The day passed pretty fast. Mrs. Moore ("Call me Lydia, please") made more hamburgers (also from scratch) and then went into the room they called "the library", where she was working on a word processor and a card catalog of some kind. Billy watched her for a while, then he and Charley watched a science fiction film on the cable.

"Why do you call him Dad and her Lydia?" Billy asked Charley.

"It's what they like," Charley said. "Well, you know, they grew up in the sixties, but Dad kind of reverted to his pre-hippie mode. I guess having a kid brought on a sudden maturity attack. Sometimes I really wish she'd be comfortable being called 'Mom.' She hates being old, I guess."

"She's not old," Billy said. "She's totally cool." He envied Charley and decided that one day, when he knew him better, he would lecture him on not knowing how lucky he was.

In the late afternoon Charley's friends started to arrive. He'd seen them around but never talked to them. There was this guy Sean, who was young but seemed to have a lot of money. Today he was waving his father's Sears card around. Then there was Walt Alvarez, who was dressed as what passed for punk in their conservative school, and had a razor blade hanging from his left ear. His sister Maria came with them too. Billy could tell that Charley was very attracted to her. Today she had sprayed a blue streak into her hair.

Charley took her arm and led her out by the pool for a while. Walt and Sean looked at Billy with antagonism.

"Business to take care of!" Walt said. "That's what he told us. That's what made us miss out on our evening. Who are you anyway?"

"I'm Billy Binder."

"Oh, you're the guy we saw on the—" Sean started.

Before Billy could answer, Charley and Maria came back inside. Maria said, "Listen, guys, it's cool for Billy to join us."

Billy listened as the four of them argued for about fifteen minutes about what they were going to do next. Charley wanted to go to the iceskating rink in Pompano Beach, because "it's probably the coolest place within a hundred miles of here." Sean announced that he'd called them and they were closed because their air conditioning had broken down. They discussed a couple of other alternatives, but no one could agree.

"Well, I guess it's down to the usual," Charley said at last.

The usual was that they would go down to the mall and hang out, and then they'd most likely go to see a movie.

They argued about which movie for another half hour.

Maria wanted to see a humorous car-chase movie; Sean wanted to see a space opera that they'd all seen three or four times already. Walt, of course, wanted to see a mad slasher movie.

Eventually, Walt won. Billy saw why. He could see that Charley wanted to do it because he thought that a scary film might help him in snuggling up to Maria. Maria gave in because she was used to giving in to her brother. Sean agreed because he was the youngest. And Walt kept proclaiming that his dad was the *Post* movie critic and therefore everyone should just trust him.

"Isn't it rated R?" Billy said.

"Don't be such a nerd," Sean said. Charley and Maria turned on him with a baleful stare. Billy saw they were trying to protect him. He fought off a natural impulse to shake off their help.

At length the group piled into Charley's car. Billy observed the others but didn't participate. They were giggling and they all seemed to like each other so much, even though they never stopped arguing. It was another world to Billy, one that didn't seem quite real somehow.

Although the movie had lots of gore, it wasn't all that interesting. The blood looked like ketchup and Billy could tell that the violence was faked. He knew the real thing from experience.

Maria was sitting between him and Charley. When Billy glanced over, he saw that Charley seemed pretty frightened after all—so much for his hope that

Maria would cling to him in terror—but that Maria was watching with detachment, as befitted the daughter of a film critic. Now and then, along with the rest of the audience, she'd scream, but she wasn't frightened, she was just joining in the fun.

Toward the end there was one of those scenes where the slasher chased a couple of screeching teenage girls through the forest in the middle of the night, wearing a funny mask and waving an axe. It managed to be quite suspenseful. At the climax Billy realized that he was holding Maria's hand. Normally he would have thrust it away in panic—physical contact always panicked him, as people found out within seconds of first meeting him—but instead he found himself holding on tight.

She squeezed his hand back.

It made him feel weird inside, because she wasn't one of the princesses in the Fallen Country, she didn't need to be pulled out of the snow or to have her fetters smashed.

He didn't think too much about the rest of the movie. Once, just once, he looked over and caught Charley staring at him oddly. Was it because of Maria? But Billy hadn't meant anything by . . . hastily he dropped her hand and he folded his arms.

After the movie the arcade was still open.

"Hey," Charley said, "this dude really jams at *Dragonrider.*"

Billy made an aw-shucks face, but, as they crowded into the arcade, which was doing a brisk business, he elbowed his way toward the game. He was determined to smash his way through to the Fallen Country tonight. Something about these people . . . suddenly he couldn't handle it anymore. He wanted to escape to something familiar.

The kid who was playing before them got out. "Anyone got a quarter?" he asked no one in particular. "Well later, I'm history."

Billy slipped inside the booth. The seat was so hot that he had to sit way forward. Sean thrust a token onto the console and Billy used it.

"I'm gonna show you something," he said to all of them as they clustered by the side of the booth. But he really meant Maria. He was going to break through so they could all see the one true place, the kingdom where he belonged.

He started playing.

He played brilliantly. Monster after monster was wasted in dazzling high-res. But he just couldn't build up enough anger to burst through. He played more feverishly now, thinking, "I can't have lost it, I can't have . . ." but there was nothing. Just graphics and more graphics. No desolate wind, no dragon of snow and crystal, no sunless gray sky.

"You turned it over," he heard Sean saying. "Awesome!"

He'd been playing for forty-five minutes. And the Fallen Country had not come. Disappointment gnawed at him. Now he'd have to go back and cope with embarrassment and confusion again. He'd never been this confused before, in the days when there was only pain.

•••

Charley dropped Sean and the Alvarezes off first. They were neighbors.

Maria kissed Billy on the cheek and said, "You know, Charley was overdoing it a bit when he gave me this whole lecture on how I had to try to understand you, because of how you'd suffered, how I had to be nice. I would have liked you anyway. You don't say much, but there's something . . . *big* about you, inside."

Then Charley walked her to her front door and they stayed out there for about five minutes.

When he came back, Charley said, "Do you want to go back to your house?" When Billy didn't answer, he said, "No. It's late. And . . . well . . . you know."

Charley's room didn't have bunk beds, so Billy slept on an inflatable mattress. He expected they'd be up half the night talking and watching old movies, like they'd done at his house, but he became very tired as soon as his head hit the pillow.

Charley sort of talked at him for a while. "You like Maria? A bit better than a snow princess, huh? Yeah, I could tell you liked her. She liked you too, she told me. I'm not jealous. Well . . . I _am_ jealous. But . . . hell, you think we'll ever survive adolescence? I'm so confused. . . ."

Billy, on the edge of sleep, grunted.

"I noticed, don't think I didn't notice. You didn't manage to conjure up that illusion of yours, that thing of snow and cold and dragons and hydras. You were going to do it, to show off, but it just wouldn't come. I'm the only one who's glimpsed it, that's why I know what you were trying to do. But . . . that's a _good_ thing, isn't it?   I mean, maybe your mind is beginning to heal . . . maybe I'm doing the right thing."

To heal. . . .

Charley said, "I'll tell you a secret. I know where Dora lives." Charley told him about how he'd followed her all the way to the kid-proof condo. "It's almost like a fairy tale . . . she's like a princess too scared to come out of a tower, or something."

"Some princess!"

"This is reality, Billy." Billy could barely hear him now, he was so tired, but Charley rambled on. Billy closed his eyes and counted lions leaping through hoops of fire.

He thought about the game that wouldn't transform itself . . . the gate that wouldn't open into the Fallen Country.   He just hadn't been angry enough to burst through.   There had been so many new emotions in the past twenty-four hours.   He thought, "People have been trying to help me: Dora, Charley, now Maria, too . . . and I've been reacting as if they were trying to shut me in a cage, I've been roaring like a wounded lion.   But maybe"—another lion jumped, then another and another—"friendship isn't a new kind of cage . . . maybe it's a way to freedom."

But in the middle of the night, in his sleep, he sat up suddenly and said, very distinctly, "But I still have to face the Ringmaster.   And no one will come with me."   Charley, who hadn't been able to get to sleep, heard it.

•••

But he didn't mention it to Billy the next morning. Later, to his mother, when they were alone, Charley said, "We've got to stop that man. Before it's too late to pull him out."

Lydia Moore smiled and said, "That's why I told you to help him.   Because beneath your cool-dude exterior there's the kind of kid you really are, the kid who's my son."

"Thanks, Mom," Charley said.   His Mom didn't flinch or make a wry face as she usually did when he called her that. She must really be proud of him, he thought.

It was another piece of magic Billy had wrought.

Chapter Thirteen
The Kids' Revolt

Sunday morning the Moores went to church, the same church where the story had begun for Charley and his friends. Charley's parents simply assumed Billy was coming, so he borrowed some of Charley's clothes and went.

It was a bland, fairly dull experience for Billy, but he did what the others did and no one noticed him particularly.

Afterwards the kids sneaked up to the belfry, as they'd done before, to hang out while their parents socialized.

Billy listened while the others argued about where they were going to go next week. Tuesday was the last day of school, with summer school coming up only ten days later for all of them except Sean.

"I can have the car for two, maybe three days," Charley was saying. "We could go down to the Keys."

"I want to go to Disney World," Sean said.

"It'll cost too much. Besides, we're getting too old for that stuff now," Charley said.

"I can get money," Sean said.

"But can you get your parents to let you go, little boy?" Walt said, taunting him.

"Of course! Everyone trusts Charley."

"What do you think, Billy?" Maria said, coming up to him.

Billy wasn't looking at the others at all. He was looking out of the window at the steeple, remembering. What must have it been like to see a boy on the steeple, a boy covered with snow? It must have spooked them.. He heard them say his name and said, "I don't know. I guess I don't have any say, really, do I?"

"Sure you do. You're one of us," Maria said.

Walt said, "I guess that makes it official!"

Billy had almost forgotten how to smile. But he did it now. He felt awkward about it, guilty almost.

Maria said, "Billy, when you smile you look almost presentable. Cute, even." She went up to him at the window and touched him, very lightly, on the shoulder. He turned around and tried to smile again. He hadn't promised the Snow Dragon not to smile, but smiling was almost as hard as crying. "Like, I really like you," Maria said.

"Dude!" Sean said.

Billy said, "But I don't even know if I *can* go." Stark was going to come back sometime. Perhaps he was waiting for him now, a shadow in the doorway, his belt in his hand.

"So what?" Maria said. "We'll smuggle you out." So the situation was the reverse of what it was in the Fallen Country. He would be the one in chains waiting to be rescued.

"You make it sound so easy!" he said. This was a new world and he didn't know the rules. At least in the Fallen Country you knew what to expect. He was happy and frightened at the same time. He started to panic. He looked at the faces of the others, so enthusiastic, so welcoming . . . and for a moment they were transmuted into the faces of a circus audience, laughing as the whip cracked over the leaping lion . . . he couldn't take it suddenly. He had to leave. He turned and ran down the steps before the other kids had a chance to call him back.

•••

Maria said, "Go after him, someone!"

Charley said, "No. We have to talk something over." He held up his hand. The others tensed. He cleared his throat. Then he said, "Okay. You've all had a chance to see him, the way he is. I admit I thought he was just another nerd at first. Then I spent the night at his house on Friday. He lives in a nightmare all the time and he can't wake up. And we can't leave him there or we'll be as bad as that madman."

"What did Dora say?" Maria said.

"I really thought she was going to do something about it. Sometimes she seems to understand everything, other times—" He told them about the child-proof condo he'd seen her go into.

"You're saying she's pretty cool most of the time," Maria said, "but in the end she's not one of us."

"It's up to *us* to save him," Charley said.

"Let's nuke Stark's house," Walt said.

"What about the cops?" Sean said. "I mean, they're supposed to protect us from child abuse, aren't they?"

Maria said, "I agree with Sean. We should report it."

Charley said, "That's legal stuff, grownup's business. Dora will have to do it."

Walt said, "Well, let's go there now and beat up on her until she agrees to our terms."

"Yeah," Charley said. "It's time for us kids to revolt."

"Storm the Bastille!" Maria said.

"I see you like to watch old late-night movies too," Charley said, overcome by a rash of warmth toward her. She moved closer to him, laughing. *"Vive la révolution!"*

"What's he talking about?" Walt said. "I say nuke the bad guys, like totally nuke 'em."

•••

As they approached the railings of Dora's condo complex, though, Charley felt his resolve weakening. He tried to quell this with a burst of anger, fantasizing as he pulled into the street about what he might say to Dora: "You threw Billy's problem into my lap . . . it's your responsibility, not mine. . . ."

It was too late to prepare a speech, though, because Dora was standing at the gate, apparently dropping some letters into a mailbox. She looked up. Charley stopped the car and the four kids approached her. Charley was steeling himself to say something resentful when she smiled at them.

"So you've uncovered my little secret," she said.

"Why not?" Charley said, losing control of himself a bit. "In the day you suck out all *our* secrets . . . and at night you hide away. . . ."

"Like a kind of reverse vampire?" Dora said, laughing. Sean and Walt and Maria laughed with her, and Charley felt a bit foolish. "You think I could really afford a place like this, on the salary of a counsellor just out of college? It's my grandparents' place. They're away, on permanent vacation. I get postcards from them: Bangkok, Paris, the Bahamas. But, okay, I confess: sometimes it's good to know that kids are not going to come battering down my door . . . that I can be alone. I guess you guys are going to invade anyway."

Charley persisted, "We have to talk about Billy."

Dora stopped smiling. "Yes, Billy."

"We've talked," Sean said, "and we've agreed—"

"It's gotta stop!" Maria said.

"Call the cops," Walt said.

She looked at them. Charley could tell she was disturbed by the idea of a direct, dramatic solution. He realized, "They're as perplexed as we are, these grownups. They don't know everything."

"When I agreed to listen to him," Dora said, "I promised him I'd never tell. My little room was to be like a confessional, like a black hole. His words."

"But you can't keep a thing like that secret! You wouldn't talk like that if you'd seen drop down from the sky, if you'd had to pull him, frozen stiff, out of the sea." Charley didn't mean to say what he said next, and when it said it he felt he was somehow betraying Billy: "I've been inside his secret kingdom. It's not just his anymore. It's not a secret anymore."

The other kids looked at him weirdly. Only Dora knew what he was talking about. "You've been inside?" There was anxiety in her voice, but also a kind of longing.

"Oh, never mind." But he couldn't retract it now. "But just call the cops, okay? Then it'll be out of your hands. You can go back behind your wall and be safe again." Charley had never been so critical of adults to their faces before. And the strange thing was, she was taking it without protest. "I'm leaving childhood further and further behind," he thought, "I'm becoming their equal."

Dora was looking at him in a new way. "She respects me," he thought. And then he saw that Maria was taking it all in, and that Dora's respect for Charley had made a big impression on her.

At last Dora said, "Thank you, Charley, for making me see."

"Just do something, and do it fast," Walt said.

"So you're on our side, then." Maria said.

"It's not a question of sides!" Charley said, and Dora nodded to herself. "It's a question of nobody could deserve what this kid has to live through and we're all he's got and if we don't do this no one will."

"But we have to think of Billy first," Dora said. "What's to become of him afterward? A foster home?"

"We'll cross that bridge when we get to it," Charley said.

"And what about Billy's feelings?" Dora said. "This man is destroying his life, but in a way, Billy really cares for him."

"Yeah. Getting hit on is what passes for love in his life," Charley said bitterly.

"We have to do this carefully," Dora said. "You said something about taking Billy away on a trip once."

"Disney World," Sean said.

"This needs to be done while Billy's out of the way. We have to cooperate. You get him out of the way and I'll go to the police. When you get back, it'll be over."

Charley brightened when Dora said this. "Thank you for having a plan," he said.

"Thank you," she said. "You're right; I have been afraid get more deeply involved, afraid this thing was too big for me."

The kids turned to go toward Charley's car.

As Charley got into the driver's seat, Dora shouted after him, "What do you mean, you pulled him frozen stiff out of the sea?"

Charley said, "I don't know if I should say more about it . . . the Fallen Country, I mean. Maybe he'll take you there one day."

She stared at him curiously, perhaps wondering if he was having her on. As he drove away, though, he became convinced that all of them would visit the land of cold and desolation before it was over.

And that their journey to Billy's secret kingdom would somehow change their lives, maybe forever.

Chapter Fourteen
The Sea of Ice

Billy had fled the belfry in panic. But he didn't want to go home yet, either. He walked away from the church. His sneakers stuck on the melting asphalt as he crossed the plaza. He walked. He couldn't go home. He'd have to wait until really late, when Stark was asleep, maybe.

He walked around. He was half in, half out of the Fallen Country. The mall was swathed in mist and he could see outlines of castle spires in the storm clouds that streamed in the sky. There were piles of dirty snow when he walked along the beach. Lions pawed at sewer gratings in the sidewalk, but when he bent down to set them free they had melted into rivulets of dirty water. He stared at the summer sun but his eyes didn't water.

Evening fell. Where was he going to go? He was tired, so tired. The Fallen Country was just out of reach. As it had been that day when he'd been showing off his skill at the arcade.

He didn't know what time it was when he reached the house. Midnight maybe. He listened at the door; he didn't hear anything. Stark's motorbike, chromeglittery in the moonlight, leaned against the kitchen sill.

Gently, wincing as it creaked, he eased the door handle open and slipped into the house. It wasn't quite dark; the TV in the living room was on, but the screen was blank, and the set fizzed. It was like snow.

In the armchair, maybe asleep, was Stark.

Billy tried to sneak past him, but Stark spoke. "Billy, Billy." Billy froze. There wasn't any anger in Stark's voice. "Where you been, Billy-boy? I looked for you, God I looked."

Billy didn't move. In the dim light he saw that Stark's eyes were open, but he didn't seem completely awake. Maybe he was hypnotized by the snow on the screen. Maybe he was talking in his sleep. His eyes stared dead ahead.

Billy didn't say anything.

"Come on, Billy-boy," Stark said. "Come on, I ain't gonna hurt you." His voice was quiet, soothing, the way you might talk to an animal. Billy thought: "The way he used to speak to his lions, perhaps. After he'd whipped them and they were down and they knew he was their master."

Stark said, "I looked for you all over, man! I looked in the dungeon . . . at the hydra gate . . . in the plain of stone lions . . . in the castle of the princess. . . ."

Billy couldn't help himself. He blurted out, "So it is you! Waiting for me at the heart of the Fallen Country. You've known all this time it wasn't something I made up."

Stark said, "Billy-boy, don't say a thing, don't make me wake up."

Billy waited.

Stark sat for a long time. His breathing, heavy and rhythmic, was the only sound in the close, humid air. At last he said, "It doesn't have to be this way. We could be a great team. You and me. Kings of the Burning Cold." His voice rose, raspy and frightening. "Kings, you and me! It was all for you."

"All for me?" Billy said, angry. "You *hurt* me! Not just my body, but the me inside. You taught me how to hate."

"Hate will make you strong." At last Stark seemed to see Billy. His eyes glowed with a cold blue fire. Billy shrank from his gaze, retreated into the corridor.

As he went into his room he heard Stark say, in a despairing moan, "But I didn't ask to be hated. And I didn't ask for the cold to seep all the way into my heart."

•••

Monday morning Joan was raving because Stark had disappeared. Billy knew that the great confrontation in the Fallen Country would be soon now. Because the two worlds were blurring into each other. He looked from the school bus window and saw a blizzard no one else could see, and shivered while the rest of the kids sweated and grew ill-tempered.

It was also Billy's last session with Dora before school closed down. The day was a sizzler, and so was the session. When he charged into her office, his eyes were blazing with rage. "He knows about it!" he shouted. "He knows it's real, he's a part of it. It's coming to a head soon, I know it is!"

She was taken aback. She asked him, "What did Charley mean, when he told me he had to pull you out of the sea?"

She was trying to ignore him! Billy thought angrily. Sullenly he sat down. "It was his own fault. He wasn't strong enough to stay with me. Anyways, how'd you know about it?" Charley had given him away . . . no one could be trusted, not anyone. "He chickened out. Otherwise we might have gone over to the other side."

"You mean, both of you into the Fallen Country?"

"No, no," he said. "Over the Sea of Ice . . . to the other shore . . . that's the next mission."

"That's something new," she said. "You haven't talked about it before."

Billy told her what had happened, from the time she and Charley left the hospital until the time Charley saw Billy plummet into the ocean:

•••

One moment the nurse was administering the Demerol into the tube that dangled above his head, and the drug was rushing into his veins and he felt himself sinking, sinking—

The next moment the bed became the dragon's back, the whole room dissolved into the cold familiar landscape, and they were soaring, high, high, high. "You came!" Billy shouted. "I thought you'd never come, I thought I'd lie there in that hospital ward forever!"

"We must hurry," the Snow Dragon said. Its wings beat noiselessly against the whine of the high wind. "There's work to do."

"Work?"

"Yes! Below! Look!"

And Billy saw children in the snow beneath, all trudging, trudging northward.

"Where are they going?" he said. They were coming from all directions, their paths joining in a tortuous road that snaked up to the horizon, where he could see, shrouded in mist, a great gate.

"They are doing what you are doing. But you must lead the way."

"North?"

"Yes. The Ringmaster's fortress lies north of here. You want to reach him, don't you?"

"Of course! Of course!" Billy said, remembering his anger and the pain he had left behind on that hospital bed.

"You are to lead them. You are to open the gate."

No sooner had the dragon finished speaking than Billy saw the many-headed monster burst up from a snowbank beside the gate. He knew what to do; slaying monsters was a regular part of his excursions into the Fallen Country. He reached into his store of anger and pulled out a sword. It glowed cold blue, and its hilt was inlaid with crystals of ice. They fought. Again and again the dragon dove and the sword slashed the air. Billy's anger sparked against metallic flesh. The monster did not roar, but whenever he swiped off one of the monster's heads there would come a whistling sound as the wind raced through its empty body cavity . . . and at least two more heads would grow in its place. They fought on, as the children cowered behind dunes of snow and waited. "It's useless," he cried. "I'll just grow tired, and then I'll have to go back to the world above."

"You must try," the dragon said.

Billy was about to cave in from exhaustion when he turned and saw Charley standing beside him. And it gave him hope. Together they fought, with Charley shouting advice and telling him the beast was named hydra, and showing him how to conquer it by burning the neck-stumps. It had never occurred to Billy that these monsters might have names, that a stranger might know what they were. Perhaps Charley was the companion he needed . . . he knew he couldn't reach the Ringmaster alone.

But Charley soon started to fade from the Fallen Country.

"Save me," Billy said, feeling the tiredness setting in, overwhelming him.

Below them he could see the hydra on a rampage now, the children scattering in fear.

"Why?" he cried out. "Why must I lead them, where are we going?"

The dragon said, in its still small voice, "I will show you."

And turned its face upward, to where the sun should have been, and soared.

A huge city sprang into view . . . with minarets of ice and cathedrals of snow and tall skyscrapers like popsicles. The city was on the edge of a sea. But what an ocean? The waves moved sluggishly, more like molasses than like water, and when the dragon glided down near the surface he saw that it was packed almost solid with chunks of ice.

"The whole city will come to meet you when you lead the army here," the Snow Dragon said. "It is a city of captives . . . of caged lion . . . for a thousand years they have brooded, waiting for one who will lead them. Look, farther to the north . . . do you see anything?"

"Only a thin pale outline, a cloud maybe."

"Another continent."

"Shall we go there then?"

"I cannot fly there. There is a wall of force that surrounds the northern continent. Only your anger can penetrate it. With a bridge of anger such as you can build, Billy Binder, all the Ringmaster's captives can follow you across to his fortress . . . and perhaps you will defeat him . . . I hardly dare hope . . . and then . . ."

"What then?"

"I have heard, Billy Binder that inside the Ringmaster's stronghold there's another gateway . . . a way out of the Fallen Country . . . a path to freedom."

"Then there's no choice. We have to go there."

"Yes."

"I want to do it now!"

"No. You don't have the strength anymore. Your store of anger is much depleted after the battle with the hydra . . . you must go back, replenish it."

"Now, take me there now, you have to!"

They flew out over the sea. The northern continent was clearly visible now, a thing of icy crags and snow-capped mountains and glaciers and frozen waterfalls. Billy saw that it was even more bleak than the southern continent. But he hardened his heart and sought to become one with the numbing cold. "Keep going," he said. "As far as you can."

They collided into the forceshield. It was like rebounding against an invisible trampoline in mid-air. Lightning, whip-shaped, flashed over their heads. Billy heard low mocking laughter from far away. He didn't know whether it was aimed at him.

"All right." Billy stood up and faced north. "I'm going to build that bridge."

He started. He dredged up all the hatred in his heart. Slowly the rainbow of ice began to form. The forceshield started to give way a little . . . then, with a sound like the cracking of ice on a river in the spring, the shield began to burst . . . he could see the splinter lines forming, almost like the shattering of a video screen. "Come on! We can go through now!" he cried, urging the dragon forward. "Come on!" They ducked through a fissure in the barrier, then—

"No!" Billy screamed.

Where was the dragon? Falling, he wrenched his body around in time to see the barrier reform and the dragon get caught in it like a fly in a spiderweb.

He hit the water hard. He was thinking, "It should be soft, I always imagined it would be soft to fall into the sea, but it's harsh, it's painful, it's like being punched all over by Stark."

Billy didn't wake up until he heard Charley's words, on the scorching sand at the beach near Boca Blanca, "If you don't wake up, the Ringmaster will win. . . ."

•••

"Pretty dramatic, huh?" Billy said. "And a great finish to an fascinating bunch of sessions with a schizo geek."

"You know I don't think that of you."

"You gonna write a book about me?   If you do, don't forget to change my name."

"I told you, what happens here is just between you and me. "Everything's going to be all right," She didn't sound too convincing. Something was going on, something outside Billy's control!   Charley blabbing to her, and now this "everything's going to be all right" bullshit. Billy knew from experience that nothing ever turned out all right when people said it would. That was something they said to cover up their fear.

"Wait," she said. "There's one thing I promised Charley I'd do."

"I was right! You two are in it together . . . you're plotting something."

She picked up the phone. It was a speakerphone, and from the tune the touch-tone played, Billy realized she was calling his mother. He shrank into himself, panicking. "Joan?" she said. "I wanted to ask you about the possibility of Billy going on a trip with some of his schoolmates, Charley Moore?   I can vouch for—"

Joan interrupted her. "He's gone off somewhere now, I don't know when he's coming back. Do you think it's another woman? He was so angry when he left, Billy was defying him. It's terrible without him, I can't get to sleep at night."

"You should cut down on the coffee," Ms Marx said angrily.   Just like a grownup, to blame it all on nutrition or caffeine when the problems were in your heart, not in chemicals.

"You'll never understand, will you? But Billy can go wherever he wants. It doesn't matter now."

"He'll be back in a couple of days."   Then, warily, she added, "I'll take the responsibility."

Those words moved Billy somehow.   No one had ever said before, "I'll take the responsibility."   It occurred to him that his own stepmother had never said that. His feelings about Ms. Marx were getting more and more mixed up.   On the one hand she seemed to be abandoning him, and on the other....

All he could say was, "Thank you, Ms. Marx. That was a great help.   But our time's up."   He was too nervous to stay. He wanted to get away.

"Wait a moment—"

He waited for her to finish.

She said lamely, "I wish there could have been more I could help you with."

He paused at the door.   They confronted each other for a moment. He said, "How can I let you help me when you still don't even believe me?"

Billy saw that she was struggling with herself, but she couldn't lie, even to reassure him.   "No, I can't really believe your stories, Billy."

"But *when* you believe . . . oh, then we'll go places, you and me."

He saw that methodically, Dora Marx had been shredding his file with a pair of scissors.   Then she let it drop to the floor.   "End of school year-—case dismissed!" he said bitterly.

The digital thermometer on his door read 103°F. "I hate the sunlight!" Ms. Marx said passionately.   "I wish it would snow."

Chapter Fifteen
The Yearbook

At seven in the morning, Tuesday, Billy heard a car pull into the driveway of his house. He jumped out of bed and ran out. He ran into his mother in the hall. "It's friends of yours," she said, "lots of them."

Billy flung open the front door.

"Are you ready?" Walt shouted.

"But we still have school today!" Billy said.

"Who cares?" Charley said. "Last day. Nothing's gonna happen anyway."

Billy ran into his house and threw some clothes into a shopping bag. Then he put on his sneakers and bolted out before his mother could stop him.

As he jumped into the back seat with Walt and Sean, he heard his mother muttering, "I guess it's OK, as long as it's the last day of school—and that counsellor, whatshername, cleared it with me."

Billy realized that she was too preoccupied with Stark's disappearance to bother with him. "Keep on driving," he said. Charley zoomed out onto Federal and then, after a few miles of traffic lights, turned sharply onto the Florida Turnpike.

"It's going to get hot soon," he said, "and the air-conditioning's not too hot . . . uh, cool."

The sun was rising. They had to roll down the windows. Then they had to shout at each other to be heard.   It didn't make any difference anyway, because they were all talking at once.

Along the turnpike is the Florida tourists know and love: the orange groves and the hotel chains and the endless billboards advertising Disney World. Billy had seen the turnpike only once . . . when they'd driven down from up north, on their way to settle in Boca Blanca . . . and he couldn't remember it. It was a new adventure for one whose long-distance travel had lately been confined to riding on dragonback.

After about an hour they pulled into a gas station, and Maria, who was sitting in the front seat with Charley, said, "I guess it's time for the announcement."

"What announcement?" Sean said. Clearly he was only pretending to be puzzled.

They all turned on Billy. Involuntarily he flinched; it was a natural reflex for him. "Hey, stay casual," Maria said, "we got you a present."

She opened the glove compartment and pulled out something that looked familiar. . . a book, bound in brown leatherette.

"What are you guys doing with that—" Billy began, but Charley put up his hand for silence.

"I stole it from your house," he said. "Sorry. I should have told you."

Maria handed it to him.

Billy said, "So what? I don't care," and started to throw it over the back seat, into the hatch. But Maria grabbed his arm.

"Aren't you going to open it?"

Billy didn't see why, but he did it anyway. Then he gasped. "It's not mine; you must have picked up the wrong one."

"Look again," Charley said.

Billy read:

To Billy, who I wish I'd known in ninth grade. You really do look cute when you tidy yourself up. Love, Maria.

Roses are red
Violets are blue
Your mother farted
And out came you! YOUR FRIEND WALT

Quickly Billy flipped the pages. There were all kinds of signatures in the book now, from his teachers, from the school's basketball star. "I ran around all Monday morning getting this stuff!" Maria said.

"Makes you feel almost human, doesn't it?" Charley said.

"I guess." Billy realized that these things were important to them, and that they'd gone to a lot of trouble to make him feel like one of them. He began to feel happy. He looked at the others' expectant faces and said, "Thanks."

"Speech! Speech!" Walt said.

"Come on, give the boy a break," Maria said.

Charley paid for the gas and they got back on the turnpike.

"By the way," Billy said. . . .

"YE-E-E-S?" everyone screamed out at the same time.

"Where are we going, anyways?"

"Oh, to Disney World. Didn't anyone tell you?" Sean said. "That's what we decided on. Money talks." He pulled a C note from his pocket and waved it around. "Nyah, nyah. Spoiled rotten, that's me."

"Hey, careful with that thing!" Walt said. "We got the windows rolled down, remember?"

•••

Billy had never been to Kissimee before, although he knew that this small town near Orlando housed not only the fabulous Disney World but also a whole bunch of other "worlds": Ocean World with its shark exhibit (which had had a starring rôle in *Jaws 3-D)* and, of course, Circus World. . . .

Billy felt a prickle of fear go through him when they passed a vast Billboard with a picture of a clown. But no one commented on it. He heaved a sigh of relief.

Everyone knew exactly what they wanted to do at Disney World: they'd all been there dozens of times. "If we ignore Epcott," Charley said, "and just concentrate on rides and stuff, we can do the whole place in maybe six hours." They parked, got on the monorail, and rode into the Magic Kingdom. Billy was amazed to see that they had the whole park memorized and that they made their way from ride to ride swiftly, without any malingering. It was definitely an express tour.

"We'd better do Space Mountain now," Sean said, "before the crowds really start."

"Yeah," Charley said. They were all walking fast now, sticking to shaded pathways when they could.

Then, after twenty minutes in line, they were inside. Billy sat behind Maria in one of those two-seater rocketships. Holographic stars whirled in the imitated night sky. Comets danced. They shot out of the launching tube and flew up into the darkness. Maria squealed. She felt warm as Billy clasped her to him. She shook with a kind of crazy joy as they fell, still in darkness, as the coaster curve swerved and brought them twisting against gravity. He felt her exuberance, a vibrant, thrilling thing. He had not felt this way on the back of the dragon.

He was shaking as they emerged into the sunlight.

Other rides followed. He couldn't keep track of it all. The colors, the vistas assaulted his senses. The other kids were running now, trying to beat the crowds. They knew this kingdom as well as he knew the Fallen Country; knew the short cuts, the places where you could cut around barricades. He ran too, losing himself in their excitement. They yo-ho-hoed their way through the Pirates of the Caribean, they oohed and aahed through the haunted mansion with its laser holography, they screamed their way down the precipices of the Thunder Mountain Railway.

"None of them are really good rides," Charley said, "if you rate them just as rides, you know, measure the velocity, count the curves, that kind of thing? But the *scenery* is radical."

"Yeah," Walt said. They stopped to buy frosties. The sweat was pouring down all their faces. Maria had a big cup of diet coke. When a bee settled on her hand she dropped it with a shriek and everyone within range got sprayed. One of the attendants nearly jumped out of his Mickey Mouse suit.

"Really cooled us off," Charley said. They all laughed.

The day wore on.

"Let's go somewhere else," Sean said.. "I'm bored."

"Wait a minute, you were the one who insisted on coming here," Walt said.

"Well, let's go look for a motel or something. We can bum around some more tomorrow," Charley said. "You're right, the heat's getting to us."

"My head! My head!" Walt said, pointing to a helium balloon as it wafted by.

•••

They drove around aimlessly for a while. The afternoon seem to stretch and stretch. They stopped for fast food and drove around some more.

They passed a billboard that showed circus elephants.

Billy said, clutching the yearbook, "This has been a really happy day for me. Thanks. And it all began with this yearbook. It's the day of the yearbook."

Even Walt beamed at this.

"It's probably been the happiest day of my life," Billy said. He wanted to make sure they really knew, that he wasn't just making it up. He snuggled against the half-open window, letting the warm air tousle his hair.

They passed by another circus billboard.

Walt said to Charley, "You know what you were saying earlier? About how the scenery in those rides is really awesome but the rides themselves aren't that thrilling? Isn't there somewhere around here with, like, more exciting roller coasters?"

"Yeah," Sean said. "The Daredevil."

"That's in Circus World," Walt said.

"What are we waiting for?" Sean said. "I still got money."

"No, I don't think so," Charley said.

Billy pricked up his ears.

"Why not?" Sean said. "I want to ride a really *good* roller coaster, Walt's right."

"No!" Charley said.

It suddenly occurred to Billy that Charley was trying to protect him. He knew that Stark claimed to have once been a lion tamer. He probably suspected that Billy would have something against circuses. Billy felt embarrassed. He didn't want Charley to feel he had to protect him.

"It's okay," Billy said quietly. "I can handle it."

"What's he talking about?" Sean said, completely oblivious to the heated emotions around him.

Charley said, "Do I have to say it aloud? For God's sake!"

Walt grabbed Sean and whispered something in his ear.

Sean's eyes widened. "Oh," he said. "Sorry, Billy."

Billy said resentfully, "What is all this? You don't have to baby me. I'm tough, you know. I'm not going to run off screaming just because—" He stopped. A memory surfaced from almost eight years ago. The circus. The snow. The flier. The lions. Stark. And he said, "I think I am destined to come to this place."

Charley said, "Now that's just what I was trying to avoid. I mean, we didn't bring you here to remind you about . . . you know."

Maria said, "Maybe we should go, though. Maybe when he sees, you know, a real, big-time circus, where they care for the animals properly and all, he'll feel better about—"

"About 'you know.'" Billy was bitter. "You guys can't even bring yourselves to say it. But, like, it really doesn't matter to me. I can tell the difference. Besides . . . I'm supposed to face reality, right? It's supposed to cure me of my . . . fantasies. My lies." He looked straight at Charley. He could tell that Charley could see his eyes in the rear view mirror. "My lies," he repeated, knowing that Charley had seen, however briefly, the Fallen Country, even if he tried to deny it.

Maria said, "It's ruined! And we tried so hard." She seemed on the verge of tears, and Billy could tell that Charley was upset. And because Maria had done for him what none of the princesses in the Fallen Country had ever done, Billy didn't want her to be sad.

"Don't cry," Billy said. "Nothing's ruined. And I appreciate what you did, I really do."

There was a long, appalling silence for about five minutes. It seemed that, without being conscious of it, Charley had been driving toward Circus World the whole time. Because they could see it all of a sudden, a city of tentlike structures rearing up in the distance....

"Well?" Sean demanded. "Are we going in or aren't we?"

"I don't know," Charley said.

But he didn't stop driving.

As for Billy: he was remembering that distant day ever more vividly. He remembered how he'd seen the sunshine through the tent-flap in the TV commercial, how he'd imagined that Karney Park would be transformed from winter to spring when he emerged from that circus tent. Maybe he hadn't been imagining things. Maybe he'd seen a vision of today, with the sun still high and the air sticky with the fragrance of fresh oranges.

Chapter Sixteen
To Free the Lions

The first thing they did in Circus World was to rush toward the Daredevil, a ride where you start up high and you're slingshotted out and the car zings right into a three-sixty and then you're suspended, defying gravity, for a perilous moment before being zapped back the way you came. For a while Billy thought he would be able to escape having to confront the circus itself, whose big top billowed up in the background. More sights and sounds as the kids ran for the giant roller coaster: little children smiling as they strained to see at the edge of the porpoise pool, and plaster elephants, garishly colored, guarding the gateways.

Sean and Walt stopped at a concession stand to have clown faces painted on. Maria giggled as they emerged with bulbous red noses and huge pouting lips. Then they rode the Dardevil. Billy closed his eyes the whole time. Charley was right; though it lacked the spectacle of the Disney World rides, it had more of the pure thrill of just falling, having your stomach turned inside out, sheer screaming.

"Maybe I shouldn't be afraid," he thought. This wasn't the world of the Ringmaster, wielder of pain. This place was all fun and laughter and bright colors. As the coaster roared, the wind rushed over him and caressed him, soft and warm.

This was the beautiful thing he'd imagined eight years ago. Not the seedy circus tent standing in the muddy snow. "This is awesome," he said, as they rode it for the second time.

Maria was sitting beside him, and she smiled and said, "I'm glad you came, Billy. I'm so glad I know you."

"?" Billy shrugged. She held his hand as they fell together. Charley, sitting behind them, made some sarcastic comment, and they all laughed.

Later they went to a demonstration of circus flying. They just caught the tail end of it, a blur, twisting figure that spun madly in the air before he-she-it collapsed into the net beneath. Then the announcer called for a volunteer from the audience.

Billy stood up.

The announcer pointed at him. "Over eighteen?" Billy nodded, just to see if he could get away with it. To his astonishment they called him up to the platform. And he was climbing a rope ladder, and they were attaching a training harness—a "mechanic", the announcer told the audience—to him.

And then he was actually standing on the trapeze and they were swinging it out, out over the audience's heads! He squeezed his eyes tight shut. He was a bit scared. But he felt the mechanic pull taut and knew that he was safe.

But he didn't open his eyes, not just yet.

Instead he thought of the boy he'd seen so long ago ... first by the lion's cage, nursing his bruises ... then in the air, suspended by magic, his body arcing to a distant slow music.

He remembered how he'd envied that boy his ability to turn pain into beauty. "Maybe," he thought, "that's why I'm here."

The trapeze swung, back and forth, back and forth. Somewhere a snare drum rolled ... crescendoing ... the crowd gasped. "At last," he thought, "I can be like that nameless boy—"

And he leaped, thrusting himself into what he imagined to be the curve of an aerial somersault ... for a split second he was weightless, free, like a spirit ... he closed his eyes but he could still see, he was caught up in the memory ... he was in the other place now, the circus of long ago. The young flier was somersaulting towards him as he dangled, upside down with outstretched arms. It was so real, so real. The other boy straightened, reached up, shouted "Catch me, Billy Binder, catch me ..."

"I can't!" Billy shouted. He looked around wildly. The circus tent was empty and snow was pouring in through rips in the canvas. "I'm not a real trapeze artist ... I'm just me, Billy."

He could see into the boy's eyes. They were empty, soulless. He said, "You're one of them now. One of the things of the Fallen Country; You're not human anymore—" And he couldn't catch the boy and the boy was sucked into the whirlwind darkness below, and Billy was screaming, trying to wrest himself free of the Fallen Country—

The mechanic jerked him taut! He was hanging over the net now. He was back in the world of Charley and Maria and their friends. The audience was applauding. "We have a brave volunteer this evening, folks!" the announcer was saying. "He has actually attempted the dreaded triple somersault! Luckily, the mechanic prevents all accidents and makes the training sessions safe even for a beginner."

He felt himself being gradually lowered. He felt faintly embarrassed about the whole thing now. But the others clustered around him and made much of him.

"You really had us scared!" Maria said. "But of course you knew you'd be OK, with that thing attached."

"I was pretty scared myself," Billy said.

"You didn't look scared," Sean said. "Hey, do you think they'll let me try something next?"

"No way," Charley said. "Your mother'll waste me if I don't get you home in one piece."

•••

As the sun started to set, Maria said, "I just have to sit down. It's finally starting to get to me."

"Is it still the best day of your life, Billy?" Charley said.

"Definitely," Billy said. He tried to forget about his momentary trip into the Fallen Country.

"My feet, my feet!" Maria said. "Someone pay attention to my feet, like I'm totally exhausted."

"I guess we should go in there," Walt said, pointing at the big top.

Billy tensed. It had been in the back of his mind all along, the feeling that this day had been just too enjoyable, that something terrible must be waiting for him at the end of it. He looked at the lines of people pushing their way into the tent, laughing, chattering people. Sean and Walt were already trying to jump the line. "It can't be that bad," Billy thought. It was like doing those aerobatic tricks with that mechanic on your back. Sort of unreal. Nothing to it. He dismissed his misgivings and followed them inside.

They were letting in the lions as they sat down near the front row. These weren't mangy, whipmarked lions . . . they seemed healthy and happy, and they roared mightily. Their trainer was an attractive woman ("the world's only female lion tamer!" the announcer rhapsodized) who wore a skimpy, sequined outfit and waved a short quirt around.

"This'll be OK," he said, determined not to act like a nerd.

Maria said, "I told you. The S.P.C.A.'s got nothing to complain about on these guys." She sat down beside him, between him and Charley. Billy could see that Charley was getting upset about the rapidly growing friendship between him and Maria, and that he was trying not to show it, to act casual. Billy didn't want to offend Charley, so he didn't answer Maria, and edged away from her on the bench.

He turned to watch the lions.

He kept telling himself, "It's make-believe, it's not like me and Stark." But already he felt the anger building up. And he thought of the lions in the Fallen Country. What had the dragon said? *A city of captives and caged lions . . . at the edge of the Sea of Ice.* "To free the lions," he whispered. Had Maria heard him? He didn't think so. The circus band burst into a tango, blaringly hypnotic, and the lions leaped from pedestal to pedestal as the trainer danced around them. . . .

Then, after a dramatic drum roll, they brought out the burning hoop. The announcer said that Frodo the Jungle King was going to leap the hoop in a single bound.

Billy started to shake. Maria tugged at Charley. "What are we supposed to do?" she said. He felt her terror. The crowd's roar melded into the howling of the cold wind—

Charley was leaning over, shaking him by the shoulders. "Don't leave us . . . don't go back into your Fallen Country. . . ." he was saying.

Billy cried, "What do you mean? Don't go back there? Do you think I ever left it? Do you think I'm not there now, at this very moment?" And he stood up. A few people stared at him curiously, but turned their attention back to the show.

Billy got up. He started stepping over the benches, elbowing people aside. Someone shouted, "Excuse me, sir, could you sit down, please?"

And Billy was standing in a bubble of the Fallen Country, in the middle of a blizzard, hurling darts of jagged anger at the bars that held the lions in—

Charley got up and followed Billy, reached into the bubble, his arms were half in the heat and half in the pelting snow, he seized Billy by the shoulder and tried to pull him out, but—

The bolts of anger were sparking against steel now, the cage was cracking. Someone screamed. The hoop flew up into the air as though yanked by a wire. It burned against the dark fabric of the tent, above Billy's head, like a halo. A lion was pawing at the side of the arena. More screaming now. Charley strained against the pull of the Fallen Country and Billy oozed out into the aisle. A lion was licking at his sneakers. Billy stood quite still, without visible emotion. "Let's get out of here!" Charley yelled. People were jostling madly, trampling each other. A voice over the hubbub kept repeating, "Stay calm, please, stay calm."

The lion turned, roared.

"Stay calm, please, stay calm—"

A shot rang out. The lion crumpled against the side benches.

Maria and Charley were pulling Billy out now, merging with the crowd as it bottlenecked out. People were crawling under the benches and emerging from the scaffolding. They heard a voice, not quite calm, over the din, "Please return to your seats . . . the cage bars have not been broken . . . the lion has merely been stunned with a sleeping dart . . . no cause for alarm . . ."

Some members of the crowd were going back inside. The entrance was jammed. Somehow, amid all the confusion, the whole group managed to assemble on the path outside. "Let's blow," Charley said, "I don't feel like sticking around, I don't feel like trying to explain what happened."

They were all hysterical by the time they made it back to the car. Only Billy seemed unmoved by it all.

"Did *you* do that?" Sean said, awed.

Billy said, "I guess you don't want to know me anymore."

"Oh, nonsense," Maria said. "It's neat you can do things like that."

"He was free," Billy said, "for a few seconds anyway." He wondered whether he would ever be able to say the same for himself.

•••

They cruised around looking for somewhere to crash. After they pooled their money they realized they didn't have enough for any motel they'd ever heard of, so Charley drove out of town, and they watched the billboards for room night prices. About five miles out they started to drop, first into the thirties, then down to about $25. "I guess we'll just have to cram into a roach motel room," Charley said, and they pulled into something seedy-looking. It was dark. A sign flashed, on and off,

Bryan Webb's Motel and Laundromat   and Maria commented, "I've seen worse."

Billy said, "I've seen <u>much</u> worse. When we were moving down to Florida from up north. Long time ago." His voice still showed no emotion.

Charley parked where the people in the motel office couldn't see and went in a got a single room. Then they all piled in. Sean started to jump up and down on one of the beds. Walt turned on the TV. "This is primitive!" he said. "No MTV, no HBO, no nothing."

"For twenty-five bucks," Charley said, "it's all we're getting."

He turned to watch Billy, who was sitting in a corner all by himself. He was getting fed up with the whole thing. He hadn't asked to be Billy Binder's babysitter. He was still angry at Dora for—as he saw it—foisting the whole situation off on him. And now Maria was paying Billy so much attention. Oh, he knew she was sorry for him, and of course he was too, but—

The TV suddenly died. Walt started pounding at it. Nothing happened. "Damn!" he said.

"Oh," Charley said, "I see you flunked the Arthur Fonzarelli School of Appliance Repair."

"That' ain't funny," Walt said, turning on him.

Charley looked around. Everyone was really tense. And it was because of Billy. Damn it, why did Billy have to appear in their lives? Everything was so neat and organized before.

"Damn television," Walt muttered, kicking it. It sputtered to life for a moment, then died again. "What are we going to do? I'm not going to sit around discussing the meaning of life."

Sean said, "We could tell ghost stories."

"I'm spooked enough as it is," Maria said, sighing.

A long silence . . . you could feel the tension building up more and more. There was going to be an outburst of some kind any moment. Charley just knew it.

"I'll tell a story," Billy said at last. "Better than that. I'll *show* you guys a story. Better than any TV show. Come with me."

They stared at Billy, fascinated. They had already come to the realization that there was something mysterious, maybe supernatural, about him. Each of them had his own idea of what had happened down at Circus World, but they knew Billy had had something to do with it. And Charley, who knew that Billy's secret world was so powerful that it could spill out into reality and draw others into it, knew what must happen next.

"Come on!" Billy whispered urgently. "You want to see magic tricks, don't you? And deep down inside, you *know* I got some kind of weird power."

"Wait a minute," Sean said. "Go easy. Like, I'm still young enough to be scared by this stuff, remember?"

Billy said, "Here. Maria. Take my hand."

She came to him, slowly, her eyes wide.

"Charley."

He took her other hand.

"Sean—'cause you're the littlest. You don't want to be on the end. Now Walt. Take up the rear. Now don't let go. Everyone quiet now, quiet, quiet."

There was a crack of thunder outside. Sean gave a little squeal, then stopped himself. Billy flung open the door of the motel room.

"Have you ever been really angry, friends, really angry? Have you ever wanted to wish yourself into another country?" Billy said, very softly. "But you don't have to be angry. Well, maybe a little, to help me. But I got enough anger for all of us. You thought Disney World was a magic kingdom, didn't you?" Though he never raised his voice, Charley had never heard such intensity. "I'll show you a real magic kingdom."

"Is it really magic?" Sean said in a tiny voice.

"It's really magic," Billy said. And he laughed bitterly.

He led his followers out into the snow.

Chapter Seventeen
Beyond the Hydra Gate

The Snow Dragon hovered overhead. Billy didn't hesitate, but ran up the sky towards it on a staircase that he built, one step at a time, from his anger. His companions followed him. Sean slipped, dangled, caught the bottom step and hauled himself up hand over hand. Billy didn't look back.

"You have brought others," the dragon said.

"Yes," Billy said. "These are my friends. Through me, they've felt the rage too. They can lend a little bit of power to us."

The snowy earth split open. The hydra's heads snaked up, smoking; ahead was the gate. They were all on the back of the dragon now, Sean and Maria and Charley and Walt. Walt was saying, "This is a trip, man, this is totally weird."

"Be quiet!" Billy shrieked. "Help me! Be angry! Feel the anger. Feel it flow through you." He let go of Maria's hand. He reached into the air and snatched a sword out of the snowstorm. He thrust it into her hand. "No time to explain," he said. "You'll just have to use it." He reached into the blizzard and plucked out more weapons. A burning firebrand that glowed with cold blue flame. "Charley . . . since you gave me the idea." A slingshot for Sean. "Use snowballs," he said. "Pack them hard." For Walt a mace with spikes of ice. "That's as close to heavy metal as I can manage," Billy said, tossing it into his hand. "Now—"

Up they soared! And the hydra came. It had more necks than ever before, and those necks twined and writhed and belched tongues of green fire. Laughter cracked like a whip in the air.

The dragon swooped! Careened into the icy wind! "Told you!" Billy shouted. "Come into _my_ magic kingdom, I can give you a better ride than Space Mountain!"

Sean screamed as one of the hydra's necks lurched over the dragon's back. "Wield your weapons!" Billy cried out, and Walt swung the mace of ice and beat the neck back and Billy lunged forward and sliced it off with a lance of force that burst out of his outstretched hands and Charley leaped up to cauterize it with his firebrand. Sean ducked another head, then scooped up snow from the ridges on the dragon's back and pressed it into a snowball and sent it flying with the slingshot. Maria ran forward with her sword and flailed at the monster. And always Charley ran to burn the headless necks before they could grow new heads.

"What next?" Billy said to Charley, who had known the beast's name and known how to conquer it.

"I think in the story he buried the remaining necks under a great stone," Charley said.

They fought on.

As abruptly as the battle had begun, the hydra shuddered and fell. The dragon landed beside the smoking body. Billy reached into the air for a shovel and began to bury one of the heads. The others found their weapons transforming themselves into shovels too. As they worked, the hydra's body began to shimmer . . . soon it was a mere outline in the snow-drenched air . . . and then the outline was gone.

"Where?" Maria said softly.

And, without seeming to have moved at all, they were standing at the gates to a huge fortress or walled city. From within came howls and moans and cries of pain and the clanking of chains.

"Not just one princess," Billy said, "but thousands of captives. We've got to get the gate open. You've got to help me."

"How?" Sean said.

"Think of all the bad things that have happened to you that weren't your fault. Banish all other emotions . . . just think of the anger. Let it grow." Billy held his hand out. Maria clasped it. They all joined hands again, as they had inside the motel room. "Think of getting rid of all your pain forever," Billy said, "of the cold and feelingless and dark. . . ."

He gripped Maria's hand harder.

The gates groaned. They were tall. When he looked up, the tips of the railings were completely swallowed up in the swirling mist. He concentrated hard for a moment, then whispered, "Now." He voice was almost lost in the wind. But the others heard him. He could feel Maria's hand tense in his own and he could feel a line of force forming, as though a live wire linked the five of them.

The gates trembled. He put his shoulder against the cold steel and shoved. "Every step's bringing me closer to him," he thought. And thought of the stunned lion lying in the circus aisle. "He was free. But they made him numb again, they took away his moment. The Ringmaster doesn't want us to feel

free." The hate was building up. He could feel the
gate giving way, turning into a clear, shuddering,
gelatinous mass. "We're coming through!" he cried
aloud. They pushed their way through. The gates
had becoming like foam. They were running into the
snow on the ground, seething, frothing.

They stood in a great castle hallway. The
moanings came from all sides. "The dungeons," Billy
said. "Let's start there."

"This is neat," Sean said. He still didn't realize
what was going on; he was just in it for the ride
really.

"We'll split up." Billy drew, from the air, five sets
of keys, oversized, old fashioned keys. They were
made of ice. He gave one to each of the others. And
they spread out over the hallway, into the dozens of
corridors than branched out from it.

Billy stood alone for a moment, then he turned
into a passageway. The walls were stone and dank.
Here and there was the skeleton of a child or of a
young lion, handcuffed to the ice-slick stones. A
babble of wailing voices came from ahead, in the
darkness. There was a grating. He found a key that
fit the lock.

They came pouring out, the prisoners of the
Ringmaster. They were children with sunken eyes
and hollow cheeks, thin as ragdolls. And Billy broke
their chains, one by one, and they crammed into the
passageway to the surface. But Billy crossed the
dungeon and found a stairwell on the other side that
led even deeper. Mud and snow crusted the walls,
and there was no light except what Billy could
conjure up himself out of the air.

Lower and lower he went. There were more
princesses and princes too, and he cut their chains
with a karate chop. There were men and women
with sallow faces and whip marks. He went lower,

half climbing, half sliding down a terraced ramp slippery with slush.

A murmuring came from below, like the rushing of waters.   It was an underground cave.   The ice crystals on the walls sparkled like diamonds.

There were lions here, hundreds of lions . . . lions like the ones he had seen in the circus of his childhood.   Their manes were shorn.   The lionesses lolled listlessly among their cubs.   They all bore marks of the Ringmaster's torture.   "You're going to be free," Billy whispered fiercely, "all of you, every one. I swear it. You're going to go up there and see the light of a real sun and run in the tall grass, like . . . like in Africa."

They lions did not stir.   He walked among them, prodding one after the other.   One of them looked at him and a pathetic miao escaped his throat.   "Oh, who has stolen your roar?" Billy said.   It was the same question he had asked the Snow Dragon.

None of the lions answered, but all turned toward him at the same time, as though acknowledging him their leader.   And when Billy said, gently, "Come then . . . out of this terrible place," they all rose and gathered behind him, pawing the snow and shaking their unkempt manes. "I'll find a way out," Billy said.

He looked around him.   The way he had come was steep; he didn't think he could climb up again.   A quiet rumbling came from above, like a distant avalanche.   Sheets of ice were cascading down the opening.

"There's got to be a way out!" Billy said.

He turned resolutely toward the darkness.   The lions stirred, shifted, fell into place behind him.

"I have to be in control," Billy thought, "I have to be able to force an opening."   The rumbling had become a roar.   Louder now, a thunder pounding at his ears. The lions waited.

"Now!" Billy screamed.   And walked into the darkest part of the cavern, oblivious to the cold and hard stone, blasting his way through the rock with his pent-up rage.

At last he saw light: a pinprick, bluish, far away. "Come now," he cried, "run for the light, run for freedom."

And he ran to the cold light, the rock floor battering his bruised feet. The lions began to move more swiftly now.   The rocks echoed with the pounding of their paws. And Billy concentrated hard on the light, he seized it with his mind and made it burn like a blue sun, and its radiance poured into the tunnel and he saw at last that they were fleeing uphill, up to the surface of the Fallen Country where the snow was thickest....

And when he emerged he was in a plain full of the children he and his friends had liberated. Maria and Charley and Walt and Sean were there.   Sean was jumping up and down with excitement.   Here and there, through gaps in the snow, they saw a road, and far ahead, where the Snow Dragon was hovering, the silhouette of a city.

"I've seen that city," Billy said, as Maria came forward to nuzzle against a lion's mane, "while riding the Snow Dragon's back. It's the city at the edge of the Sea of Ice.   The last outpost of the Southern Continent."

The ones they had freed waited solemnly on either side of the road to the city. The lions had broken ranks and were circling and rolling their heads in the snow. But still they did not roar. Nor did the people cheer, but stood as if awaiting punishment.

Billy said, "Don't you understand?" He walked up to one of the captives, a old woman with white hair, now dandruffed with snowflakes, and said, "You don't understand, do you? You're free now, you can go."

"The Ringmaster no longer rules?" the old woman said.

"I don't know. But I'm going to fight the Ringmaster. I'm going to lead all of you to his stronghold . . . and find the way out of the Fallen Country for all of you. That's why I came here," he said firmly.

"You are Billy Binder . . . who will be king of the City by the Sea of Ice . . . the liberator," the woman said, her voice mechanical.

"You must rejoice," Billy said, "even though you're not used to it anymore. It will come back to you. I promise."

The old woman turned to some of her companions. And they began to raise their voices in a hymn of some kind; it was in a language Billy didn't know, but it sounded ancient. Their voices quavered and were sometimes quenched by the wind's ceaseless wuthering. Billy didn't know whether it was a song of joy or a dirge; it sounded too alien.

The five companions from the world above began to walk toward the city. Lions preceded and followed them. The dragon flew over their heads, spreading its wings as an umbrella against the snow. People lined the road. They had no flowers to throw, so they threw shavings of ice and giant snowflakes.

It seemed that they were in the city almost immediately. The crowd that followed them was immense. They were on a float, being drawn by mythical beasts, unicorns and winged horses down a broad avenue. Children appeared at windows and pointed, staring; but they uttered no cries of jubilation. The throng grew.

"It's like being in a real-live movie," Sean said. "It's totally cool."

"It's more than that," Maria said softly.

Still silent, the followers of Billy Binder seemed now to number in the thousands. They stretched endlessly down the avenue. At the limits of his vision they blended into the gray landscape. "Did I accomplish all this?" Billy thought. His heart lifted a little. But then came more pain. For he knew they were not truly free. They never would be until he vanquished the Ringmaster, until he found the way out of the Fallen Country.

At last the procession—was it a triumph or a funeral?—reached the sea. Icebergs clashed and unclashed on the frosty waves. The snow fell heavier than ever here.

The people waited. Billy knew they had once been like him, fueled by their terrible anger; now it had all been bled from them, and they were almost as lifeless as the snow itself.

Billy spoke in a small voice; but for a few moments the wind was hushed, and his voice carried across the crowd-packed beach. His four friends from the world above stood by him. He was glad they had come, glad they had helped him. But there was more now. The sea . . . the sea had to be crossed.

"What'll you do?" Walt said.

"He'll have to part the sea," Charley said. "like in *The Ten Commandments.*"

"Casual!" Sean said.

"I don't think so," Maria said. "I think it will break his heart."

"You're right," Billy said. "To part the sea . . . yeah. Charley, you're the one who's read books and heard stories and seen movies. You know the world better than me. You knew about the hydra, too." He was amazed at how Charley was always able to come up with the answers, and how familiar the answers seemed.

The crowd swayed forward, hungry for any scrap of emotion that might fall from him, for like vampires they had drawn strength from his life force. Even as I, Dora, had done, knowing his reality to be more vivid than my own. And Billy faced the sea, faced the crystal gaze of the Snow Dragon, and tried to separate the ocean into two walls of icy water. It was there, he knew, somewhere. It had to be. But he was so drained. . . .

"Please help me," he said, turning to the four companions. "It took so much out of me to free the lions and to break out of the dungeon. I need your help. Wish with me. Concentrate with me—"

Sean said, "I can't, Billy. This is so real, it's getting to me. Can we go back now?"

Already he was fading. . . .

"Please!" Billy said, almost choking. The Sea of Ice churned, blurred before him.

Walt was saying, "You know we can't stay here, Billy."

"But you came here with me . . . you must have the anger in you, somewhere, locked up, waiting."

"No, Billy," Charley said. "You asked us to concentrate on our rage, our pain . . . but what kind of pain did we have to offer?"

Sean, almost invisible, said, "I thought of maybe getting grounded if I hung out with you guys too much."

"I thought of flunking algebra," Walt said.

"You see what I mean?" Charley said. "Big deal! We could never have gotten here by ourselves. It's your world all the way. You know what *I* thought about when I wanted to get angry? I thought of how Maria was paying too much attention to you, I thought of being jealous. It was petty and dumb. It's not the kind of thing you can use to fight the ruler of your universe." And he turned to go. "I'm sorry, I'm real sorry, Billy. We can only do so much."

"But my people—I *must* free them!" Billy cried out. As he spoke the lions around them began to rush past them into the waves. "Look, the lions are going to kill themselves. I gotta have that way through."

Walt and Sean had vanished completely now; they had just whirlpooled away into the wind.

Charley made a move to follow them.

"Charley—" Billy said.

Charley stopped. "I'm still your friend," he said. "More now than ever before. But I'm not part of this war, I don't belong." And he disappeared.

Only Maria remained. "And you? Even you? You won't leave me, will you?" Billy said.

She made no sound, no move. But Billy saw that the tears were streaming down her cheeks . . . that they were turning to ice . . . that pieces of her tears were breaking off and blowing into the sea. He remembered the first princess he'd rescued, how she had cried those precious tears for him even though it hastened the time when she would have no tears left at all, and become devoid of life, a stone.

"If you weep like that you'll become like all those people out there," Billy said. "You might as well be dead, you might as well be made of marble."

Still Maria wept. He did not know if she wept for him or for this terrible world, forsaken, desolate, with a young boy as its only hope for redemption.

"Go!" he cried harshly to her. "Go! I don't want you to turn into stone!" And he had to force himself not to cry, he had to clench back tears himself, he who had come to the Fallen Country in order to dry his tears forever.

And he found himself alone alone, and he gazed out over the speechless hordes, and he despaired of

crossing the Sea of Ice.

Chapter Eighteen
The Stone Flier

In the morning the expedition seemed to have lost its steam. Everyone just wanted to go home. For once none of them argued.

They had found Billy stuck to the bathroom door of the motel room, his hands manacled with rings of ice. They'd taken him down and laid him on one of the beds, and heaped up all the blankets in the room over him. When he started to come to, he was shaking as if he had some deathly disease. They turned off the air-conditioning. According to Charley's watch, it was only about five minutes after they had all stepped out into that snowstrewn landscape . . . it had seemed like days.

Charley kept a close vigil all night long while the others dozed off. Maria, now and then, joined him, and they talked about school and about boy- and girlfriends from their pasts; commonplace things that you talk about when you want to get to know someone better. As the night went on, Charley began to realize that this might get to be a pretty serious relationship. "I was wrong to be jealous, wasn't I?" he said. He tried to sound confident, but he had been really shaken when she paid attention to Billy.

"Billy . . ." she said. "He's a miracle, that kid."

"What do you mean?" Charley said, more nervous now.

"I mean, because he brought us together, kind of. There's power in him. Because of him, I can see . . . more of your true self, I guess. And I like what I see. You were brave to go out there. We all were, I guess. It's going to bring us together."

She kissed him then. "Wow," Charley said. Billy stirred in his sleep.

"You think it'll all be over soon?" Maria said. "You think Dora's kept her part of the bargain?" She spoke very quietly; none of them wanted Billy to hear.

"I hope. But well, you know how they operate. Adults, I mean. They'll stick him in a foster home or something until it blows over, and . . . except maybe it won't. They never know how urgent anything is. They spend their whole lives filling out forms and filing them and stacking them up."

"God, I hope we don't end up like that."

"Me too." He kissed her again, more confidently.

"I really like you," she said softly.

The night passed.

On the three-hour drive back to Boca Blanca they hardly spoke a word to each other. They were all afraid for Billy, afraid of what might be waiting for him.

At last they crossed the railway tracks and found Billy's street. Charley said, "I'm not going to drop you off, Billy, not if I see that motorbike parked outside, swear to God."

"What difference does it make?" Billy said. "Sooner or later, I got it coming to me."

There was no one parked in front of the duplex at all. Charley pulled in and stopped the car. Billy hopped out. "See you in summer school," he said. He didn't look back at them.

Charley hesitated before getting back into the car. "You want us to, uh, like come in with you, wait around in case . . ."

"No! I mean, no, thank you."

Still Charley didn't want to leave Billy alone. He noticed the depression in the gravel against the whitewashed wall of the house, and the grease stain from where Stark's handlebars had rested against it. "He <u>has</u> been back, then," Charley said. "He didn't walk out on your mom forever like she was afraid of." But he thought, "Maybe they've already taken him away."

"It's happened before," Billy said. "I knew he'd be back. He needs me, you see . . . that's the twisted thing about it. He thinks he loves me, he thinks it's for my own good . . . he really believes that, he's convinced himself. That's why it's so hard for my stepmother."

Charley began to feel even more guilty. He said, "It's so unfair! When I have fights with my parents, sometimes I feel like I hate them, especially if they ground me or cut my allowance or something. But they never—I mean, I know they still care about—I mean—"

"You don't have to feel sorry for me," Billy said. "And don't feel bad that you didn't come with me to the end. Maybe there's no way out. Anyway you're right, you guys don't have the anger for it, it's my battle and I have to win it my way."

"Billy, that stuff ain't real."

"I guess not." Charley knew that Billy was just saying that so Charley wouldn't think he was completely crazy. "But . . . but it's better than watching music videos all night."

"Yeah, right."

Charley realized he'd probably choke up with emotion if he hung around any longer. And that would look bad in front of Walt and Sean. So he spun around, climbed in, and peeled out of the driveway.

•••

Stark was waiting for Billy inside.

"Hah! Fooled you," he said. "I moved my bike round to the back." Stark was sitting in the living room. The TV was blaring beside the sofa, so loud that Billy could hardly hear what he was saying. And his words were coming out slurred, though Billy didn't think that Stark got drunk that often.

Billy waited.

"You little creep! You made up terrible lies about me, didn't you? And you told them to call the cops. And I was doing what's right. A lion cub'll never mind until it's had a good licking."

"I didn't tell the cops," Billy said, perplexed.

There was a hamburger commercial on TV. It was about to change into the twelve o'clock news.

"You just ask for it, whenever I see your face I know you're just begging for a whipping. I wear my arm out and I can't even get through to you."

He was pulling out his belt.

"You're not touching me," Billy said faintly. "Not in this world and not in the other world either."

"Other world, other world . . . I've had enough of your stories. You told the cops a bunch of stories. Ten thousand dollars bail, they said. You creep."

"Ten thou—I don't know what you're talking about!"

"They found me at the mall. They took me in. They got me for possession too, you little squealer!"

The story came out, punctuated by spurts of cursing. A bored, overworked judge had set bail in a five-minute hearing. Then Stark had gone straight home. He had been waiting for Billy for about an hour. Waiting, brooding. "I bet it never occurred to those idiots that I'd try beat you up again! They probably figured an impending trial would be intimidating. They don't understand us, do they? They don't realize I've nothing to lose now. If I'm going to hell anyway I'm gonna take you with me."

Billy turned and ran into his room. He tried to shut the door in Stark's face. But Stark had already jammed it with his foot. Billy pushed against the door, but Stark was stronger. The door flew open, smashing into Billy's forehead and drawing blood. Billy was thrown clear across the room. He tripped over the snake tank. Glass shattered, lacerating his arm in a dozen places.

"I'm gonna get you for those lies," Stark said. "I'm gonna kick your butt all the way into the Fallen Country."

It was the first time Stark had ever spoken the name of Billy's secret kingdom. It was time then, time for the final battle! "You do know the Fallen Country! That proves that it's real!" Billy cried out triumphantly. "You're the Ringmaster . . . you're the one who tortures the world . . . the adversary, the one I am destined to fight. . . ."

"More lies!" Stark said, grabbing Billy by the shoulders. His eyes were bloodred, murderous. But as Billy watched them they changed; they became cold, so cold.

The TV news announcer from the living room said: "An unexplained incident in Circus World today, when a lion mysteriously escaped from. . . ."

They both froze for a moment.

The voice continued, "A tourist at the show, Mr. Joe Siclari, had his portable video camera and we were able to obtain this footage. . . ."

"Turn on your bedroom set," Stark growled.

"Why—"

"Now!"   He relaxed his hold on Billy almost imperceptibly, just enough for him to reach over and push the on/off switch.

The picture was grainy but recognizable.   There was the cage.   There was the busty girl who had been controlling the lions.   There—the camera was handheld, and the picture shook violently from its owner's agitation—was the lion running up the aisle. And there, unmistakably, was Billy.   His arms were upraised, his face was contorted in unspeakable rage, and from his hands came sparks of brilliant blue light that zapped over the heads of the audience and showered the bars of the cage—

"You dared!" Stark said, hopelessly drunk now. "You dared to show your power in the world above!"

"So you admit it!" Billy taunted.   "You admit that I haven't been lying—"

"Our war was an ancient quarrel, private, not of this world—"

"If I'm crazy then you're crazy too—"

Stark pushed Billy down on the floor.   "This time I'm gonna kill you," he said.   "It doesn't matter any more, let's not pretend anymore."   Billy tried to fight him off at first.   But then he just said hoarsely, "You can do anything you want, you jerk, every time you hit me you send me flying farther and farther into the Fallen Country and I can defeat you there, I can, I can, I can."

Splinters from the broken terrarium sliced into his hands, his back, his arms.   Billy screamed.   Then Stark started punching.   Billy could feel hot blood spurting from his nose, his lips.

But he couldn't feel any pain.   The minute he had seen that first blow coming he'd bolted into the numbing snow, he had called for the dragon to come to him.

The beating went on and on. He felt nothing, knew nothing; in the world above he had lost all consciousness.

But in the Fallen Country he rejoiced, because he had arrived so strong with anger that he now had the power to part the Sea of Ice with a single thought. "My people will be free," he shouted at the prisoners as they followed the lions into the roiling ocean. "Free, even if I have to die for it."

•••

No sooner had he spoken than the ocean parted. A wall of water and fractured icebergs towered on either side of a road of freezing slush. Leaping onto the back of the Snow Dragon, Billy flew to the head of the throng. The sea was strangely silent, insubstantial. Fog tendriled up from the ocean bed and wove its way around the people and lions as they marched soundlessly. They seemed more like ghosts than people, and they did not smile. They moved in a single mass, like a single graphic on a video game screen.

The Snow Dragon flapped its wings and cast a gray shadow over the people. On and on they ran. Lower and lower the dragon flew, until they were almost level with the ocean floor, glistening with crushed ice.

"Why are we falling?" Billy said.

"My wings ... the snow...."

It was true. So much was falling that it was building into dunes against the ridges of the dragon's back, clogging the fissures of its wings. "You won't be able to fly at all soon," Billy said.

"No . . . we're getting closer to the Ringmaster's inner domain . . . where the snow is like lead." When Billy stretched his hand out, each snowflake felt heavy, it pounded into his flesh, although he was to numbed by cold to feel any pain from it. The dragon went on, "When we reach the other shore, I will not be able to fly at all. . . ."

"Then how will I reach the Ringmaster?" Billy said.

"I do not know."

Lower they fell. When Billy looked to either side the walls of water seemed so tall that they almost met at the zenith of his vision. The sky was a tiny slit of gray.

At long last they reached land. A great plain that inclined slightly upwards to the north. Everywhere, in the snow, stood stone lions. The blizzard went on. The people and the lions followed Billy out of the sea, and the sea closed silently behind them.

"North, we must continue north," Billy said.

But now the dragon's wings were dragging on the snow, and its breath was a tongue of ice . . . uphill they went, the people sliding in the slush, the lions leaping over the backs of the lions of stone.

"They're not going to make it!" Billy whispered.

He saw what lay ahead. The plain ended abruptly; they had been climbing along the top of a plateau. A twisted rocky outcropping stood at the edge of the plateau, the highest point of the incline. The people were collapsing, exhausted, where they stood. "My anger—it's got to be enough for all of us—it's got to be!" Billy cried. And the dragon shuddered as it crashed onto firm snow.

"Poor Snow Dragon, can't you go on?"

The dragon said, "I am so heavy now, and so exhausted . . . only once before did I even come this close to the Ringmaster's stronghold. . . ."

Billy said, "No, be strong for me, be strong."

With Billy still on his back, the dragon clawed its way uphill. "The outcropping!" Billy said. "When we reach it, perhaps we can rest. . . ."

At last the dragon's body came to rest against the tower of stone. It heaved its haunches hard against hard rock and dislodged a ledge full of snow. "This is the end for me," it said, and spoke no more for a long time.

The snow piled up on his back. After a time it hardened into a slick pathway, and Billy was able to clamber up to the ledge. The cold snow seeped into the holes of his cutoffs. In front of him there seemed to be a wall of solid snow. He couldn't see beyond a handspan past his face. He stuck his hand out and it brushed against something firm. He started to scoop away the slush with his arms.

It was a human face.

He began to dredge feverishly away. The face became recognizable beneath his fingers. Suddenly he knew who it was.

"It's him again," Billy said. "The one I met so long ago. At the circus." He began to shovel madly now. "It's the flier"

"Yes," said the dragon, its voice vanishingly small in the wind.

"So he came here too! And this is how he ended up."

"Yes. Turned to stone."

Billy saw him now. He was a boy of marble, his face frozen in an expression of concentrated anger. "He almost made it to the end, didn't he? How much further is there to go? Tell you, you have to tell me!"

"I don't know . . ."

There was the statue now, dark against the dazzling whiteness of the snow. Billy remembered how he'd been, soaring, somersaulting, twisting in the air . . . compact, perfect, beautiful. And now he had turned to stone. Wasn't that what the princess had said? That they all turned to stone in the end, after all their emotions had been burned away?

At last the dragon continued: "I had hope for him, Billy Binder. His anger ran clear and true. The

Fallen Country was younger then by a thousand years, for time passes differently in our land. He too led the captive people across the sea . . . not by dividing the waters, but by building a great ship, lashing together a thousand icebergs with ropes of wrath. But it was not enough. Here it was that he stumbled. As he stood at the edge of the precipice, he saw where his destination lay. He despaired, Billy Binder; his heart burst, and he became one with the substance of the Fallen Country, cold forever."

"And you brought me here? To the brink of the cliff? Just to see this?" Billy said.

"Yes. Go back to your world, Billy Binder. Do not seek to go on. You will grow into a man. Somehow you will learn to live with what you've suffered. You'll grow up warped, but at least you won't be dead."

"Dead? Then the boy, the young circus flier—"

"Yes."

"How?" Billy said softly.

"One day, when he could stand the pain no longer, he ran to the circus tent, he climbed up to the platform, he leaped in a perfect three-and-a-half, he leaped but there was no catcher and there was no net."

"How long ago?"

"A thousand years. But in your time, I don't know. That was when the man called Stark came down from the north. He knew where you were. He tracked you down, he cast a spell over the woman who cared for you, and he became her lover."

"Then Stark is the Ringmaster?"

"Stark is but the Ringmaster's shadow, just as Billy is the shadow of Binder."

"I won't have it end here! I won't be turned to stone!"

And Billy knew suddenly that somewhere, in the world above, the beating was still going on. He could see it in the blood-red lightning that zagged across the sky. "I'm going to go on, I'm going to see what the other boy saw. And I'm going to fight it, and win." Plunging his arms up to his elbows in the snow, he felt his way along the rock wall. There was a turn up ahead, and if he could inch his way along it he would soon be looking over the plateau's edge.

Then it was that he saw his objective....

First the gulf. He was clinging to the side of a cliff so high that he couldn't see all the way to the bottom. The terrain was white and featureless; there was no way to judge the distance to the horizon. But there, at the absolute limit of his vision, was the source of the ruby lightning. Snow cloaked it, but he still knew what it was at once.

A circus tent.

Billy turned away. "Maybe I should go back," he thought. The snow blasted at his face. He edged his way back to the statue, which was already getting covered up again. In a few moments he would no longer see it. "Is this how it has to end?"

He turned to the boy of stone. "Why didn't you go on?" he screamed. And the scream echoed in the moist air. "If you'd gone on, if you'd made it to the end, maybe I wouldn't have—" It was a selfish thought. But then the boy had been selfish, hadn't he? He'd removed himself permanently from the Fallen Country . . . from every country in the universe. And the lions were still captive, and the people were still the slaves of the Ringmaster. The stone lions on the plain . . . they must have turned to stone when he had. The plain was a vast cemetery, a place of dead hopes. "Why?" he shouted at the dragon.

"He was like you," the dragon said. "In the end, his friends could not come with him. And he did not want to fight the Ringmaster alone."

"I can't cross the chasm to the circus of the Ringmaster," Billy said. "Not unless I build a bridge of anger, a longer, stronger bridge than I've ever built before."

And he closed his eyes and concentrated and wished with all his might, but only the ghostly outline of a bridge appeared, shimmered, dissolved into the snow and mist.

"I must have help!" he said.   And he started to pound at the statue with his fists.   "We could have fought him together, you and me, his victims!" His fists were bleeding now, the blood turning to ice as it oozed out.   "There's got to be someone left, there's got to be someone who will help me to the other side —"

But he was fast getting tired.   The snow weighed on his shoulders, on his arms.   He could feel the final numbness steeping him.   It was a welcome cold.   To be like stone, to be nothing more than a statue . . . not even to have to breathe.   He wanted it.   He wanted to die.

"I don't want to be alone!" he gasped.

And he began to shout out all their names: "Charley!   Maria!   Sean!   Walt!"   and finally, remembering that he'd promised her a curbside seat at the final confrontation, "Dora!"   Over and over he screamed the names.   The mountain rumbled.   His voice echoed and reechoed over the ice, a mighty clanging.   The ground was shaking.   An avalanche!   A solid wall of snow filled the sky.   He yelled the names again and again, daring them to hear him in the world above.

Chapter Nineteen
To Build the Bridge of Anger

After they dropped Billy off, the group had decided to go on to Charley's house. It was the one place where they could be assured of eating well.

It was late, well after sunset, and they'd been swimming. The evening was hot and steamy. They were lounging around the pool. None of them wanted to talk about Billy; Charley realized they'd been avoiding the subject all day. They talked about movies, about New Wave music, about sex, about drugs, about their parents. Anything so the subject of Billy wouldn't come up.

At last, after they'd been talking for about an hour, there was a lull in their conversation, and Charley said, "I guess I have to be the one, as usual."

Maria looked up. Charley hadn't been able to keep his eyes off her since she got into her bikini. "Yeah," she said, "what's going on in that house?"

"Billy'll be fine," Walt said. "They probably have Stark in a cell somewhere by now."

"I'm afraid," Charley said. "When adults do things, they have to have paperwork. And due process. Stuff like that."

"I hope they lock him up forever," Sean said. He was paddling around on an inflatable raft.

"He'll probably say he's crazy and he'll just have to see a shrink or something," Walt said.

"Yeah, but what about *afterwards?*" Charley said. "I mean, when it's all over. What'll we do with Billy?"

"Maybe we can adopt him," Sean said.

Walt said, "Don't be stupid. Kids can't adopt other kids."

"What about an orphanage?" Sean said.

"Get outa here!" Maria said. "Total gross-o-rama! You think it's like *Annie* or something, like a millionaire will just turn up and adopt him? Be serious, you know."

Charley heard Lydia's voice from inside the house. "It's on the ten o'clock news!" she was shouting.

They trooped in through the patio. Sean was dripping wet and hugged himself as the airconditioning hit him. They stood at the back of the living room and saw, on the TV, Billy and the lion.

"Awesome!" Sean said. "Do you think they'll show us, too?"

"Wait a minute. There's more," Lydia said.

There was a thirty-second item—no picture—about Stark. How he'd been arraigned, how he'd been released on bond.

"That means he's free," Charley said. "Free to find Billy and—"

Maria began to sob. Walt went up to her and tried to comfort her. Sean said, "Dude, we gotta do something."

"Listen!" Sean said.

Outside, the howling wind. "There's no tropical storm forecast," Charley said.

"It's not that kind of storm," Walt said, going back to the patio for a look.

The kids looked out. The sky was dark. Palm trees swayed. The wind was icy cold. "The swimming pool!" Charley cried.

It was freezing up before his very eyes. He walked out. The wind gusted in his face. He had to fight the wind to reach the edge of the pool. The others followed him. They were shivering. There was frost in Maria's hair. They huddled together by the diving board. . . .

"Look!" Maria said. "In the ice."

They looked down. They saw castles of snow with rainbow borders . . . a sprawling plateau strewn with broken stone lions . . . they saw a young boy falling from a trapeze, falling into an abyss of utter darkness . . . a mountain of snow collapsing . . . a dragon crushed beneath an avalanche.

And a voice, faint against the roaring of the wind: "Charley! Maria! Sean! Walt! Dora!"

"We can't go!" Sean said. "I'm scared and I want to stay behind."

"We have to go," Maria said firmly. "Because he needs us. We're his friends. Maybe we can't fight his war for him, maybe we don't have enough anger. But we can be there."

And Charley, clutching both her hands because of the searing cold, knew that Maria had goodness in her, and strength. And he knew that his feeling for her ran much deeper than his infatuation with Dora and his casual flirtations with other girls. And it was because they had been there together, inside another kid's nightmare.

"Inside!" Lydia's voice from the house. "You'll freeze. This is really freaky weather. The news says it's supposed to be over 95°!"

Charley ran into the house to the kitchen phone and tried to call Billy's number. He let it ring ten, eleven times. "No one there," he called out to the living room. "Maybe things are okay."

"You know that's not true," Maria said. She was calm but insistent.

"Yeah," Charley said, "I guess I do know."

"Call Dora," Maria said.

Charley called directory assistance. "I'm afraid that number is unlisted, sir," the operator said.

"I can't reach her by phone," he said.

"What are we gonna do?" Sean said.

Maria was still crying. Charley had to do something. He couldn't stand to see her like that. He said, "We'll go there."

"Do you know where she lives?" his mother said.

"Yeah. I followed her home once."

He started to rush out the door, with the others following him. "Hey, aren't you going to put on some clothes?" his mother called after him. "Oh, never mind. Be home by midnight . . . oh, never mind, never mind!"

They piled into the Datsun and Charley peeled out into the night. He hoped he remembered the way. There was Federal, there was the first turn, the second . . . yes! The long white wall, unearthly in the moonlight. Like the wall around a mediaeval castle, he thought. He slammed on the brakes. They crowded around the gate, an ornate thing of spiked iron railings. There was a buzzer. Charley pushed it.

Someone turned up: a watchman of some kind. "Hey, can't you read? No kids allowed here! Damn pranksters. . . ."

Maria said, "We've gotta see Ms. Marx, it's an emergency."

Charley looked through the railings. Sweat was running down his eyelids. The whole scene was swimming, shimmering. There was a fountain in the middle of the courtyard, and low buildings on three sides. Hardly any lights were on. They were most retired people here; they went to bed early.

"It's always an emergency," the guard said. "Get out."

"A kid may die," Sean said.

"You're not even wearing shirts," the guard said disgustedly. "And what's that in your ear?" he said to Walt.

"A safety pin," Walt said.

Charley suddenly noticed that it was snowing in the middle of the courtyard. That the fountain was turning to ice. "Look!" he said, with such urgency that the guard turned. He stared.

"Is this some kind of practical joke?" he said. "I'll have to call maintenance. How did you get that by me?"

But Charley didn't listen to him. He was staring at the snow. A dark shape was forming in the snowfall, the shadow of a young boy.

Sean saw it at the same time. "Billy's here."

The guard noticed it. "So one of you did sneak by me, huh?" He turned to chase after Billy. "Hey, no kids allowed, you hear?"

The four kids gathered closer to each other. They stared at Billy. He was little more than a wavering outline. A ghost. "Is he here or is he in that other place?" Maria whispered, awed.

"I don't know," Charley said. "I guess they overlap."

"I'm scared," Sean said. The guard had gone off somewhere, to find help perhaps.

"It's okay," Charley said. "We all are. But we have to wait here and see what happens. He needs us. He needs Dora, too, I guess."

"She's sort of like the last piece in a jigsaw puzzle," Maria said.

"Don't chicken out this time, Dora!" Charley whispered to himself. The shadow that was Billy had reached the door and seemed to be siphoning itself through the crack above the threshold.

•••

"She's dreaming," Billy thought. He stood in the foyer, outside her door. Snowflakes danced before his eyes. He could see her dreams. He was in her dreams, somehow, or her dreams were leaking out into the world, or it was all running together in the Fallen Country.

He saw her twisting and turning in her bed, he saw vague images from her dreams: dragons' wings, leathery and hung with icicles ... she was trying to remember if her father had even beaten her. What a question, she was telling herself, half-awake now. Of course her father had never . . . or had he? She couldn't recall it, but ... suddenly it came back to her. Billy saw it with frightening clarity, as though he were right there in the mind of a little girl, lying there thinking, "Why is he taking this out on me, this has nothing to do with me, nothing at all. . . ."

The emotion was so strong that Billy had to withdraw from Dora's mind. His pulling away jolted her awake.

She sat up in bed.

Listened.

Outside ... a hurricane building up? Or was it ... could it be ... the beating of giant wings?

Billy, ear to the door, heard the air-conditioning give up with a wheeze. An eerie silence fell in the apartment. It was going off in the whole building. It started to grow uncomfortably warm, although Billy shielded by the numbness of the Fallen Country, hardly felt it.

Outside . . . against the shuttered windows . . . it
<u>was</u> the beating of wings, huge wings whose flapping
set the banana trees to swaying!

It was time to confront her.

He knocked.   Then he said faintly, "I'm cold, I'm
cold, Ms. Marx."

"But children are not allowed here," came Dora's
voice. She knew who it was then. She must have felt
him in her dream. "How did you get past security?"
The door opened. Billy saw her for just a moment,
pulling her sweat-soaked bathrobe tight around her
shoulders, in the small, dusty living room. Then he
collapsed into her arms.   "Billy," she said, "for God's
sake, what are you doing here? Oh, my God, it's like
hugging a snowman, you're so cold, so cold."

"I killed the hydra and freed the lions from their
prison! I parted the Sea of Ice!" His voice was frail,
defiant. "I saw where the one before had gone, I saw
him turned to stone . . . I'm ready for the Ringmaster!
But I have to have help."

"He's too strong for you," she said. "He'll kill you.
Try to stick it out for another day or two. It's out of
my hands now, I've talked to the police—"

"I'm not talking about Stark! Stark is nothing. I
mean *him*."

She was murmuring, half to herself, "The kid's lost
control completely. He's slipping out of reality, going
into fugue as the shrinks call it. I'd better keep him
here, keep him warm, who knows what he'll try—"

"Look at me, woman! This is what you've been
hiding from, isn't it?" he shrieked. He ripped open
his tee shirt. There was blood. There were scars.
And blue bruises.   Red white and blue, like the
American flag. But his eyes were dry. "Let her
weep," he thought. "Not me."

More welts were forming on his skin. Fresh scars burst out and the blood oozed from them. She said, "How are you doing that?"

He said, "I'm not here right now. I'm still back at the house. You see me because you are seeing into the Fallen Country, because a tiny piece of the Fallen Country has projected into your apartment...."

"I can't believe that, I can't!" she said. "Or I'll go mad."

"Try," he said. "Ms. Marx, you're all I have now. I'm going to go back to the Snow Dragon and the cliff at the edge, forever maybe. Or until I kill the Ringmaster."

"No!" she cried. "I know the real world is unbearable for you. And I know the cold hard beauty of your imaginary world. But I just can't let you run away from reality. I just can't let you hide inside yourself for ever."

"Believe me!" he shouted. "Come with me!"

She said, "All right. All right." she crossed into the bedroom and quickly pulled on a pair of jeans and a sweatshirt. "I can't believe I'm doing this."

"Just humor me. Pretend you're going along with my fantasy until you can get me down to an emergency room."

She was shepherding him out of the door now, down the steps, across the courtyard where the fountain had dried up, into the car. She was really hustling him. He said, "You're scared someone'll see you with a kid, aren't you? That they won't let you live here anymore."

"I admit it," she said. "Come on."

As they pulled out onto the highway, it began to snow.

•••

"Look!" Sean shouted. "That old VW. It's coming out."

"They're in it! Where are they going?" Maria said.

The four of them had crowded into Charley's car to see what would happen next. The gate opened and they saw Dora's car pull out, wheezing and clanking. The snowstorm seemed to follow them.

"Let's go!" Charley said.

"Where?" Walt said.

"How should I know?" Charley said.

"Aren't you scared?" Sean said.

"Why should he be?" Maria said. "If Dora can do it so can we."

"I can't believe we're driving into a snowstorm and we're still in our swimsuits," Sean said.

Charley paid him no attention. They tore into the blizzard.

•••

Dora was panicking. She fumbled for the wipers. Billy watched her solemnly. The snow grew from powder-fluffy to great big blinding blizzard sheets. She stomped on the accelerator and slithered. They couldn't see the road at all.

"I knew it," Billy said. "I knew you had it in you to come with me. I understand your secret fears, the pain you think you're hiding so successfully. All the while you thought *you* were taking the lead." They careened through the thick whiteness.

They stalled out. Dora pushed hard on the door handle, cursing the old clunker. When she got the door open the snow piled in, drenching their faces and flooding the car floor with chalky ice.

"Out of the car now," Billy said.

"But we'll freeze!" she said.

"No," he said firmly, "we'll be fine. You don't want to lose control of the fantasy, you don't want to go crazy like me. But it's *our* fantasy now." He scooted across her lap, his torn tee shirt flapping in the wind. Then he was walking into the billowing whiteness;

he was striding, oblivious to the wind. The cold didn't touch him at all.

"Be angry!" he yelled back at her. "Anger will keep you warm."

Dora started to follow Billy. "Soon you'll feel nothing at all," Billy said. "Welcome to my kingdom. It's hell, but it's mine. It's what I see and feel." The wind lashed their faces. He heard her cry out his name, but he was too intent to answer. All he thought of now was the Ringmaster, waiting for him at quest's end. And the way to freedom for his people.

At last, in the whirling snow, he saw two pinpoints of pale blue fire . . . the Snow Dragon!

The storm subsided a little. The dragon hulked over the edge of a cliff. One of its wings, stretched out and piled high with snow, seemed to be broken and bleeding. It shook a snowdrift from its back. The sky opened and the lightning-whip cracked. But the dragon didn't notice.

"Now do you believe?" Billy shouted at Dora. "Now do you see? Don't say it's all in my head now!"

She believed now. She had seen. He could tell. The numbness of the Fallen Country had seized her, drugged her; he no longer sensed the naked pain he had seen in her dream.

Softly, he called out: "Snow Dragon."

"You've brought another?" the dragon spoke slowly, and only to Billy.

"She's been hurt too, Snow Dragon!" Billy said. "Only she doesn't see it sometimes. She hides it too well."

And Billy led me, climbing up the neck of the dragon until we reached the ledge where the stone flier stood. The dragon stirred; the wing came down, lashing the snow and sending up flurries for a moment. Billy held out his hand for her and they went on. He looked out over the plain saw where the prisoners of the Ringmaster stood, thousands in number, humans and lions. There was the distant sea, and beyond it another shore. Then, ahead, the chasm that Billy had seen earlier.

"Now," Billy said, "my bridge of anger. Hold my hand. Feel it with me." His voice did not waver. He stood and faced the gulf. He gripped her hand tightly. He began to dream his bridge into being.

At first there was nothing. Then the whip, cracking in midair, over and over, and the dragon shuddering into stillness behind them. The dragon's blood had seeped into Dora's clothes. Clouds gathered around them. Soon they couldn't see anything. They stood in thick darkness. Billy couldn't feel anything except Dora's hand, clenched, firm.

Then the clouds cleared! A bridge grew in the air, a suspension bridge with great ice columns sprouting from the mist below, a silver bridge edged with rainbow. A pathway of living ice began to form at his feet. It thrust up in an arc across the sky. From somewhere terribly far away, he could hear mocking laughter, and the shrieks of a bloodthirsty crowd.

"The circus," Billy whispered. "Don't be afraid."

There was the bridge. It stretched behind them now, over the dragon's prone body and down to the crowd, who were even now beginning to file up. "Can you sustain all those people?" Dora said.

"That's why you have to help me. I have to free them all. Be angry, Dora, please be angry."

He felt her trying to help him. A little spurt of anger here, a dash there. He felt it all flowing into the bridge. But almost all of it was his. "There is no anger like mine," Billy cried out.

The bridge hung there there. Girders glittering in the sourceless light. It was only boy-wide in places, and it thinned with distance into a point. And now and then, where the mist was less dense, he could see the outline of the circus tent that was his goal.

"You're exhausting your anger!" Dora cried, as the bridge wavered. The first of the hordes had reached our level and he saw their eyeless faces. The bridge groaned with their weight. "You won't be able to keep it up," Dora said, "come home with me, come home."

"Never!" he cried. "Not till he dies, that's the only thing that'll kill my anger." He stepped onto the icy road. "Are you coming?"

"I—" The bridge swayed.

"We don't have all day!" Billy screamed.

She hesitated for just the tiniest moment. The bridge was shaking now. Billy could see girders buckling and the pavement dissolving into mist. . . .

"Yes. I'll come."

"Come on then. Run with me." He turned. Already their combined fury was fuelling the bridge, making it firmer, easier to run on.

"Look!" Dora cried.

Billy stopped for a moment. The bridge groaned. Behind the crowd of captive souls . . . another car . . . its hood weighed down with ice.

"Your friends are coming! They haven't abandoned you at all! Billy, your friends are going to be with you at the end! Because they love you."

He heard the screech of Charley's car as it swerved through the crowd. "They're really coming," he thought. "They do love me." It was a strange idea, new and frightening even. "I don't have time to think of love!" Billy shouted. "Only of hate. Of revenge. Love won't let me kill the Ringmaster, and killing the Ringmaster is why I'm here."

He concentrated on the bridge. His anger made it strong. It would stand against the Ringmaster's power. His friends were right behind him now. He could see their faces through the snow-fogged windshield, full of concern. He was proud that they had come. But he pushed his joy deep into himself and allowed only the rage to come out.

Billy exulted. In the world above he was only an abused child. Here he was the leader of an army. He had brought these people down from the world above. His sneakers pounded the thin ice. Behind him the prisoners shuffled. The lions murmured, for they could not yet remember how to roar. The car skidded and squealed over the ice.

"I'm powerful!" Billy thought. "I'm king of the wind and the snow."

They ran on. The air whistled with the whip and the wind; beneath, the sea crackled and clanged with the collisions of countless icebergs.

Chapter Twenty
The Ringmaster

Charley and his friends had been driving blind. The car was spinning madly. Sean was clutching Walt in panic. Charley took his foot off the brake and tried to steer into the skid. Snow had piled up on the windshield and the wipers were clogged. "I can't see a thing!" Charley said. "I don't know the way, it all looks the same—"

Then Maria had touched his arm and said, "Look. There's some kind of bridge up there." Charley saw it over the mist. And running along the bridge, as though they were part of a Special Olympics marathon or something, were the lions and the prisoners they had freed from the castle beyond the Hydra Gate.

"We'd better follow them," he said.

"That bridge is nothing but ice, thin ice," Maria said.

"Yeah, I know," Charley said. "But it'll hold. I can feel it." The sky split open for a moment and they saw the whipcrack of the lightning.

He turned the car in the direction of the bridge. "There's no road," he said. But the moment he spoke he found himself tailing the crowd. The bridge shook.

"Billy's out there!" Sean shouted. "And Dora!"

"Faster!" said Maria.

Walt looked out of the back window and said, "Look, it's dissolving, man, the bridge is melting right behind us. You better hurry."

"I'm going as fast as I can!" The wipers were moving jerkily now. He could see ahead a bit. He looked up at the rear view mirror and saw that it was true, the bridge behind was being swallowed up in mist. He stepped on the accelerator, felt the tires whirring on the ice. "We're going to crash into those people!" The car careened into the crowd. They fell like bowling pins.

"Why can't we just go back?" Sean said. "Last time we were here, we just drifted back into the real world."

"We're stranded here," Walt said, "until it's all over."

"What? What's over?" Maria said.

"The war," Charley said, "between Billy and the Ringmaster."

They were gliding now . . . the people blurred . . . suddenly Maria put up her arms and screamed, "A snowbank!" The wheels spun. The car crashed into a mound of snow.

"We're stuck." Charley tried the ignition several times. It coughed and sputtered and then didn't react at all. "Let's get out of the car."

Shaken, they climbed out. The car was halfway up the snowdrift, so they had to jump down onto the snow. "Where are we?" Walt said.

"We've arrived. Look." Charley pointed. There was a circus tent ahead. He couldn't tell what it was at first because there was so much snow piled over it that it had lost its shape. People were streaming into the entrance. "Come on," he said.

"I'm scared." Sean was shivering.

"Don't be.   We've been brought here to witness something important. As far as the Fallen Country's concerned, this really is going to be the greatest show on earth." There was an evil presence in the tent.   It grew stronger as Charley led his friends toward the entrance.

But he felt a strange exaltation too. "We can win this thing," he thought.   "We're here to help Billy, together we can do it, somehow."

They entered the tent and a clown dressed in a skeleton tee shirt and baggy pants ushered them to front row seats.   "For you, special treatment," he said. He had beady eyes. Charley didn't like the way he cackled. A band was playing wild music. Then, abruptly, it stopped.

The announcer's voice, reverberating over a drumroll: "Ladies and gentlemen . . . children of all ages past, present and future . . . brought to you for your special delectation . . . the ultimate battle between good and evil!"

The drumroll went on and on.   Charley heard voices all around: "What's going on? When will the Binder come? Where is the Ringmaster?"

"I can't stand it!" Sean screamed.   "I wanna go home now."

"Quiet," Charley said. "He needs us."

The drumroll went on and on . . . bombarding his brain . . . drowning his thoughts . . . they waited.

•••

Billy had been running ahead relentlessly, and Dora had to keep up or she would be stampeded by those who followed behind.   He stopped for a moment to let her catch up. They ran neck and neck. He wasn't even tired yet.

The bridge soared up steeply. Billy was gasping now. When would it end? He lurched forward. The bridge seemed to be folding up before his eyes. The sky was splitting down the middle. The sky was just canvas, and the canvas was shredding, and they were running into a circus tent.

The walls were flapping and the sun and moon and stars were all painted on the canopy above them.

Billy shouted, "So that's where they all are! The Ringmaster stole the sun and moon and stars and bewitched them into the canvas! That's why nothing shines in sky of the Fallen Country."

The lions and captives were filing into the tent now, filling the rows of seats. Clowns were capering up and down the aisles. Vendors with skeleton tee shirts were selling hot dogs. The floors were of snow, and the seats were banks of ice. This wasn't just a three ring circus. There were countless rings, stretching to infinity and in them bony children with terrified expressions were leaping through firehoops. Their hair was long and tawny and flew behind them like the manes of lions. There were seals with planets whirling on their noses. If they dropped one the entire world would be annihilated. There were elephants trampling with earthquake feet, trumpeting whole thunderstorms from their trunks.

Then he saw his friends. They were already seated. He said to Dora, "I promised you a curbside seat, didn't I?"

Dora said, "Don't you want me to come with you?"

Billy said, "You told me a terrible truth once. You told me that in the end I was the only one who could fight the Ringmaster. You said, 'You have to play the cards you're dealt.'" He led her to the bench and she sat down next to Charley.

Maria said, "We came, Billy.   We heard you calling."

"Thanks," Billy said.

Dora protested, one more time: "I ought to be there with you. Maybe I failed you before, but I think an older person should be there to—"

"No, Dora," Billy said softly. "It's time I grew up, it's time for me to leap through the hoop of flame, and I'm the only one who can do it."

Maria said, "We love you, Billy Binder." She moved closer to Charley; perhaps she was a little afraid of Billy's intensity.   Billy saw that she and Charley shared something different, something special. He was pleased for them; he felt that somehow he had brought it about.

But now he strode through the chaos single-mindedly, seeking out the center. He called out the name of his enemy: "Ringmaster! Ringmaster! I've come for you!" His voice was tiny in the din. He edged his way forward. And then he saw him.

He was a little man in a leather jacket with bare, tattooed arms.   He was dancing as he waved the whip.   His eyes were cold and expressionless, like snow that has never thawed.

The face was Stark's face. Then it changed. It was Dora's face and Charley's face and Joan's face and the face of the young circus flier.   Then Billy's face. A template of human faces.

The Ringmaster bowed to the audience. He began to speak very quietly. "Children of all ages."   He laughed. "That's what we are here. Forever." There was even a little of the Snow Dragon in his voice.

Billy stood his ground. "Come out and fight," he said softly. "I'm not scared of you." He caught sight of Charley and Maria and Walt and Sean and Dora in the front row. "They're rooting for me!" he thought. "Fight me!" he said more boldly.

"Fight! Why? You have come here just as I knew you would: you, Billy Binder, the strongest and bravest of all my children."

He stepped out of the ring. He advanced toward Billy.

He cracked his whip: once, twice, three times.

Worlds whirled! Children sprang! Blood spattered the sand! And then, like clockwork winding down, everything fell into slow motion. Until he cracked the whip again.

"I've been expecting you, Billy Binder," the Ringmaster said.

"I'm not your child!" Billy cried out. Suddenly he remembered the first day Stark had come to the house, the first time he had beaten him. It had been because he'd screamed "You're not my father." It was the same thing all over again.

"I hate you," he said, "you're not my father, you never will be."

And there came mocking laughter from the stands. He spun around to look at the audience. But they were the same ghostly people who had followed him from the southern continent, the same spectral lions pawing the air. Then . . . in a moment . . . all their faces changed . . . to <u>his</u> face! The face of the Ringmaster! And they all laughed in unison, as though a single hand animated them.

"So come and get me," the Ringmaster said.

Billy reached out with his rage. A fireball sprang from his hand. It shot out at the Ringmaster and shattered harmlessly at his feet.

"You've got it all wrong!" the Ringmaster said. "You haven't come here to kill me at all. I sent for you, Billy Binder. You were specially bred to rule with me in the Fallen Country. One day you will be a great Ringmaster—all that rage, all that pain. I sent my shadow to the world above so that he would torment you. If you suffered enough, your anger would drive me to seek me out. I even made my shadow into a lion tamer, so that you would know me right from the start."

"And the young flier?"

"Bah. One of my failures. Forget him. The future's you and me, kid."

"No!" said Billy. But he was beginning to see the pattern of his life.

"I gave you the gift of anger, Billy Binder. So you could build a pathway to me."

"No!" Billy shrieked. "I came to find the gateway to the outer world, so that all the ones you've captured and tortured can finally escape!"

"The gateway?" The Ringmaster laughed and drew a circle in the air with his whip . . . and the circle flamed, and within it was a void. "There's your gateway. Do you want to reach it? But first you'll have to become a shadow of a shadow. Like Stark. Like all the others."

"Did you torture Stark, too? Like you tortured me? Was he an abused child once?"

"You got it, kiddo!" the Ringmaster said. "Now, fight. Eventually you'll give up. And then you will know who you really are. And you'll go back out into the world as my shadow."

"I am not like you," Billy said.

"Have you never heard the old cliché, 'Inside every child abuser hides an abused child?' Didn't your foolish counsellor teach you that?" He turned to Dora. "You fool. Why did you come here? After I absorb Billy Binder into myself, I'll swat you down like a fly. And all Billy's airheaded little friends."

More darts of anger flew from Billy's hands. The Ringmaster dodged them. Billy rushed at him. He blinked out. Laughter from above somewhere—

Billy jerked up his head. The Ringmaster was swinging from a trapeze that was suspended from a cloud. Behind him shone the artificial sun. "Oh, Billy, Billy," the Ringmaster said. "You could be such a good Ringmaster. Just like me. I have no pain. I only dish it out now. Your anger only makes me greater, only binds you more to me! That's the true meaning of your name, Binder, Binder. Yes, you're my son all right. Be free, Billy Binder, free like me!"

Billy thrust a lightning bolt of anger at him. The Ringmaster absorbed it and grew tall. His head burst through the top of the circus tent and still he grew . . . and the snow billowed around us through the rent in the canopy . . . and still the worlds danced and the children screamed.

"Dora! Maria! Charley!" Billy screeched at last, and turned to them. He could see the tears spurting from their eyes, hardening into ice as they hit the freezing air. They couldn't move. They were rooted to the snow of the arena. They were already becoming statues, just like the flier.

"Oh Billy . . ." the Ringmaster said, his voice quietly seductive, "how can you turn your back on all this? It's more than you ever had in the world above. Here you too can wield the whip and make a thousand universes dance with pain. And you never have to feel the pain yourself, no, never again."

Billy couldn't believe that he had come so far only to learn that he was going to be just like the Ringmaster. He screamed in rage. A blast of anger exploded from him. The Ringmaster absorbed it and grew some more.

Billy was exhausted now. He knew he couldn't go on fighting. And to fight was to make the Ringmaster ever stronger. "I have to give in," he said. He seemed shrunken, spent. "I'll stay with you here forever. But on one condition."

"And that is?"

"I want them all to go free. I brought them here. They came here because they felt something for me; they thought they could save me somehow. So let them go. All but me. Send them through the gateway. You can keep me as a hostage. But free the others. Please. Let something good come of all this. Or else I'll fight you until I die, and then you'll have to grow a new shadow and nurture him until he can find his way to you again."

"Huh. That's a new one."

"It's the only deal I'll make."

"Oh, all right. Have your way. It doesn't make a lot of difference either way."

The gateway, ringed with fire, glowed in front of us. Billy said, "Open the gate." His voice was so faint. "I'm going to die," he thought.

The Ringmaster pointed the whip at the gate and lashed at it a couple of times. Slowly shapes began to form there. Billy looked inside and saw, for an instant . . .

Another whip. The face of another Ringmaster in the sky on the other side of the gate. And another gate there, and another Ringmaster, and behind him another and another. . . .

"They'll never get out now," he thought. "There's no way out. The gateway is a fraud; it just leads to more of the same. . . ."

Suddenly Charley began to yell hysterically at the Ringmaster. "I hate you, Ringmaster! There's no reason for you to exist! You're senseless; you've made the universe into something twisted and horrible. We're not leaving! I don't care what Billy says. We're going to stay here and help him fight you. Until the end of time. If we have to." He rushed forward and flung herself at the Ringmaster and began to pummel him with his fists, over and over, until the Ringmaster flicked his whip around his neck and brought him crashing to the icy floor.

"Tough guy, aren't you?" the Ringmaster said. "Maybe I'll come after you one day."

Dora said, "You're nothing but a common bully. You're nothing, you're no one."

Charley's friends clustered around his prone body. "Go for it, Billy, cream him," Walt cried out. Even Sean, little Sean, ran up and spat in the Ringmaster's face.

And Maria shook her fist.

"Scum!" the Ringmaster said, dismissing them with a wave of his hand. "Go, stay, I don't care. I've got what I want."

Anger! Billy thought. He reached further and further into his heart, trying to pull out the last shreds of rage.

"Strike me down!" the Ringmaster taunted him. A thin smile played on his lips, a joyless smile, as Billy dredged up all his reserves of rage and readied himself for his last onslaught.

But at that moment Billy remembered Stark, crushed and hurt because the rich patrons of the club despised him . . . Stark sitting in the living room talking in his sleep and saying, "I didn't ask for the cold to seep all the way into my heart."

Billy saw a vision of himself twenty, thirty years in the future. Sunken, pathetic, collapsed into a sofa, his heart a stone. "That's what he wants me to be," he thought. "He's not the king of the Fallen Country. He's a victim too."

And Billy said, very softly, "I don't have any anger left."

And the Ringmaster's face grew very pale, and there was fear in it at last. Because Billy had been drained of anger, and he had not been destroyed.

The Ringmaster said, "But you _must_ hate me! I bred you to hate me. I followed you, I beat the hatred into you—"

"Just as they did to you!" Billy said, remembering the time he'd asked Stark about his childhood and Stark had beaten him senseless. Of course . . . that was Stark's way of answering his question.

And Billy turned his back on the Ringmaster and walked away. His voice was still faint, but now it was calm and confident. Those who had come with him from the world above were silent; Charley was coming to now, his head cradled in Maria's lap; Dora held the other two boys close, one in each arm. "Don't you see?" he said to his friends. "I could have been like him. He's not even the real Ringmaster. He too is just a shadow. He dances to the whip of a higher Ringmaster. And so on, and so on. Where will it end? How can I hate him? He is right. We are alike. I almost became him. How can I hate him?"

Dora said, "Inside every child abuser hides an abused child. That's what they teach us counsellors when they train us. How did you manage to understand that, Billy?"

"You'll never understand it in your gut," Billy said to Dora. "But I do. Because it happened to me." He turned to the Ringmaster and said, "I won't hate you. No. I pity you, Ringmaster. I don't forgive you. But I understand what drove you."

The Ringmaster snarled once, like an untamed lion.

"You think you're free and that the world dances at the end of your lash," Billy said. "It's not true. You're a prisoner too. I came to Fallen Country to liberate the captives. I have to set you free too, even you."

"Don't . . ." the Ringmaster said. There was anguish in his face now. Then he began whining and cajoling. "Don't pity me. I can't survive on pity. Pity will destroy me. Hate me, hate me, my son, my son. Stay here with me."

But Billy, walking resolutely away from him, said, "How can I stay here? The Fallen Country is only a fantasy."

"Look," Maria whispered, pointing at the Ringmaster. But even as Billy and the others watched, the Ringmaster had begun to dissolve into a shimmer of circus colors, into snow that was rapidly turning to rain.

Chapter Twenty-one
The Circle of Fire

"Quick!" Billy cried. "Hold onto me! Or you'll get sucked away!"

Tightly he grasped Maria's hand.   Maria linked hands with Charley.   They formed a chain with Dora at the far end.

The whole universe was being sucked into the circle of fire that still hung in the air. The circus was whirling.   Planets and suns were catapulting into the hoop.   Children fell screaming. Lions leaped through the hoop and never emerged from the other side.   And now the storm was bursting through the tatters in the canvas and we were drenched in rain, warm rain that pelted so hard it hurt, it hurt . . . "I can feel it! It's hurting me!" Billy shouted those words for joy. To know pain meant that feeling was returning to the Fallen Country.

The tent had collapsed into a few shreds of canvas and was being pulled into the fiery hoop. Suddenly they were standing in an open plain. Everything was all blurring together. Billy saw the hydra fall into the whirlpool of darkness.   He saw princesses floating serenely into the void.

"The Fallen Country is closing in on itself!" he said. "Don't lose me, help me to get home."

They had to get out of there fast, before the entire kingdom closed in on itself. "Grab Sean, we're losing Sean!" The chain reformed as they gripped each other tighter, falling into the whirlpool darkness.

The bridge of anger drifted by, distorted into a line of brilliant color. Castles and palaces crammed themselves into the hoop of flame. Billy remembered what he'd said at the first session with Dora: "Like a confessional? Like a black hole?" That was how the circle of fire seemed to him.

Abruptly they were facing the two cars, neatly parked side by side, floating in the melting snow. . . .

"Grab the car!" Billy said.

He held his hand out and collided with the hood. Rain was sloshing down the window. The car stood motionless, something familiar in the midst of the turbulence. Then he saw the Snow Dragon moving slowly toward him. Billy nuzzled against its wing. "It's true, isn't it?" Billy said. "That he's my father."

The dragon didn't speak. Billy went on, "And you, Snow Dragon? If the Ringmaster's shadow in the world was Stark, who was your shadow, Snow Dragon?"

The dragon's eyes sparkled. "If he's my true father, are you . . . my mother?" He realized that he'd always thought of the dragon as _it_ before. Because in the Fallen Country everyone was an _it_, even people. Billy said, thinking of Stark again, "It's strange how he hates himself so much. When he goes around tormenting those kids, he plants in them a little shred of something that could . . . destroy him. He works for and against himself. Like, he's dancing to the Ringmaster's tune and yet secretly working to sabotage him at the same time. I don't have a real father and a real mother. But I know who they are, here in the Fallen Country."

The rain cascaded down. They couldn't see anything but the dragon and the halo of fire that burned ahead of them.

"Billy, you know there are no emotions here," the dragon said. "But the snow is fast melting. When the spring comes, the Fallen Country will be closed to you. The shadow won't come for you again. I'm part of the shadow too, you know. I'm the part that seeks the shadow's own death, the left hand that does what the right hand dares not know. You've killed us both. Him by your compassion, and me by fulfilling my purpose."

"I can never come here again?" Billy said.

"No," the Snow Dragon said.

And then she roared. Her roaring rent the sky as sunlight broke through gaps in the thunderclouds. The rain was burning hot. It slicked the dragon's skin and made her glisten. She roared and roared again, for she had not roared in a thousand years, and the sound was both of heartache and joy. And she spread her wings and took to the silvery air, and was gone, like a dream, like a half-stirred memory.

"Get into the car," Dora said to Billy.

He obeyed, turning back to see the crazy churning of the Fallen Country for the last time. He heard Charley's Datsun start up too, and then they burst out into the world the others knew so well, the world of concrete roads and tourist hotels, of beaches and of fast-food restaurants, and they were racing down Federal Highway back into Boca Blanca, toward his house.

It was raining hard here too. He couldn't see more than a few inches past the windshield, but he didn't care. Somehow Dora found her way to Billy's house, and they saw, getting out of the car—

A circle of fire against the driving rain! The gateway hovering above the road! And bursting out of the circle, crashing against the wall of the duplex house, a motorcycle. And on the bike, a dark figure with a face like a skull, and a leather jacket that was already on fire. The circle spat out a few more spurts of fire. Then it closed, shrank into a single point of light, winked out.

They ran from the car. The walls were already on fire. How could it burn so, in the middle of this rain? As they stood there, too stupefied to do anything, Charley's car pulled up and all Billy's new friends got out. Charley shouted, "We were there, we saw it all, we've won!"

Dora said, "He faced his trial in another kingdom, and he's met the end that he chose for himself."

The house was only smoldering by the time the fire engines came. They rushed in and carried Joan out on a stretcher. Then there was another stretcher, a covered one.

"He's dead," Billy said.

"I guess people are going to say that he just couldn't stand the idea of facing it in court," Maria said, coming up to Billy. "They'll say he killed himself, he just crashed his motorbike into the house, huh?"

"I killed him," Billy said.

"Thank God for the rain at last," Walt said, stretching his arms out and looking up with his eyes shut and letting it run all over his face.

Sean said, "And we're in our swimsuits! We can play in the rain!" He stretched out his arms and started to dance wildly up and down.

"You're crazy!" Walt said.

"No I'm not! This feels awesome!" Sean shouted. All you could hear was the rain. It was up to their ankles now. The heat wave had broken, in spades.

Walt watched Sean for a long moment with a mixture of envy and disdain. Then he said, "Oh, what the hell," and joined in.   Soon Maria was rolling around like a wild animal in the flooded driveway. Only Charley, of the gang, made no move to join them. Perhaps it wasn't dignified.

The rain had put out the fire now. Debris from the house was floating out onto the street. "Look at all that junk," Charley said. A wastepaper basket made from an elephant's foot rolled by.   "Hey, there's things in your life you just got to flush down the toilet."

"They look sort of like Sioux Indians or something," he said.

"Maybe it's a rain dance," she said.

"Kind of late for that, ain't it?" he said.

They didn't speak for a while. The rain plastered Dora's sweatshirt against her skin. She didn't seem to care about being wet.

"Yeah," Billy said again, "I killed him."

Yes. He had found his way into Stark's soul. And he had understood it; he had felt compassion for it; in giving it peace, he had destroyed it. He had set Stark free as well as himself.

Dora said, "We all dance to the lash of a Ringmaster deep inside ourselves.   We're all his children, and until we stumble into our private Fallen Countries and find him and make our peace with him, we'll never be able to live with our pain. Oh, Billy, how can you forgive me?   My job was to understand, but instead it was you who understood. I was like a little Ringmaster myself, coaxing you until you danced out your pain for me in my office. But I never believed. Until too late."

Billy said, "Of course I forgive you. You're the only one who ever asked me to."

The sirens were still screaming.   Dora moved closer to him, awkwardly trying to shield him from the noise.

Charley said, "Hey, dude, we thought we were going to rescue you. But in a way it was you who saved us."

Dora said, "Yeah. I thought I'd learned everything about kids when they trained me for this job. But you set me free. You taught me to be brave."

Charley said, "You saved me too. From what my Mom called 'a certain lack of compassion.'"

Maria, sopping wet, cried out, "We love you, Billy. Come on, come and boogie in the rain."

Charley said, "What'll you guys do with Billy? Don't tell me you're still thinking of sending him to an orphanage."

"Maybe we can all adopt him," Dora said. "After all, we've been through a lot together. But we're all going to have to work something out with Joan." Then she said, only half kidding, "Maybe I'll adopt him."

Water was streaming down Billy's cheeks. He couldn't tell if it was rain or tears. Against the smoking house, the other kids danced, the warm rain slicking their tan, slender bodies.

"But you'll have to give up that child-proof condo," he said.

"Who cares?" Dora said. "I'm a big girl now."

And Charley said, "What's important is you're coming back to our world. Where you belong. And we'll be with you all the way home."

"Home. . . ." Billy knew that he was crying now. Because the water on his lips tasted salt. He couldn't even see his friends through his tears. "I don't know what home really means, I've never been home in my whole life!"

"Breakin' in the rain!" Maria chanted. "Come on, you guys!"

Dora said, "What the hell. I can be childish if I want. Thanks to Billy." Laughing, she joined the others.

Charley still didn't move. At last he said, "I guess, if an old maid of twenty-two can still act like a kid, I can too." He started to move toward the group. Billy watched them wistfully, not quite daring yet to become one of them.

"Are you ready for the real world?" Charley called out to him.

For a few moments Billy said nothing. He heard the music of the Fallen Country in his mind: the desolate whistling of the wind, the sighing of the shifting snow. He knew now that the inner and outer worlds touch each other in a thousand places, and that wherever he stood he would always be within a hair's breadth of the Fallen Country.

The real world! In the Fallen Country you didn't have to feel. There were no colors, only the endless white. It was all different here. How wet the rain was! And the fresh smell of it! And the colors: the emerald of the swaying palms, the red and yellow and ash-gray of the smoldering house. It was as if he was seeing them for the first time.

He watched them dance. Dora a bit stiffly. Maria lithe, almost like a ballet dancer. Walt doing a robotlike electric boogie. Sean leaping wildly. Charley trying to keep up with Maria, entranced by her every movement. Just one more step away from the Fallen Country! Billy's tears mingled with the driving rain.

"Yes," he said. "I think . . . I think . . . I'm almost ready now."

One more step.

—Boca Raton: Alexandria: 1980/1985

PART THREE

The Libretto

The Snow Dragon is a chamber opera created to take advantage of more intimate performance spaces with small orchestra pits. The composer has based his libretto on his short 1982 short story *The Fallen Country*, which was original published in the anthology *Elsewhere* from Ace Books. The story was also adapted into a young adult novel by the same name published by Bantam in 1986. The stage work derives from the original short story rather than the novel.

The opera centers around the relationship between Dora Marx, a jaded, middle-aged children's counselor who has lost her sense of direction, and Billy Binder, a physically abused young boy whose rage is so powerful it has opened a doorway into another world. But the Fallen Country is not a colorful kingdom of adventure where boys ride dragons and rescue princesses. It is a place of perpetual cold, whose citizens have lost the ability to feel, ruled by the Ringmaster, a sadistic demigod.

Defeating the Ringmaster in the fantasy kingdom is the key to overcoming Billy's problems in the real world, but that is easier said than done. Dora must put aside the comfort zone of her complacency and truly believe Billy's stories, so that she can follow him into the Ringmaster's kingdom ... and find redemption for herself as well as the boy.

Of the original story, award-winning children's book author Jane Yolen has said: "Somtow manages to combine child abuse and fantasy in such a way as to provide an avenue of healing... " In the 1980s the book was frequently recommended by child therapists.

The Snow Dragon is the Thai-American composer-author's seventh opera. "In writing this work," the composer says, "I hope to bridge many genres. This work connects opera and fantastic literature, speaks directly to young people in an accessible style which sacrifices none of the subtleties of 'classical opera'. I also aim to create a work on a scale that is easily transportable, in order to bring this world into venues beyond the traditional opera house."

The music of *Snow Dragon* reaches across genres. Young people will recognize the the eerie tropes of fantasy and horror film music which make the score very accessible to an audience new to opera. It's also melodically inventive — one of those rare creatures, a modern opera whose tunes can be hummed.

The Snow Dragon: characters and orchestra

Billy Binder *boy soprano*
Dora Marx *mezzo-soprano*
The Snow Dragon *dramatic soprano*
Peter Stark *bass-baritone*
Joan Straczynski, Billy's mother/Princess *soprano*

*Chorus: nurse, policeman, citizens of the Fallen
Country; off-stage soprano voice*

musicians

WINDS

1 flute player doubling alto flute, piccolo
1 clarinet player doubling e flat and bass clarinets
1 oboe player doubling English horn
1 horn
1 trumpet player
1 trombone player (tenor and bass)

STRINGS

1 violin
1 viola
1 cello
1 double-bass
1 harp

PERCUSSION & KEYBOARDS

1 lead keyboard player, occasionally doubling
percussion
1 secondary keyboard player doubling percussion
1-2 percussionist/sound effects person

two electronic 88-key sampling keyboards should be
used. Both should contain a classical grand piano
sample. The following patches are also called for:
celesta, chamber organ, circus calliope, string/synth
pad - the sound required is a shimmering sound
close to that of a real string section, but with a slight
synth haze to it.

The Snow Dragon

The action of *Snow Dragon* moves between reality and fantasy, and between past and present, with a cinematic fluidity, and sometimes within the space of a few bars of music or even a single chord. Because of this, props and set pieces should be minimalistic and multifunctional - for instance, a couch in Dora's office could be a bed in Billy's house or a stone wall in the Fallen Country. It is important not to tie any scene too closely to a location, in order to maintain the fluidity to switch perspective, or go from dialogue to interior monologue.

The stage has two levels. Downstage (Area A) anchors us to the physical world and it usually represents Dora's office, Billy's house, or a street. The downstage area is divided from a slightly raised upstage by a huge "frame" that functions sometimes as a window, sometimes as a doorway, sometimes as giant screen in which images and thoughts can be projected. Behind this frame is Area B, which serves sometimes as a window into fantasy or memory, and sometimes as the landscape of the Fallen Country.

Scene divisions are not meant to be hard-and-fast. Locations should meld into one another and the music interludes that play between scenes can be used visually in the manner of slow dissolves. There should be no attempt to take the stage directions that describe things flying through the air and cinematic effects literally. Instead, all the magic available to live theatre, with illusions, projections, and symbolism, should be used to tell the story.

The Fallen Country should be shown as gray and colorless, either through very desaturated lighting effects or the use of grainy black and white projections. It should be in stark contrast to the real world.

ACT ONE

Orchestral Prelude

At the beginning of the opera Area A is completely dark. A cold luminescence flitters in Area B. It might be a snowstorm. A music of eerie desolation plays. Slowly we make out a boy standing in a blizzard. He is dressed for summer, with a torn teeshirt and cutoffs. We do not see his face, but it is Billy.

Slowly it grows more light. A ladder is being hoisted up and rescue workers are trying to pry Billy loose. He is frozen. The workers lower Billy down from the roof and he disappears from view. The sunlight fades again, as though someone were lowering the shades in Area A.

Scene One

A light comes on in Area A and we see that it is Dora, darkening the sunlight that was streaming through her window. Dora returns to her desk.. She is looking through some notes or files. There is a thermometer on the wall which reads 92°F. Dora looks up from her work and wipes the sweat from her face with a tissue.

DORA

It's hot here,
So hot.
There's a heat wave,
And no sign of a breaking storm.
It's hot here,
So hot,
But deep inside of me
Somewhere
It's snowing.

Each weekday from nine to five
I sit here.
Each hour on the hour
A child comes
and from the child's mind
I coax
his dreams, his nightmares,
his terrors, his torments,
his traumas, till the child
dances in pain,
here in this room.

And when they have danced
to exhaustion
I try to heal them
to build a pathway
a road to peace.

But where is my peace?
Where is my redemption?
Who has stolen my roar?

It's hot here,
So hot,
And somewhere deep within me,
Somewhere, somewhere
It is snowing.

In Dora's office, the telephone rings.

> DORA
> (picking up the phone)
> Yes. Yes.
> (she looks through her files)
> ... found clinging to the steeple.
> Frozen. Yes.
> (she puts it down.)
> Here comes another one
> lost in some inner world.

Billy is standing in the doorway.   They look at each other.   She looks at the file.

> DORA
> Hello, Billy.

Billy doesn't answer.

> DORA
> My name is Dora Marx.
> You can call me Dora,
> Or Ms. Marx.
> Whichever makes you feel
> more comfortable.

> BILLY
> I think I'd prefer Ms. Marx.
> But you can call me Billy
> ... if you like.

DORA
You don't say anything.
Why are you here?

BILLY
They said you could help me.

DORA
How do you think I can?

BILLY
I don't.

DORA
They found you this morning —
frozen.

BILLY
Clinging to the steeple, frozen stiff,
in the middle of a heat wave.
I was on TV.

DORA
Are you hurt?

BILLY
Frostbite.

He extends his arms. Dora moves towards him.
They come a little closer to each other, but still far
from touching.

DORA
But I see something else.

BILLY
Just the cold,
the bitter bitter cold.

DORA
No. There are bruises.
Marks. Scars.

BILLY
Fell off my bike.

DORA
No. Other marks. Older marks.

BILLY
No!

They turn away from each other. The two characters
sing an interior monologue, never looking at one
another, but their intertwined arias build into a
passionate duet.

BILLY
Should I tell her?
Dare I trust her?
She could betray us.

DORA
It's a classic case
a statistic.
Abused child,
escape into fantasy.

BILLY
My rage
push, push,

my rage inside
I am the power
that fuels the unseen world.

DORA
But Billy's fantasy feels so real
it turns his blood to ice
and makes a snowstorm
in the tropic heat.
The scars of fantasy
burn so deep
He doesn't have to think
about those other scars,
the scars of an abuser.

BILLY
Can I tell her?

DORA
Will he tell me?

BILLY
Secrets, secrets...
buried in the cold —

DORA
Secrets, secrets...
buried in the cold —

BILLY
in the burning cold —

DORA
— the burning cold.

Dora turns to Billy.

DORA
Tell me, Billy …
tell me who hurts you.

BILLY
I can't.

DORA
How often?

BILLY
I don't know. Every day.

DORA
But you never cry.

BILLY
No. I promised.

DORA
Who? Promised who?

BILLY
… the Snow Dragon.

DORA
Who is the Snow Dragon?

BILLY
I knew it!
You're supposed to be trying to help me,
But all you want
is to hear my lies.

DORA
Do you lie, Billy?
Is that why he hurts you?

> BILLY
Yes! But I'll never stop, never, never.

The temperature in the room appears to have been rising and the thermometer bursts.

> BILLY
I'm sorry, I didn't mean to —

> DORA
It's okay, Billy.
In this room
You can tell all the lies you want,
here in this room,
just between you and me.
Nothing can ever escape this room,
nothing.
I promise.

> BILLY
Like from a black hole.

> DORA
Yes.

> BILLY
Good.

> DORA
So what were you really doing?
Up there,
straddling the steeple.

> BILLY
I was rescuing a princess.

Blackout.

Scene Two

A brief, violent intermezzo plays. As light returns to
the stage, we see that we're no longer in Dora's
office, but she is walking somewhere, in an ill-
defined limbo of a space, while behind her, projected
or mimed within Area B, we see a kind of surreal
acting out of the images in her mind.

> DORA
> And so he starts to tell me stories.
> The stories!
> The envy of any clinical psychiatrist,
> of any researcher with a pet theory.
> Stories with mythic resonance,
> stories we've all heard,
> stories plucked from
> the garden of archetypes ...
> but of course I don't believe them.
> I'm paid to listen
> not to judge.
> And my nightmares
> are not to be shared with the children.

Dora takes a key out of her purse. A doorway has
appeared in Area B. She goes inside.

Scene Three

Area A transforms into the interior of Billy's house.
Billy is playing a video game.
There is a knock on the door. Billy's mother Joan and
Stark come in. Stark is handsome. His arms are
tattooed with dragons.

JOAN
(switching off Billy's TV)
Let's turn this off now.

BILLY
But Mom — I was just
getting to this cool new level and—

JOAN
Not now.
This is important.
Billy, this is Stark.
He works in the circus.
He's a lion tamer.
He wanted to meet you.

BILLY
I know you. I've seen you before.
You're bad. Go away.

STARK
Relax, Joan.
'Bad' means 'good' in kids' talk.

BILLY
I've seen you in my dreams.
You're the Ringmaster,
with a whip of burning cold.

JOAN
He isn't usually like this,

BILLY
Get away! Get away!

STARK
I'll talk to him, Joan.
Man to man.
Because from now on
I'm gonna be kind of a father to him.

BILLY
You're not my father!

JOAN
He's never had a father.
        (to Billy)
Now, Billy, be nice.

BILLY
Don't wanna be nice.

STARK
I'll deal with this, Joan.
Kids are like lion cubs;
you gotta tame them.
In the jungle they're wild things,
mindless. But a man
can mold 'em, make 'em do tricks.
I'll talk to him.

He waves Joan dismissively away.

STARK
Man to man.

JOAN
You two make friends, now.

She leaves and Stark slams the door shut. Stark
takes off his belt.

STARK
And now you're getting a licking.

Billy shrinks back and closes his eyes. Stark lashes
out with the belt. Billy scurries away.

STARK
I am your father.
Say it. When I'm through with you
you'll be dancing at the end of my whip,
you'll be leaping through fire.

Billy faces Stark, his face beginning to set into a mask
of insensate rage.

Scene Four

Stage goes to black. In the darkness, the orchestra
goes into a frenzy, spurred by the sound of the whip.
As the orchestral interlude dies away we are back in
Dora's office. Billy has been speaking to Dora.

DORA
And then — how many times? —

BILLY
Every day.
But then I found the path
to the Fallen Country.

DORA
How did you find it?

BILLY
I was angry.

Scene Five

The stage darkens again and the music wells up, with
angry weals of sound building to a terrifying climax.
And then we're in Billy's room again.

In the foreground, as though we are seeing the story
through her eyes, we see Dora, watching, not part of
the action.

Billy has been playing a video game and we see,
within the frame of Area B which is now like a giant
monitor screen, a dreamlike vision of the game ... a
fleeing princess ... the shadow of a white dragon.
Billy is playing with increasing fervor, almost
becoming part of the game. Then he thrusts aside
the controls, switches of the screen, which now has
become a window frame. Billy climbs over the frame
and out of Area B.

> DORA
>> He tells me one night
>> the anger burst at last,
>> and he escaped from the window
>> and biked into the night....

We see Billy crossing the stage on a bicycle. As he
cycles the lighting becomes cold, moody, dismal. The
music takes us to a different place, eerie and
haunting. The mundane world becomes one of
fantasy.

> DORA
>> And he barely noticed the cold
>> and the blizzard
>> and the mountain of snow.

Billy's bike runs into some kind of snowdrift. Snow
fills the stage.

> DORA
> A dead, sourceless light
> played over vistas of whiteness.
> It didn't feel like the world at all.
> And in the distance
> in an impossibly far horizon
> stood a castle....

As she sings, we see the outlines of a castle in Area B.
And there is what seems to be a huge snowdrift or
mountain of ice, only as we focus, it resolves into the
body of a dragon. Billy struggles to move the bike
further, not realizing that it isn't snow, but the
bicycle is stuck. Then comes the voice....

> DORA
> Then came a voice....

The eyes of the dragon open, and we at last that the
mound of ice is part a huge creature. But it sings, it
has a still small voice.

> DRAGON
> Billy Binder
> Welcome to the Fallen Country.

> BILLY
> What are you?
> Send me home...

> DRAGON
> You have no home.

BILLY
Yes. You're right.

DRAGON
Billy, Billy, are you thinking
That a dragon ought to roar?

He tries to roar, but an empty, whining sound comes
our.

BILLY
Oh dragon
Who has stolen your roar?

DRAGON
Billy Binder
you have come to the Fallen Country
because your anger
opened a pathway here.
In the Fallen Country
there are no emotions,
no love or hate
no sun or moon
the world is muted
by perpetual snow.

BILLY
What do you mean?
I couldn't have biked that far
not to another country.

DRAGON
It is your anger
that has brought you here.
Anger is strength.
We need your anger,
for we cannot feel

such anger, such pain,
such hate.

BILLY
Who has done this to you?

DRAGON
You know him.
You have touched his shadow.
He is the Ringmaster
with his whip of burning cold.

BILLY
Stark —
I should take you back to my world —
let's kill him, together,
you and I.
I'll make him give back your roar
You'll spew out flames
you'll burn him up,
I know it,

DRAGON
Poor Billy. You cannot kill the Ringmaster,
He slips from world to world
as easily as you.
But slowly, slowly, we can sap his strength.
Your anger can build bridges
Burn pathways through the snow.
Try it, Billy.

Billy concentrates all his anger into a flame that flies
across the stage. A path in the snow forms showing
traces of greenery beneath.

DRAGON
Yes! You see!

> You are the Binder.
> You and you alone
> one day
> will bind the Ringmaster
> and free our world.

In Area B, we see Stark standing in the costume of a circus Ringmaster, brandishing a whip. Behind him, lions are leaping through hoops of fire.

BILLY

Stark!

DRAGON

No!
Stark is but the shadow of a shadow ...
and it is a shadow of a shadow
that has followed you
all the way to your world.

A red weal opens up on the dragon's flesh.

BILLY

He's hurt you.

DRAGON

No.
I have no feelings.
We have no pain here.
Your anger is all that exists,
Your anger and the Ringmaster's rage.

BILLY

Take me to him.
I'll conquer him,
I'll kill him for you,
I'll save the Fallen Country.

DRAGON
Many children come here,
They dream they will shape their anger
into a bridge that will reach
the Ringmaster's heart
and topple the circus
where he wields his whip.
That time is not yet to be.
Ride me now, Billy.
We'll have adventures.

BILLY
What sort of adventures?

DRAGON
This is a fantasy world, Billy —
What kind of adventures would you like?
Shall we battle pirates,
save a princess?
Ride me.

Billy leaps onto the Dragon's back. Music of flight
wells up from the orchestra. Lighting and effects
suggest that they are flying through the air. We see
townspeople, gray and disconsolate, pointing at the
sky,

CHORUS
The Binder rides at last!
Save us! Save us
According to the prophecies,
Save us, Billy Binder!

The action moves cinematically, through a
combination of movement, lighting, and projection.
We see chained humans. As the dragon wheels

overhead, bolts of flame descend from the sky and shatter their chains.

CHORUS
Save us, Billy Binder!

A combination of smoke and lightning allows us to see Billy atop the mists, with the dragon's face showing through the carpet of cloud.

DRAGON
You see, your people need you.

CHORUS
(in the distance)
Save us, Billy Binder!

As the dragon flies about and the sky is shot through with bolts of flame flung from Billy's hands, we hears off-stage cries from the chorus....

CHORUS
The Binder has come
to set us free....

We come closer to the castle we saw earlier. We see a cage on the castle walls. Inside the cage there is a chained princess who is played by the singer who plays Joan.

BILLY
That's my mom!

JOAN/PRINCESS
(expressionless)
Save me, Billy.
Save your kingdom.

BILLY
Does he hurt you too?

JOAN/PRINCESS
Save me, Billy.
Save your kingdom.

Billy starts to cry.

DRAGON
You will never need to cry again,
From now on
you will save your grief
your anger
to use here in the Fallen Country.
Listen to me,
For I am the Snow Dragon
the last dragon of this world.
The Ringmaster has defeated all the others,
but I survived
but purging myself of all
that made me dragon:
my rage, my fire, the shimmer of my scales.
I have waited so long for you
that I have lost the the capacity
to feel joy at your coming.
Dry your tears, Billy Binder
Dry them for the last time.
Promise me.

BILLY
I promise.
I know why I was brought here!
I see what I have to do!
I have to be the one,
I have to defeat the Ringmaster!

Scene Six

The scene transmutes itself into Dora's office. Billy is lying on the couch, shivering. Dora, who has been observing, now moves in closer to Billy. His spasms slowly subside.

> DORA
> I liked your story.

> BILLY
> It wasn't a story.

> DORA
> No, of course not.

Billy gets off the couch and makes for the door. For a moment he stands in the doorway.

> DORA
> See you next week.

> BILLY
> Sure, Ms. Marx.

The light slowly fades as Dora sits down again, lost in a private well of loneliness.

ACT TWO

Orchestral Prelude

The second act begins with a music of white-hot anger and vehemence. We should imagine terribly violent things happening. The music transforms into a bitter, sarcastic circus organ waltz. As light slowly fills the stage we see in Area B images of lions leaping through flames, of a laughing Ringmaster ... but sometimes it's Billy leaping through the hoop of fire.

Scene One

Billy is flying on the back of the dragon. We are approaching the icy castle that we saw in Act One, where Joan/Princess is caged.

> CHORUS
> (running around in the landscape far
> below)
> The Binder rides at last!
> Save us! Save us
> According to the prophecies,
> Save us, Billy Binder!

> BILLY
> There, there, is that where the princess is?

> DRAGON
> Yes. She is imprisoned in the keep.

I can't go any farther.
You have to do it it, Billy.

> BILLY

How?

> DRAGON
> You have to build it,
> the bridge of anger.

Billy climbs down from the dragon's back and stands on a rocky precipice.

> BILLY
> Yes. I feel the anger.
> I feel the hate.

As Billy concentrates, a bridge of ice begins to form, stretching all the way to the distant castle.

> JOAN/PRINCESS
> (in the distance)
> Save us, Billy,
> save your people.

> DRAGON
> Your anger, Billy!

> BILLY
> My anger! My hate!

The bridge forms, reaches all the way to the distant castle, and ...

Billy is climbing the bridge of anger. In Area B, he has reached the turret with the caged princess. We see the dragon wheeling overhead. We see the caged princess.

> BILLY
> I'll save you.
> Don't be afraid.

He concentrates and her chains and the bars shatter. Joan/Princess steps out of the cage. She does not smile. She walks towards him.

> JOAN/PRINCESS
> Thank you.

> BILLY
> That's all?

> JOAN/PRINCESS
> What did you expect?

> BILLY
> I thought that —

> JOAN/PRINCESS
> That what?
> My hand in marriage
> and half my father's kingdom?

> BILLY
> I guess.

> JOAN/PRINCESS
> Oh you are all alike
> You battered kids that climb
> through the icy window of our kingdom.
> One rescue and you think
> you've saved the world.

I will walk away
and tomorrow he will capture me again
and you will find me again
in another castle
in another cage,
and you'll save me again,
And he'll come again.

BILLY
But I've come to kill him!

JOAN/PRINCESS
You can't.
I know you really want to.
But he is more real than you ever will be.

BILLY
But I *am* real!
Because I can feel pain!

JOAN/PRINCESS
No, you can't.
There is no pain in the Fallen Country.
Try, Billy.
You are numb here, quite, quite numb.
The only fuel is anger.

BILLY
No! I *can* feel! I *can* feel!

Billy tries to hit himself, but we can see that he feels nothing.

JOAN/PRINCESS
There is no pain in the Fallen Country
and you can stay here forever if you want,
you never have to leave,

to feel pain, ever again.

Suddenly we hear the sound the Ringmaster's whip, the roar of a hungry crowd, and the bridge begins to crack.

> JOAN/PRINCESS
> I told you he'd be back.

Billy tries to grab onto the princess. We see the whip swinging in the sky and then the princess leaps into the void.

> BILLY
> I can't — hold the bridge up —
> any longer —

The dragon swoops down, trying to catch the two of them, but Billy trips and falls. The lights whirl as they plummet.

Scene Two

Downstage left there is a hospital bed. Billy is asleep, on an IV, and his face appears bruised. Upstage and far right, we see a sofa and part of a waiting room. The two areas are separated via lighting so that scenes can simultaneously be shown to be taking place inside and outside Billy's hospital room.

On the waiting room sofa, Joan and Stark are seated together. They do not look at one another. A nurse enters Billy's room, makes some annotations, adjusts the IV, and then comes back out and exits upstage right.

> STARK

I want him of there. Get him checked out.

JOAN
This time
you went too far.

STARK
Bones will mend, Joan.
But the child within the bones
he's the one I need to bend,
for his own good.
Kids, you gotta break them
so you can put them back together
right.

JOAN
How can I trust him?
Oh, he's not human.

STARK
Trust me.
        (he kisses her quickly)
I'm going in to see him now.

JOAN
Wait up.

STARK
No, no.
It's got to be just me and him, see?

JOAN
Make peace with him.

STARK
Oh yes. But on my terms.

Stark rises and goes through to where Billy is lying.
During the subsequent scene between Dora and
Joan, he hovers over Billy's prone body, like a
vampire waiting to feast. Joan sits in the sofa, staring
worriedly at the entrance to Billy's room.

Dora Marx comes in with a nurse. She sees Joan. The
two women look at each other. The nurse goes looks
in on Billy's room.

> NURSE
> He's with someone.

> DORA
> I'll wait.
> (to Joan)
> Are you his mother?
> I'm Ms Marx. I'm the counsellor
> the school sent him to.

> JOAN
> Counsellor? Is Billy in trouble? —

> DORA
> He missed his morning appointment.

> JOAN
> Appointment? What appointment?

> DORA
> Mrs. Binder —

> JOAN
> Straczynski. Joan.
> (puts out a hand)
> I didn't know he was seeing a counsellor.

                    DORA
Don't you realize that your child
is a victim of domestic violence?

                    JOAN
                  (toneless)
He rode his bike into a tree.

                    DORA
             (indicating the entrance)
Is that the man?

                    JOAN
Yes.

                    DORA
You let him be alone with him?

Meanwhile, in the other room, Stark begins to speak
to Billy, at first whispering in his ear, in an aria that
becomes increasingly emphatic and violent.

                    STARK
Billy Binder ...
Billy Binder ... I know you are listening.
You think you can hide
in your frozen world
but you know
I am there too.

                    BILLY
                  (murmuring)
No ... no ...

                    JOAN
What can I do, Ms. Marx?
He is not a human being.

He is a force, a wind, a storm.

DORA
Excuses! You *can* stand up to him,
You *can* save your child
and yourself. But instead of that
he speaks to me of castles in the snow
imprisoned princesses
who dare not speak —

JOAN
I know I could end it
but it's like I'm in cage
like I'm gagged
and unable to speak.

DORA
Get rid of this man.

JOAN
I can't! I can't!

STARK
Yes! When I call
you must come!
I wield the whip
and the world obeys!
Oh, you must leap through fire
into the heart
of the eternal cold
Oh, Billy, know
this ultimate despair
for I have come to the world
to fetch you,
to bring you to your true self....

> BILLY
>
> You're not my father.
> You're a bad dream.

The two conversations build in intensity until they become a full-blown operatic quartet.

> JOAN
>
> He's a monster, not a man,
> and even if I got rid of him
> what about Billy's lies?
> Will they end?

> DORA
>
> You say he's not human
> and that makes it easier
> on yourself.

> STARK
>
> Come! Come!
> This is where you belong!

Billy sits bolt upright, finally completely awake.

> BILLY
>
> Stark!
> I will kill you!
> I will avenge them all,
> all the creatures
> in the Fallen Country!

> STARK
>
> You are mine
> For all eternity,
> mine,
> in the Fallen Country!

Stark leaps up towards the frame of Area B, behind
which we can see a billowing vista of the Fallen
Country. He pulls out a whip and cracks it in the air.
Bill rips out his IV and stands on the bed, summon
reserves of power from deep inside himself. The bed
becomes a ring of fire.

> DORA
> Something's happening in there.

> JOAN
> Ms. Marx — please —
> protect him! —

Dora and Joan run from the waiting room into Billy's
room. They are just in time to see Stark leaping
through the frame and into the Fallen Country. The
wind whistles. A spectral hand bursts out of the
frame and drags Billy into the vortex.

> JOAN
> Billy!

She tries to reach through the frame but it is solid.

> JOAN
> I told you.
> I told you, he's not human.

> DORA
> No! he is!

Blackout.

Orchestral Intermezzo

We hear a music of flying.   We hear the off-stage
cries of the citizens of the Fallen Country.

> CHORUS
> The Binder rides at last!
> Save us! Save us
> According to the prophecies,
> Save us, Billy Binder!

Scene Three

In another part of the stage we see Dora, slowly
making her way home, as she did in the first act. As
the bridge of anger forms, Dora sings to herself.

> DORA
> Illusion! Fantasy!
> Do I dare believe?
> What I saw
> in a hospital room
> Plumes of fire
> a blizzard through the window
> blasting the summer heat
> do I dare believe?
> What can I do, the mother says?
> What can anyone do?
> All right. Enough.
> Time to do my job.
> Time to call the authorities.

She takes out her mobile phone.

> DORA
> Hi. This Dora Marx
> from the school.
> I want to make a report....

Yes, yes. An abuse report.

The music wells up for a moment, drowning out her
words. She hangs up the phone and puts it away.
She has reached a the shadow of a doorway. She
fumbles with a key and goes inside

> DORA
> It's out of my hands now.
> Here is my hiding place
> my private little Fallen Country
> after all day spent
> among children's traumas
> I come home to a adults-only condo
> where children are forbidden.

She goes inside.

Orchestral Intermezzo

A wild, cascading, churning music plays.

Scene Four

As it subsides, Joan unlocks the door of her house.
The lights come slowly back on revealing the living
room of Billy's house. Stark is asleep on an armchair,
covered with a blanket. He isn't himself. Joan is
looking at him nervously. He doesn't answer.

> JOAN
> But - you disappeared in the hospital -
> you leaped into another world.

She touches him, He is clearly not himself.

                         JOAN
                   This isn't you.
                   It's a shell.
                   You're somewhere else.

We hear a thunderous knocking.

                         VOICES
                   Open up. It's the police.

She opens the door. Dora and a police officer enter.

                         JOAN
                   (reproaching)
                   Ms Marx. You've turned us in.
                   Wasn't there some other way?

                         DORA
                   They are not here to arrest anyone yet.
                   They just want to ask a few questions.

                         JOAN
                   (pointing)
                   My son isn't here. You can look in his
room.

The police officer exits in the direction of Billy's
room. Stark does not wake up.

                         DORA
                   I am sorry.

                         JOAN
                   I came back and found Stark like this,
                   Not awake, not asleep.
                   Where has he gone?

                    STARK
                 (murmuring)
          Billy....

                    JOAN
          Stark ... the police are here.

Stark doesn't respond

                    JOAN
          The police, Stark.

                    STARK
                 (in his sleep)
          Where have you been, Billy-boy?
          I looked for you all over ...
          at the Hydra Gate ... at the Plain of Stone
                 Lions
          in the castle of the Ice Princess....

                    JOAN
          He's raving —

                    DORA
          No. Those are places
          in Billy's stories ...
          places in the Fallen Country.

                    STARK
          We could be Kings together, man
          Kings of the Fallen Country.

                    DORA
          It's all true.

The police officer comes in.

POLICEMAN
Ma'am,
Could we ask you some questions?
Maybe it's best without your husband.

JOAN
Sure ... this way.

She leaves with the policeman.

STARK
(still asleep)
I didn't ask to be hated,
I didn't ask for the cold to seep
all the way into my heart.

Dora is left alone with Stark. She looks at him and
realizes....

DORA
The Fallen Country exists.
Anger has made it real.

Suddenly the wall bursts open and Billy crashes into
the room, as though he had just plummeted from the
bridge of anger in the Fallen Country.

BILLY
Wake up, you monster!
Maybe I can't kill you *there,* but here
you're just a human being.

He leaps at the sleeping Stark and begins to pummel
him with his fists.

DORA
Not now, Billy! Let the police handle it!

Stark wakes up abruptly and his blanket falls to the floor. And we see he is the Ringmaster, the Stark in the Fallen Country. He pulls his whip out of the chair cushions and brandishes it.

> BILLY
> I can't fight him alone, Dora —
> I need someone to believe —
> It's gotta be you.

Joan comes out of Billy's room but now she is the princess. Stark's whip curls around her body and drags her up towards the frame of Area B. Behind the frame we see the outlines of the Fallen Country. Stark pushes Joan/Princess into Area B and she is caught in a whirling storm of gathering darkness.

> BILLY
> It's gotta be you, Ms. Marx.

In the far distance, through the mists of Area B, we see the Snow Dragon hovering. Billy gets sucked into the vortex.

Scene Five

We move into a chaotic sequence of scene shifting now, as castles and images of circuses fly through the air. In ghostly monochrome, we see chained children and adults moving through the darkness, fearful always.

> CHORUS
> We are the citizens of darkness,
> we do not feel,
> we do not weep,

We do not know.
We do not hope.

DORA

I feel it now
building within me
the frustration of my wasted life
my anger
my self-hatred.
Billy grasps things
that I can only read about
in journals, in statistics.
I've been so sure of myself
so sure of my ability
to coax those traumas
from those children's minds.
But Dora, Dora, where
is *your* peace?

I cannot compress
the shadow substance of my dreams
till it becomes diamond-hard
till it becomes truth.

Now I must choose,
Now I must believe,
Or I will never be more than
a dried up, bitter woman
who has never lived.

Now I release my rage.
Now I shall step into
the Fallen Country.

CHORUS

We do not know.
We dare not hope.

Scene Six

The storm has cleared and Dora stands in a desolate landscape. Lions made of white stone guard the emptiness. Far away we hear the sound of a circus.

Ahead of her stands Billy, reaching towards her from Area B.

> BILLY
> Dora, Dora!

> DORA
> I can't reach you ...

A stairway of ice seems to form. Dora begins to climb. She is buffeted by wind and wild cascades of light.

> BILLY
> Stay angry, Dora ...
> Stay angry and stay alive.

Billy pulls her up.

> BILLY
> Stay with me, Dora.
> I'm going to end this now.
> Stark! Stark!
> I'm coming to kill you!

We hear Stark's laughter and the sound the whip. The line of chained inhabitants of the Fallen Country moves, shadowy and broken, through the snow. Far away we hear the eerily cheerful sounds of a circus.

DORA

Keep calm, Billy.
I'll stay with you
through everything.

BILLY

Yes. Believe.
You're all I have, Dora.
I'm not coming back
until one of us is dead.

DORA

Aren't you afraid?

BILLY

No, but you are.
Don't be afraid. Be angry.

And then we hear the Snow Dragon moving through
the sky. The dragon lands beside Billy and Dora.

DRAGON

You have brought another.

BILLY

She's been hurt, too.
Only she hides it too well.

DRAGON

Come then.

His wing extends onto the stage and Billy helps Dora
to climb. They look down from the dragon's back.
There is an endless line of people shuffling slowly
towards some distant place.

                         CHORUS
            Ah, ah, ah.
            The Ringmaster calls.
            We dance to his lash
            of burning cold.

As we move through the air we see in Area B a circus
tent from which the music of the calliope pours out.
The dragon comes to rest on a cliff and we see the
bridge of anger again.
                          BILLY
            My bridge of anger ...
            It's holding. I'm going to cross over.
            Follow me if you dare.

Orchestral Intermezzo — segueing into Scene Seven

Billy and Dora cross over the bridge of anger.
Around them, behind them, the enslaved citizens of
the Fallen Country too are all making their way to
the same place. The stage transforms into a huge
circus tent. The ceiling is full of stars and moons. In
Area B we see the enslaved citizens as a grim
audience. In the center ring, Stark wields his whip.
Joan/Princess is his assistant, dressed in a spangled
costume, chains attached to her wrists and feet.

                        ANNOUNCER
            See the Dominator of the Desperate
            Darkness
            making the lions leap!
            See the King of the Cowering Creatures
            pushing the beasts through the flames!

We see Stark brandishing his whip. We see shadowy
creatures leaping. Joan/Princess gestures for
applause.

The bridge of anger bursts into the circus tent.

> BILLY
> The sun and the moon and the stars
> They're here ...
> you stole them and stitched them into that
canvas —

> STARK
> Ah. You're here at last.

> BILLY
> Princess, be free.

He releases the princess from her chains, but she
does not leave.

> STARK
> She does not want to be.

> DORA
> Get out of this boy's mind —
> you've done enough damage.

Stark sends out a magic bolt that sends Dora reeling.

> STARK
> This is not your business.
> Billy, what's *she* doing here?

> BILLY
> She's someone who believes.

Stark cracks the whips. The lions dance.

BILLY
But she's not the one who will defeat you.
I'm the one who can leap
through the hoop of fire.

STARK
Good, good.
You came as I dreamed you would
you, the strongest and bravest
of my children.

BILLY
I'm not your child!

Stark cracks the whip.

STARK
Say it! Say I'm your father!

The images around them go haywire. Stark's
demoniacal laughter fills the air. Lions leap and
claw. Stark whips the princess and she herself leaps
from a hoop of fire, screaming from the pain. Billy
hurls flame at Stark.

BILLY
I'll kill you first.

They fight using bolts of magic fire and ice.

STARK
You have it all backwards
You didn't come to kill me
I sent for you.
I bent you and I broke you
so I could build you up in my image
so we could rule together

as father and son
here in the Fallen Country
for ever.

            BILLY

No!

            STARK

The Stark I released into your world
the Stark you think hurt you so much
— just a shadow. I am your real father
who gave you the gift of anger
to bring you to me.

            BILLY

No! I came here to free these people
to open up a gateway to the real world
to let them all escape you!

            STARK

We are alike.
You too will wield this whip
and make a thousand universes
dance with pain
and never feel the pain yourself.

He twirls his whip. Behind, in the Area B frame, a
dark window appears. It is completely void.

            STARK

There's your gateway, Billy —
emptiness and more emptiness
utter desolation.
Abandon hope, Billy Binder.
You are mine.

> BILLY
> I'll never be like you!

He sends another bolt of energy into the dark gateway. For a moment we see an image in the heart of the darkness ... another Stark.

> DORA
> You're senseless!
> You screw up the whole universe!

She rushes at Stark, who turns to her and slowly she starts to turn into a sculpture of ice. It is happening to everyone — to the audience, to the princess, to the lions. Stark rages and rampages. But Billy stares only at the void.

> BILLY
> That's enough, Dora.
> I have no more anger left.
> Stark, I pity you.

> STARK
> No. You *must* hate me.
> I bred you to hate me.
> I beat that hatred into you.

> BILLY
> Dora ... mother ...
> I could have been like him.
> You see, Stark too dances
> to the whip of a higher Ringmaster.
> And behind that Stark there is another
> Stark.
> Each Stark is but a shadow of a shadow.
> How can I hate him?
> He's me.

STARK

No! Not pity.
I cannot survive pity.
Pity alone can kill me.

BILLY

I pity you
I take away your spell
I turn my back on you.
I won't be defined by you.
The Fallen Country
is an illusion.

STARK

Billy — my son —

Slowly, deliberately, Billy turns his back on Stark. As
he does so, the ice begins to thaw.
Stark begins to fade a the artificial suns and moons
in the canvas tent top begin to shine with real, warm
light. A breeze springs up.

The Snow Dragon appears ... seen clearly for the first
time.

SNOW DRAGON

Billy,
It's time for you to go now.
Soon,
the Fallen Country will be closed to you.

Dora and Joan slowly come to life. Each of the
characters begins to sing for himself alone at first,
the music building and blending into a quartet.

BILLY

It's strange
He really was my father.
It's strange
how the Ringmaster plants
in all his kids
a little shadow
that works to destroy him.

SNOW DRAGON

Oh, Billy, I too was part of the shadow,
the part that seeks the shadow's death.
You have killed us both
Stark with your compassion
and me with the gift of love.

JOAN

Am I really free?
Has my son really shattered
the chains that bound me to the darkness?
How long is the journey now?
I am afraid, afraid to be unchained.

DORA

The snow is melting.
The world is turning.
As therapists we learn
that inside everyone who hurts
there is a child who once was hurt.
Billy lives
what we only read in books.

SNOW DRAGON

The world you made
was beautiful, Billy,
beautiful and terrible.
I have not roared in a thousand years,

now I shall roar.

The dragon roars, a sound of infinite power and
heartbreak. The Fallen Country fades. We return to
Billy's house. Stark is being led out of the house in
handcuffs. Joan watches him leaves with a mixture
of fear and longing.

She moves toward Billy. They look at each other but
do not speak. Slowly, Joan turns and walks slowly in
the direction that Stark has been taken off in.

> DORA
> She has a journey too, Billy.

> BILLY
> Yes.
> But she'll come back.

He stands alone, downstage, isolated in a pool of
light.

> DORA
> You understood things I never understood,
> I, whose job is to understand.

> BILLY
> I killed him. *I* killed him.

> DORA
> Yes. You found the path to Stark's soul
> and in daring to understand it
> daring to give it peace
> you destroyed it.

> BILLY
> You can write up your fancy explanations,

your report about my craziness
my psychosis. But you know what really
happened.

> DORA
> The inner and the outer worlds
> are congruent in a thousand places;
> wherever we stand
> we are within a hair's breadth
> of the Fallen Country.

> BILLY
> You know. You saw.

> DORA
> Now I must do what I am trained to do.
> I must close in on your fractured soul
> and I must heal it.

> BILLY
> Yes. You must.

> DORA
> O, Dora, damn it,
> who has stolen *your* roar?

Billy doesn't answer.

> DORA
> Billy, if I hug you
> will you flinch? O Billy,
> let me.

> BILLY
> Sure.

She makes a tentative step towards him. Slowly, before she can reach him, the lights fade to black.

END OF THE OPERA

About the Author

Once referred to by the *International Herald Tribune* as "the most well-known expatriate Thai in the world," Somtow Sucharitkul is no longer an expatriate, since he has returned to Thailand after five decades of wandering the world. He is best known as an award-winning novelist and a composer of operas.

Born in Bangkok, Somtow grew up in Europe and was educated at Eton and Cambridge. His first career was in music and in the 1970s he acquired a reputation as a revolutionary composer, the first to combine Thai and Western instruments in radical new sonorities. Conditions in the arts in the region at the time proved so traumatic for the young composer that he suffered a major burnout, emigrated to the United States, and reinvented himself as a novelist.

His earliest novels were in the science fiction field but he soon began to cross into other genres. In his 1984 novel Vampire Junction, he injected a new literary inventiveness into the horror genre, in the words of Robert Bloch, author of Psycho, "skillfully combining the styles of Stephen King, William Burroughs, and the author of the Revelation to John." Vampire Junction was voted one of the forty all-time greatest horror books by the Horror Writers' Association, joining established classics like Frankenstein and Dracula.

In the 1990s Somtow became increasingly identified as a uniquely Asian writer with novels such as the semi-autobiographical Jasmine Nights. He won the World Fantasy Award, the highest accolade given in the world of fantastic literature, for his novella The Bird Catcher. His fifty-three books have sold about two million copies world-wide.

After becoming a Buddhist monk for a period in 2001, Somtow decided to refocus his attention on the country of his birth, founding Bangkok's first international opera company and returning to music, where he again reinvented himself, this time as a neo-Asian neo-Romantic composer. The Norwegian government commissioned his song cycle Songs Before Dawn for the 100th Anniversary of the Nobel Peace Prize, and he composed at the request of the government of Thailand his Requiem: In Memoriam 9/11 which was dedicated to the victims of the 9/11 tragedy.

According to London's Opera magazine, "in just five years, Somtow has made Bangkok into the operatic hub of Southeast Asia." His operas on Thai themes, Madana, Mae Naak, and Ayodhya,have been well received by international critics. His most recent opera, The Silent Prince, was premiered in 2010 in Houston, and a fifth opera, Dan no Ura, will premiere in Thailand in the 2013 season. His sixth opera, Midsummer, will premiere in the UK in 2014.

He is increasingly in demand as a conductor specializing in opera and in the late-romantic composers like Mahler. His repertoire runs the entire gamut from Monteverdi to Wagner. His work has been especially lauded for its stylistic authenticity and its lyricism. The orchestra he founded in Bangkok, the Siam Philharmonic, is mounting the first complete Mahler cycle in the region.

He is the first recipient of Thailand's "Distinguished Silpathorn" award, given for an artist who has made and continues to make a major impact on the region's culture, from Thailand's Ministry of Culture.

Books by S. P. Somtow

General Fiction

The Shattered Horse
Jasmine Nights
Forgetting Places
The Other City of Angels (Bluebeard's Castle)
The Stone Buddha's Tears

Dark Fantasy

The Timmy Valentine Series:
Vampire Junction
Valentine
Vanitas

Moon Dance
Darker Angels
The Vampire's Beautiful Daughter

Science Fiction

Starship & Haiku
Mallworld
The Ultimate Mallworld

Chronicles of the High Inquest:
Light on the Sound
The Darkling Wind
The Throne of Madness
Utopia Hunters
Chroniques de l'Inquisition - Volume 1 (omnibus)
Chroniques de l'Inquisition - Volume 2 (omnibus)

The Aquiliad Series:
Aquila in the New World

Aquila and the iron Horse
Aquila and the Sphinx

Fantasy

The Riverrun Trilogy:
Riverrun
Armorica
Yestern
The Riverrun Trilogy (omnibus)

The Fallen Country
Wizard's Apprentice
The Snow Dragon: Three Variations

Media Tie-in

The Alien Swordmaster
Symphony of Terror
The Crow - Temple of Night
Star Trek: Do Comets Dream?

Chapbooks

Fiddling for Waterbuffaloes
I Wake from a Dream of a Drowned Star City
A Lap Dance with the Lobster Lady

Libretti

Mae Naak
Ayodhya
Madana
The Silent Prince
Dan no Ura
Helena Citronova

Collections

My Cold Mad Father
Fire from the Wine Dark Sea
Chui Chai (Thai)
Nova (Thai)
The Pavilion of Frozen Women
Dragon's Fin Soup
Tagging the Moon
Face of Death (Thai)
Other Edens
S.P. Somtow's The Great Tales (Thai)

Essays, Poetry and Miscellanies

Opus Fifty
A Certain Slant of "I"
Sonnets about Serial Killers
Opera East
Victory in Vienna
Nirvana Express